UNCAGED OBSESSIONS
UNCAGED DUET

MADI DANIELLE

Copyright © 2025 by Madi Danielle

All rights reserved.

No part of this book may be reproduced in any form or by any electronic or mechanical means, including information storage and retrieval systems, without written permission from the author, except for the use of brief quotations in a book review.

This novel is entirely a work of fiction. The names, characters and incidents portrayed in it are the work of the author's imagination. Any resemblance to actual persons, living or dead, events or localities is entirely coincidental.

Designations used by companies to distinguish their products are often claimed as trademarks. All brand names and product names used in this book and on its cover are trade names, service marks, trademarks and registered trademarks of their respective owners. The publishers and the book are not associated with any product or vendor mentioned in this book. None of the companies referenced within the book have endorsed the book.

Cover Design: KBGDesigns

Editing: KMorton Editing Services

❦ Created with Vellum

To everyone who has fought a silent battle and came out stronger on the other side of it.

PLAYLIST

Powerless - Villian of the Story
LET THE WORLD BURN - Chris Grey
Angry Too - Lola Blanc
HOPE - NF
That's how you make a villain - Emlyn
I Did Something Bad - Taylor Swift
Damage - Savannah Dexter
The lonely - Christina Perri
Someone else - margo
STFD - TeZATalks
Look What You Made Me Do - Taylor Swift
Bad Dreams - Rachel Lorin
The Walls - Chase Atlantic
I Know You're Watching - Lilyisthatyou
Underneath the Mask - Royal & the Serpent
Born To Die - Lana Del Ray
FERAL - Xana
Dark Side - Iris Grey

TERMS AND ABBREVIATIONS

BJJ - Brazilian Jiu Jitsu.
Gi - jiu jitsu outfit.
Muay Thai - fighting style in MMA that originated in Thailand.
MMA - Mixed Martial Arts.
Cage - Enclosed space where fighters compete against each other.
Submit or "tap out" - When a fighter yields resulting in defeat.
Full mount - Grappling position where top fighter is on top of opponent with their legs wrapped around the opponent's torso.
Arm bar - Submission hold in MMA that hyperextends opponents elbow.
Triangle choke - Choke that encircles opponent's neck and one arm with legs.

CONTENT AND TRIGGER WARNINGS

This book has some dark themes and elements, so please take care of yourself. All content in this book is intended for audiences 18 years or older. Content and triggers include:

- Anal Play
- Explicit Sex Scenes
- Light Bondage
- Dub-con
- CNC
- Blood Play
- Somnophillia
- Cockwarming
- Attempted SA (Not by MCs)
- Primal Play
- Masturbation
- Breath Play
- Violence (on page)
- On page alcohol
- Murder
- Someone being drugged (Not MC)

CONTENT AND TRIGGER WARNINGS

- Domestic abuse, mental abuse, physical abuse (Not by MCs)
- Group Sex Scenes
- Snake Play

If any of these will cause you distress please don't continue. Do what is best for yourself and your own mental health.

NATIONAL DOMESTIC VIOLENCE HOTLINE

If you or someone you know needs help, please reach out to someone.

You can reach the National Domestic Violence Hotline at 1-800-799-7233(SAFE).

CHAPTER 1
DREW

Something is wrong.

I could always tell when I was growing up, and the same feeling of impending doom is consuming me now.

Just like the day when I was sixteen and my dad came storming into the kitchen while I was attempting to clean some of the dishes piled in the sink. I just needed a plate and a fork or spoon to use on whatever food I could scrounge up in this house.

I fucking hate it here. I hate that we live in filth and that every single day I'm just waiting for my dad to come home. He'll either be too drunk to remember that he has a son, or just drunk enough to remember he does and that he hates me.

So as soon as I hear the rickety door to our trailer slam shut, I turn the water off. I'm hoping he'll avoid coming in here and I can be invisible today.

His heavy footfalls come closer and I hang my head, the longer strands of hair falling in front of my face. I know I need to cut it soon. My hack jobs look awful and I wish that just once I could get a real haircut like the other guys at school.

I've been trying to get a job, but apparently it's hard to get hired anywhere. I just want to be able to make some money, save it up, and get the fuck out as soon as possible.

The footsteps come closer, but he doesn't say anything. I don't move as I hear him open the fridge and slam it shut again. I continue to wait, hoping he's just going to leave and go sit on the ripped and broken couch, or go to his room.

Apparently, I'm not that lucky.

"Couldn't even get those fucking dishes finished, could ya, boy?" he snarls.

"Maybe if I had some help," I murmur.

"The fuck did you say." He shoves my back, pushing me into the counter, but luckily I was braced for it.

I turn around, feeling more confident, or stupid, or just completely done with him and this life he's forced us to have. "I said maybe if I had some help. Like maybe if you didn't run Mom off, or if you were actually a functioning human."

"You ungrateful piece of shit." The first blow comes flying at me, no doubt slowed down by the alcohol running through his bloodstream. So I'm able to avoid the hit.

I stand at my full height, having passed him up this year by at least two inches. I also started weight lifting at the gym at school and have been starting to build more muscle. So when I cock my own fist back and it cracks against the bones in his face, he goes down easily.

I don't stop.

All my rage that's built up over the years. All my desires to finally see him get what he deserves. All the revenge I've wanted to get on him comes out as I continue to rain punches down into his face.

He's gargling on his own blood, and I don't stop. Not even when he stops his feeble attempts to fight back. Not even when he stops moving all together. And not even when his face is unrecognizable from my fists.

I will myself to stop, sitting back on my ankles as I look down at the unconscious man laying on the floor of our kitchen. My hands are covered in blood. His blood. Probably mine too if I'm being honest because even though I can't feel it, I know my knuckles are busted.

As I continue to stare at the man who has called himself my father for my entire life, I notice the lack of movement in his chest. Standing up slowly, I stare down at him waiting for him to move, to make a noise.

I don't know how long I stare at him without noticing any movement, but my fear kicks up. I killed him.

I took it too far, and I fucking killed my father.

The panic takes over and I need to get out of here. I'm going to go to prison for the rest of my life. I can't be here anymore.

My hands are shaking as I go to the bathroom and wash off the blood quickly. Then, I grab my old ratty backpack, shoving as many clothes as I can fit alongside my school stuff already in there.

I leave without looking back. I should probably call for help because maybe he's not dead, but if he is then I'd be caught. And that's the last thing I want.

So I close the door to the house that's been a prison to me.

I don't take the car, instead, jumping on my bike and pedaling away as fast as I can. I'm hoping all of the neighbors are minding their own business. I don't know where I'm going to go, but I just can't be here.

※

I END up finding a secluded area in a park and I choose to settle in for the night because the adrenaline has since left my body and I can feel myself crashing. Though, as I lay on the ground, resting my head on my backpack, all I can see is the mangled remains of my father's face. I know I'll never forget the sight for as long as I live.

After three days of sleeping at the park, one of the guys that I consider a friend at school offers me a place to stay on the couch in his garage. I hesitate taking him up on his offer, but he tells me his parents wouldn't mind and sleeping somewhere that isn't grass sounds nice.

His name is Jordan, and he ends up letting me stay, even after the news about my dad came out.

He didn't die.

He couldn't remember anything about the attack and somehow no one has come after me. The nightmares that have plagued me my entire life continue, with him always making an appearance. Only now, there is the added fear of the cops showing up at Jordan's and taking me away in handcuffs.

But somehow, it doesn't happen.

Jordan's the only person who knows what happened and he didn't look at me with fear. He just said he wanted to show me something.

So one night, we sneak out and go to this old abandoned building that's covered in graffiti and overgrown bushes and vines.

"What is this?" I ask.

"Come on."

I follow him into the dark building and I'm instantly hit with the smell of smoke and the lack of light. There's the sound of a crowd, and grunts with the familiar sound of flesh hitting flesh.

That's when we're met with the sight of two men fighting in a makeshift ring. I watch them trade blows, and both have blood running down their faces.

"You ever seen a fight before?" Jordan asks.

"On TV, sure, I guess."

"I think you'd be good at it."

I grimace, looking back at the two men, one looks like he's struggling to stay up, swaying on his feet while the other guy uses it to his advantage. With one more blow the weaker man goes down and the other is announced as the winner.

"What do you think?" Jordan asks.

"I don't know how to fight like that. I just... I don't know." *I shake my head.*

"What if we train?"

"The fuck do you mean?"

"I know someone, and I told him about you. He would be willing to train you, well us, if you wanted."

"Let me think about it."

He accepts my answer and as the next fight starts, we stand and watch. I find myself focusing on the way they move, the precision of their feet and how they seem to be tactical in some of their moves while others seem to be drawn from emotion. I'm familiar with that because those are the only kind of fights I've been in before.

As we continue to watch, I think about Jordan's offer and that it might be a good thing for me. A way to regain a semblance of control over my life. Especially when I learn these guys are winning money, and that's something I desperately need. I'm not sure how long Jordan's parents will be nice enough to let me stay, and I need to be prepared to be on my own.

Maybe this is exactly what I need. Maybe this will be the thing that changes my life.

I'm pulled out of my memories and back to reality by the banging on my door. This time, before I answer it, I anticipate the pissed off man that's about to greet me. This time I'm ready.

I open it, already speaking, "Max isn't here—"

"We have a problem," Caine cuts me off, and the feral look in his eyes lets me know he's serious and this time the problem doesn't have anything to do with either of us.

CHAPTER 2
ADAM

I don't think about my childhood, ever. Remembering the various foster homes I was bounced around to and from isn't something I like to recall. Sometimes, I do remember what led me to where I am today, and that's especially true when I'm laying in the quiet. Just the sounds of Athena slithering around the couch onto me, then exploring the couch even more.

She came into my life at a perfect time, just like my first coach, Jesse. I remember the first fight I won and actually making enough money to pay more than just my bills. I finally had enough to buy everything I needed to get her started, and then finally the snake I'd always wanted.

Though, I didn't make it easy to get there because I did whatever the fuck I wanted to, and hated authority. Some things never change.

The cash is slapped into my hand for my win. It's not enough, and will barely cover the rent on my shit hole apartment, but it's all I can do. It's the only thing I'm good at and I know I'll win.

I count out the money to make sure it's all here before grabbing my shit and leaving for the night, knowing I'll have to be back in a few days to make more for groceries.

As I'm leaving, I hear my name being called and normally I'd ignore it, but then he calls again. "Adam Hayes."

My head snaps up to see who keeps calling after me, and the man who's approaching me isn't familiar, but he raises a hand in a half wave.

"Do I know you?" *I snap.*

"No, but I've been watching your fights and you're good. But I think I could make you better."

I fold my arms across my chest. "Why the fuck do you think that?"

"My name's Jesse." *He stretches his hand out, but I don't take it.* "I own a boxing gym, and I think you have potential to go pro, but that'll never happen if you keep fighting in shitty places like this."

"Yeah, no thanks." *I shake my head. Fucking sketchy dude approaching me out of nowhere claiming he can make me fight better. Hard pass.*

He calls out to me again, and as I ignore him, I get on the Yamaha that I got for way too cheap—though, I was able to fix it up to get it functional again. Luckily, I don't live too far from this fight location, so I'm home in less than ten minutes.

I stash the cash I won in the box I have in my top dresser drawer before cleaning up in the shower that doesn't get warm enough. When I climb into bed, which is just a thin mattress on the floor, I'm glad it's summer in Portland, so it isn't too cold because the blankets I have are wearing thin.

One day this won't be my life anymore. Everyone has to start somewhere, and the bottom is different for everyone. Mine just happens to be pretty low. But I know I'll get to the top one day.

※

I'VE ALWAYS BEEN TALL, but lean, which has always been an advantage while fighting because I'm faster than my opponents and they always underestimate me.

That is until today when I'm paired up with a guy who outweighs me by at least seventy pounds. Still, I refuse to pass up a fight, even if it's unfair.

It doesn't take long for me to regret it because I may be quick on my feet, but the bastard is strong, and every punch he lands rattles me more than the last. I'm swaying on my feet, blood is pouring down my face, but I'll never submit in a fight. I'll continue going until I'm knocked out.

Though, that'll be a first for me.

Another hit lands and my ears start ringing. My vision blacks out for a moment and it gives him the perfect opportunity to hit me again almost immediately. I try to stay standing. I try to block. I try to fight back, but everything feels like it's in slow motion and out of my control. I can't see straight. I can hardly hear what's going on around me.

I barely register the next hit, and it's not until the world is turning on its side that I realize I'm falling. My head hits the ground and everything goes black.

※

EVERYTHING IS *cold when I wake up, and there's a beeping noise that's making the headache, currently playing like a drumbeat in my head, even worse. When I try to open my eyes the bright light is too much and I shut them immediately with a groan.*

"You're awake," a man's voice says. I don't recognize it, but I try to open my eyes again to see. Despite it burning, I refuse to close them.

That's when I see it's the man from the other night, but I don't remember his name. I can hardly remember my own at this moment though because my head hurts so bad.

"What're you doing here?" I ask, my voice hoarse and throat burning.

"I brought you here. Found you tossed aside, probably left to die by those assholes that don't care if you live or die."

"Why?"

He leans forward, resting his elbows on his thighs. "I see something in you, kid. Kinda reminds me of myself when I was young. I see your potential and I think you're wasting it on fights that won't get you anywhere except dead."

I can't help but feel like there's a catch here. There has to be because there always is. This guy knows nothing about me, and I don't know what he could see in me other than the fact that I'm a good fighter, which is true, but so are a lot of other guys.

"You don't know me."

"No, but I know potential when I see it."

"What's the catch?"

"No catch. Train at my gym, compete in real fights, and let me be your coach. Let me show you what you can accomplish," he pitches. "If you hate it, then you quit and go back to your underground fights and I won't bother you again."

I shift in the stiff hospital bed, fire burning up my side with the movement. "I don't know," I grunt.

He stands up, setting a card on the table next to the bed. "Think about it and let me know. I just hope you decide before the next time you end up almost dead."

And with that he leaves. I drop my head back against the pillow, closing my eyes once again because everything is starting to feel fuzzy again and I end up drifting off.

※

AFTER I'M DISCHARGED from the hospital and I'm laying on my flat mattress on the floor, hardly able to move and unsure of when I'll be able to pull myself up for a fight again, I make my decision.

Pulling the card from my wallet where I tucked it away I stare at the name on the card—Jesse Anderson—and his phone number.

It takes me another three days before I call him to take him up on his offer to train me. After I do, I'm still not convinced there isn't a catch. On the first day I show up to train it doesn't include a single moment of fighting, and I finally realize what the catch might be.

"I don't see how this is going to help me fight," I say after the fifth round of circuit training Jesse has me complete.

"That's because boxing isn't just about punching the other guy in the face."

"You sure about that?" I scoff.

"Another round," he barks.

I groan, wanting to argue with him before walking right out of here and go back to what I was doing before.

But I don't.

I stick with it. Despite the arguments and the misery at times, I stick with it and I trust Jesse. Eventually, when I actually get my first official fight, it's an entirely different experience than any of my past ones.

I've always been self-assured when I stepped into the ring, but this time it's a different level of confidence. This isn't about me just believing I'm the best. I'm confident in my skills I've learned, and that I'm going to be able to execute them to perfection.

"How're you feeling?" Jesse asks during my warm ups.

"Good."

"You got this, kid."

I nod. I know I've got this. The hint of nerves hits me as soon as I enter the ring, and I try to shake them off. As soon as the fight begins, I'm locked in and focused on all the training I've been doing.

I win.

Not only that, I win money and it's more than I've ever made in any of my past fights. I'm almost overwhelmed by the fact that I'll be able to afford rent, and maybe even something I've always wanted.

"How do you feel?" Jesse asks as we're leaving.

"Like I'm ready for the next one," I answer honestly.

He chuckles. "There will be more. This is just the beginning."

For the first time in a while, I fully trust someone else. Because I feel like this really is just the beginning.

There's a pounding at my door, and I wonder who it could be this late since I assume Max is already asleep, probably with one of the other guys. I set Athena back in her tank before opening the door where I'm met with Caine and Drew standing there. I look around them for the other person that should be standing with them because she would be the only reason they would be showing up to my house right now.

When I don't see her, I look at the two of them and notice the matching looks of concern and anger on their faces, so I ask, "Where's Max?"

CHAPTER 3
CAINE

Max is supposed to be here by now. I knew that I should've showed up at her work and taken her back to my house. This is what happens when I try to let her have a little bit of independence. Clearly, she can't handle it and just runs away again.

I thought we were getting better. She's been spending the night with one or more of us every night. But my girl has a knack for running and wanting to be chased. Maybe that's what's happening right now, I'm always happy to chase my little killer if that's what she wants.

I pull up the camera view in her house to see just how far she's planning to run, but as soon as I do, I'm shooting to my feet. I'm already halfway out the door when I see a man I don't recognize in her house as she attempts to fight him off.

Without stopping, even to put on my helmet, I'm racing toward Max's house, ready to commit murder. I don't know who the man is. I don't know what's going on, and all I can see in my mind is the way he had a fistful of her hair while he dragged her through her living room as she kicked and fought.

I get to her house in half the time it would normally take, and my stomach drops at what I see. Her front door is wide open, her car still in the driveway, but it's eerily quiet. I race inside, calling her name, but just like the street it's dead silent.

Her house is a mess, just like it was the other night. I check and clear all the rooms to make sure she's not hiding. I know she was here, but I can't feel her nearby and it's eating at me.

Someone took her.

When I have no other option, I pull out my phone to watch the recording from the cameras. I see Max come home, and the man is waiting here. I watch the altercation. She tries to run and he chases after her. She fights back as he grabs her and I'm proud of how she handled herself.

Until he hits her and I see red. She falls, which is when he grabs her hair, pulling her across the floor as she screams. Then they are out of frame. That's when I know she's gone.

I throw my phone across the room with a roar. I need to find her. Whoever that was has no issue hurting her and I don't doubt he would do worse. She's my girl, and I'm supposed to protect her, but I fucking failed.

I don't fail at anything.

Jumping back on my bike, I go to Drew's first since he's closer. He answers the door and immediately starts like he knows what I'm here for.

"Max isn't here—"

"We have a problem."

His face falls. "What? Where's Max?"

"I don't know. Some guy broke into her house and took her."

"What the fuck do you mean?" He yells. "Why wasn't she with one of us? Why the fuck was she alone?"

"Because she's stubborn and instead of coming over to my house right after work, she apparently went home first," I snap harshly.

"Well, what the fuck are we doing standing here just holding our dicks, let's go find her."

"Yeah? Where?" I ask sarcastically. "You know who this guy is and where he took her? Where the fuck are we going to look for her?" My voice progressively gets louder with each word because reality is really hitting me about this and we have absolutely no idea where she is.

Drew flexes his fists, clearly upset about this too. "We need to tell Adam."

As much as I want to argue, I know we need as much help as we can get right now to get our girl back. I agree easily and we head over to Adam's immediately.

As soon as we both pull up, Adam answers the door, and looks between us. I see the second he registers that we're here without someone.

"Where's Max?"

We give him the short version, including me having to tell them about the cameras.

"When the fuck did you put cameras in her house?" Adam asks.

"When I needed to have a way to see her at all times."

"You're insane," Drew grumbles.

I don't even care to argue with him because, yeah, I am insane. I'm even more insane not knowing where my fucking girl is.

Adam looks like he's as ready to kill someone as we are, but like the two of us, he doesn't know where to start.

"Show me the video," he states, surprisingly calm for the situation.

They both look at me, and I throw my hands up. "I threw my phone, it's still at her house."

"That's fine. We should go there anyway," Adam agrees.

Once we're back at Max's, I see them experience the same feelings I did when I found the trashed and empty home where our girl should be.

I pick up my shattered phone, thankfully it still works, and I pull the video up to show them. They watch and fume at what they witness.

"I recognize him," Adam states.

"The fuck do you mean?" I question, because that fucker isn't anyone I've ever seen before.

Adam pulls out his own phone, scrolling for something, and then holds up some news article with a small picture attached. I grab it from him, zooming in, and recognize Max instantly. She's more done up than I've ever seen her before, wearing some fancy ass dress. And the way that her hand is laying on a man's chest has me gripping the phone so hard, I swear I can hear it crack.

The man looks smug as shit. Plus, the way he's gripping her wrist as it rests against his chest looks tighter than it needs to. Max isn't smiling, she's grimacing but trying to hiding it.

Sure as shit, it's the man from the video.

The caption under the photo gives us a name. Carson Bradford. The worst part it the caption says who he is. Max was engaged to this asshole. I see red, my eyes honing in on the ring on her finger. A ring that isn't mine. His hands on what's mine. Him trying to take away someone who is clearly *mine.*

"She was *engaged?*" I seethe.

"She never told you?" Adam asks, and all I can do is glare at him.

"Hm, interesting," Drew looks like he's hiding a smile, but I'm too pissed off that someone who thinks they deserve to marry Max has stolen her away from us. I'll also deal with her not telling me about this once we get her back.

"We have a name, let's find him," I demand.

"How? He's from some rich ass family like Max. They don't usually advertise their homes for anyone to find." Drew rolls his eyes.

"There's always a way to find someone," I insist.

"I think I know someone who can help," Adam chimes in, and we both look at him. "You guys know Danner?"

I think about the name, and realize that's the woman that's kind of become friends with Max from the bar. "What can she do?"

"She's good with finding people."

I narrow my eyes at him, because it sounds like there's more that he's not saying, but I accept it anyway. "Alright, let's go."

"I doubt she wants the three of us banging on her door in the middle of the night," Adam reasons.

"I don't give a fuck what she wants, we need to fucking find Max!" I yell.

"We all want to find her," Adam snaps. "We *will* find her. But it's not going to happen tonight, we need to get a plan together and make sure that we're ready to do whatever it takes to bring her home."

"You think we can just go to sleep after all this?" I rear back.

"No, but we need to. We're going to find her, Caine."

"You two go to sleep then, I'm going to actually fucking do something to try and find her."

I sit on the couch because I can't go home. I can't think about leaving here unless I'm going to get her.

Adam and Drew don't leave either, but instead of sleeping, the only thing I'm able to do is watch my girl be taken over and over again. It fuels my anger and by the time the sun rises in the morning, I'm more determined than ever that nothing matters until we get her back.

CHAPTER 4
MAX

Everything comes at me in flashes.

I feel like it had to be a dream—the worst nightmare I've ever experienced.

Carson showing up at my house in Seaside. Him attacking me and fighting back with all my strength. Screaming. The pain of his hand in my hair, pulling me by it across the floor. Being tossed into the backseat of a car. Then the sharp pain before everything went black.

What's worse is I remember my eyes opening in a car, but I was unable to move my body. It all felt heavy, my arms and legs felt like they had concrete blocks attached. My head throbbed, but I looked outside and saw the familiar landscape on the way into my hometown in Texas.

I find myself willing the darkness to take me because the pounding in my head is already unbearable and I haven't even opened my eyes yet. My mouth and throat are painfully dry and as I try to turn over, every muscle in my body screams at me.

I can tell before I even open my eyes that I'm not in my bed. The hint of the ocean smell that clings to everything is gone. The weight and heat from my three large men is gone. I know as soon as I open my eyes I'm going to break down at the surroundings I never thought I would have to see again.

I don't want to face my stark reality. I don't want it to be real. Squeezing my eyes even tighter, I try to convince myself that this will all go away and when I open my eyes again, I'll be scooped up in Adam's arms instead.

Yet, when I finally peel my eyelids apart, the blank walls cause the memories to slam into me. I want to cry, but somehow manage to keep the tears at bay. It's the room I spent eighteen years in at my parents' house. All white, with nothing personal hung up. The large bed is soft and sterile, just like the entire room. Honestly, the entire house is the same way.

I want to scream, and if my throat didn't already feel like it was being ripped to shreds, I just might. Instead, I close my eyes again and wonder what I did to deserve this life. I was finally out, I was learning how to be independent. I was *happy*. And just like everything else before, it was ripped away from me.

There's a knock on the door and I ignore it. When I finally hear the knob turning, I force my eyes to open so I can see who's coming in. Not one inch of my body—or my spirit—is ready to fight anyone off, but I will if needed. Because I will get out of here, *again*. Even if it kills me this time.

I see that it's one of my parent's maids. She's younger and doesn't look at me, just drops some towels on the edge of the bed. But before she leaves the room her meek voice speaks, "Your presence is requested downstairs."

Even though it feels like swallowing needles, I retort, "Tell them that they can drag me out of here like Carson dragged me from my home."

I see her hesitation knowing she doesn't want to pass the message along, and part of me feels bad for her. I'm sure she's subjected to less than stellar treatment working here.

"I'm not going down there," I say sternly. She nods before rushing out of the room.

I know it's only a matter of time before someone else is sent up here. So I force myself to get up, my legs barely able to hold my weight. I don't bother going to the door to lock it because it never had one.

Privacy in the Barclay household wasn't allowed.

Unless you're my dad while he fucked one of his many secretary's, then I'm sure he had some privacy. Or maybe not, it's not like my mom gave a fuck anyway.

The bathroom, however, does have a lock. I make my way in there, and close myself in, making sure to click the lock firmly in place. The back of my head hits the door lightly as I tip it back, closing my eyes as I try to keep my breathing even.

I won't let this break me. I got out once, I can do it again. Deciding that it's time to start figuring out how to do just that, I start the shower and spend the entire time being pelted by the hot water, while I start to form a plan.

ONCE THE WATER is cold and my skin is wrinkled, I force myself out of the shower and back into my old room. I only have a towel wrapped around myself, but the clothes I was wearing are dirty and sweaty.

The sight that greets me in my old room is worse than the one I woke up to. My mother, Claudia Barclay, sits on the edge of the bed, the pissed off look in her eyes I remember seeing my entire childhood present. Her gray hair is dyed blonde, her makeup done to perfection as always. She's dressed like she's planning to go somewhere when I doubt she is. But of course she has to be prepared just in case. Can never be caught looking anything less than perfect. Not as a Barclay.

"You look awful." Those are her first words that she's spoken to me in months. She hasn't seen me since the day I ran out of my wedding, and those three words are the first things she says to me. Not that I'm even surprised. Her special talent of tearing me down is one she's perfected over the years.

I just scoff, rolling my eyes, walking to the closet to find some clothes to pull on. Because I don't care what she has to say to me now. I don't care about anything other than getting back to Seaside and back to my new life. Including Caine, Drew, and Adam. I can only imagine how insane they're going knowing I'm gone.

I'm not delusional enough to think they'll be able to help me. I know I'm going to be on my own for yet another escape, but I'll get back to them. I have to.

I pull out some of the T-shirts I tucked in the back of the closet, hidden away, and gently tug one on. Then I shimmy on some jeans and hear the noise of disapproval from my mother before I even see her.

"Nothing else fit, Maxine? I mean seriously, did you run off just to eat whatever you want and gain as much weight as possible?"

I grit my teeth and clench my fists. I gained muscle. What she's seeing is the fact that my body has filled out and now has strength, but to her that's considered a bad thing.

"Put something presentable on. Carson's going to be here to get you after he's done with work for the day."

That gets me to respond to her. I whirl around, fuming. "I'm not going with him anywhere."

"Oh, for the love God, Maxine. We've been over this. He's your *fiancé*."

I look around like I'm losing my mind, and maybe I have. "Are we pretending like the last few months didn't exist? I fucking left. I left you. I left him. I left this entire fucking life and I'm going to do it again."

"No"—she stands—"You made a mistake. He knows this and is willing to look past your…indiscretions. We will have the wedding, albeit smaller. You'll fulfill your duty to our family, become Carson's wife and forget about whatever it is you thought you were doing."

"I'd rather die."

"Then, that's your choice to make." She shrugs, walking toward the door like she really doesn't care if I do. "Get changed."

I REALLY WONDER if there's a way for me to escape before Carson shows up. My room is on the third floor, and the only thing stopping me from jumping from the window is how vulnerable I would be with two broken legs. Deciding that it's safer for me to find an alternative exit, I turn back and glare at the door. It looks like I don't have much of a choice—or any—in the matter. At least not for now.

The one thing I won't do, is change. I'll be damned if I let anyone here tell me what to do. Not my parents, and sure as shit not Carson. I could try and hide out somewhere in this massive mansion. Unfortunately, I'm sure anyone who works here would sell me out almost instantly and it wouldn't be worth it. They don't have any allegiance to me. I'll choose my small acts of defiance for now.

I'm going to face my reality head on, including the man that's responsible for bringing me back against my will. When my door opens again, I'm sitting on the edge of the bed, waiting. Reclined with my hands resting behind me, eyes glued to the figure now standing in the doorframe.

Carson clearly expected a different sight when he came in here because he looks around, then the slimy smile spreads across his lips when he sees me.

"Look who's awake and ready for me," he greets.

"Why'd you do this?" I can't help but ask. I thought maybe he would give up and find someone else to torture once I was out of the picture. Clearly, that didn't happen.

His smile falls. "Not here. We'll discuss this back at home."

"And you think I'll just willingly go with you?"

He steps in, closing the door behind him and my heart rate kicks up. My body preparing on its own to fight.

"You think I don't know what you've been up to? That I don't know how you've been whoring yourself out?" His smile is back. "You think you really got away from me?"

I furrow my brows because there's no way he could possibly know anything about what I've been doing.

"It was cute, your little escape attempt, and I let you have your taste of freedom. But now your fun is over and you're going to come back home with me. You're going to marry me and you're going to be the perfect little wifey I was promised."

"You can get *fucked*," I seethe.

"Aw, missed that, did you?"

I grimace because just the thought of his tiny dick makes me want to gag.

"Don't worry," he starts again. "You'll get what you want. Maybe I'll even fulfill those disgusting fantasies you had."

"You're not going to *touch me*. I'm not going anywhere with you."

"You will. I knew where you were, I know who you've been with. I can and will ruin their fucking lives if you don't do what I want."

I fight my jaw from dropping, refusing to give him any indication that what he's saying holds any meaning to me.

"Come with me right now, Maxine. Do what I say and I'll leave them alone. If you fight or run again, then I won't."

"You know nothing."

"No? Caine Aldridge, his family is a pretty big deal you know? Lots of mutual contacts. He thinks he can be some big shot fighter. I can make sure he never sees the inside of a fighting ring again, and that he has no backup family plan to come back to."

"Cage," I correct. "MMA fighters fight in a *cage.*"

"You think I care? Then there's Adam, he's the easiest target, obviously no more gym for him."

"You. Wouldn't."

"Try me, wifey."

I want to, *fuck* I want to. I want to fight; I want to push him to his limit. I can see the remnants of my struggle on his skin that he tried to cover up. The scratch marks on his neck, the bruise under his eye. I'm curious how he explained those at work.

"There's also Drew. You know he has a violent past and I have people willing to say whatever is needed to make sure he ends up where he should have been this entire time—in a prison cell."

I don't want to believe him. I want to fight this, but I can't risk the guys. I know I can't, we all may have started our relationship off in an impractical way, but I can't deny that I've started to soften for them. The feelings I have for them are impossible to deny and knowing I may never see them again is only making it worse.

Knowing that I could be the reason their lives are ruined is something I could never live with.

Which is the only reason why I stand up reluctantly and silently agree to go with Carson. The pleased smile he has as he says, "Good choice," has me doing everything in my power to not punch him in the face. Again.

I don't pay attention to my mother as we leave, but Carson says something about family dinner at *our* house this weekend. I would love nothing more than to be long gone by then.

Carson drives us away, the drive from my parents' house to Carson's is about an hour, and I look out the window the entire time, ignoring every conversation attempt he tries. All I'm paying attention to is the scenery as we pass through it. The areas between two rich areas, while everything that lies between is essentially rotted.

Whenever I drive through an old town with rundown buildings, the remnants of what once was still evident, I think about what it may have been like in its prime. That club with the writing on the chalkboard outside and the cocktail sign in the window. I wonder if people look at me the same way. What would I have been if all my pieces weren't shattered. My life altered and my feelings shut down. I guess we will never know. And just like the buildings, I need to rebuild myself. Stronger and better.

CHAPTER 5
CAINE

I don't remember the last time I was able to sleep. I've wanted to rip apart every single thing I come across since she's been missing. I've turned her house upside down, destroying it even further, looking for any clues that could possibly lead me to her.

"Seriously, Caine.. You need to calm the fuck down," Drew says, but I ignore him, continuing to search. Maybe I need to go to the gym or have a fight to get some of my anger out. I know I'm not thinking clearly, but I can't stop. I need to find her, need to bring her back here.

"Caine," Adam tries to break through my haze, but it's not going to happen.

"Aldridge!" he yells and my eyes fall on him, even more pissed off that he's using my last name. "This isn't helping."

"Well all you've done is sleep and bitch at me, so please tell me what's supposed to *help*."

He pulls his phone out of his pocket, looking at it for a second then putting it back. "It's still really fucking early, but we can try."

"What're we trying?" Drew questions.

"If whatever this is sucks, then I'm doing things my way," I insist.

"If your way is pissing Max off even more by destroying her place, then I think you've succeeded. So again, you need to calm the fuck down." Adam shakes his head. "Come on."

He walks out Max's front door, and I don't want to follow him. I feel like I should be here just in case someone comes back, with or without her. Whoever would dare to show up may have information or something for us, but I follow anyway.

We end up at Uncaged and I feel like Adam just lured me here to try and work out some of my aggression rather than do anything to actually help. Then I see a car pull up and I'm ready to fight whoever it is, until I notice the woman that steps out is the blonde that hangs out at the bar with Max. I think they're sort of friends.

"Danner," Adam greets the woman while I glare at her.

"Will you tell me what the hell is going on?" she asks, looking between all of us.

"Inside." Adam nods toward the front door, and leads us all in. Once he's locked the door, the rage is back and I'm about ready to start losing my shit again if we don't start getting some answers.

"Where's Max?" Danner asks. I let out a scoff at the fact that she's just now asking about her. She narrows her gaze to daggers and focuses directly on me.

"That's what we're hoping you'll help us with." Adam turns to me. "Show her the video."

I grumble about how we're wasting our time as I pull up the footage. As she watches, I force myself to watch it again, letting the anger fuel me even more. It's like adding more fuel to an already raging fire.

She watches the same video I have no less than fifty times, and once it's over I'm ready to throw my phone again, but I manage to keep it together. Just barely.

"Look," Adam tells her, "I know you don't talk about what you do with anyone and I respect that. But we need your help."

"Wait." Drew looks at her, then Adam, then back to her. "What do you do?"

"Right now, I'm going to help you guys find my friend," she says, seriously. "Now, tell me what all you know."

Adam explains everything he found out about Max during his research, including the family she comes from and who she was engaged to. I realize I recognize the name of her ex fiancé, well his last name. I don't know anything about the prick, but I know his dad runs some shady shit, so I'm sure the dickhead son isn't any better.

I know her family is a big deal, which is why I name dropped her to my own trying to get them off my back, but knowing the Bradfords are involved too is a whole other level.

It doesn't make things harder, but it does make me more annoyed.

Mostly because that means we can't just kill him to get her back because people would notice he's gone. I clench my fists so hard my knuckles crack.

"Think you can help us?" Drew asks hopefully, once Adam is done explaining.

"Yeah, I know I can. But what's your plan if she doesn't want to come back?" Danner dares to ask.

"What the fuck do you mean? You saw the video, she didn't want to *leave*," I snap.

"I'm just saying, if she went back home and realized she wanted to be there, I'm curious what the plan would be then?"

"Who's side are you on? Isn't she your friend?" My voice is raised and I don't care if I scare her. And because of the impeccable timing my family has, my phone goes off in my pocket and I know who it is immediately. I glance at the screen to double check before ignoring it. The last thing I need to deal with right now is them telling me to come back to Chicago.

"Yeah, she is," Danner agrees, keeping her voice level while she stands tall in front of me, even though she's only a couple inches taller than Max. "Which means I want what's best for her, whatever and wherever that is."

"You saw that asshole drag her away by her hair." I get closer to her face, trying not to scream at her. "There's not a chance in hell my girl *would ever* want to be where he is. Help us find her, and then I'm bringing her back home."

"Caine." Adam's voice has that warning tone to it again, but Danner doesn't back down from me.

"Find her, or I'm going to Texas and I'll destroy every single thing and person in my way until I find her," I declare, pushing past them and going to the hanging bags because I know I need to get aggression out before I start punching Drew and Adam.

Nothing is going to be the same until I have her back. The harder I punch the more pissed off I get that I let her go home alone in the first place. I should've been there. She should've never left my sight.

As soon as she's back, I'll never make that mistake again.

CHAPTER 6
DREW

We leave Caine to do what he thinks will make him feel better. He acts like we all aren't as desperate to find Max as he is. We are, but Adam and I are just a bit calmer about the situation. Of course I want to lose my shit and help Caine kill the man that came into her house and put his hands on her. I saw red when I watched the video. Just like when I lost it on my dad all those years ago.

Maybe when I see this Carson fucker, I'll end up killing him, I wouldn't be surprised. But for now, I know we have to be smart about this. We don't know if she's in any more physical danger, especially if we show up and try to kidnap her back.

Danner said she was going to use her connections to get more information on Max's family and this Carson guy. At least then we'll have more of an idea on where she could be other than an entire state.

Caine hasn't let up on the bag since he started working it ten minutes ago. Adam gestures me toward his office. I follow him because the only other option is to stay out here with the rhythmic noise of Caine's fists hitting the heavy bag and knowing that it will drive me crazy after a few more minutes.

Everything feels so out of control right now. There's so much I want to do and nothing that I'm able to at the same time. I want to find Max. I want her to be back here with us. Everything else seems unimportant until she's back here. With us, where she belongs.

Adam closes the door to his office behind me, and I wait for whatever he's about to say.

"We have to make sure he doesn't completely lose his shit," he tells me.

I nod in agreement. "Yeah, but have you met him? He loses his shit regularly over way less than this."

"I know. We need to get her back and we will, but he can't end up in jail along the way."

"His dad is some fancy ass lawyer, I'm sure he could get him out of whatever trouble he gets himself into." I roll my eyes. Caine's privilege isn't a mystery and I'd be lying to say I'm not annoyed that he comes from so much and throws it all away. I like fighting, but it's a necessity to me, not just something I do for fun.

It's survival, and it always will be.

Adam and I both came from nothing and that's something Caine will never understand. Max may not either, but I can tell life hasn't been the easiest for her either. And seeing the video of her being taken only confirmed some of my suspicions about how her ex treated her.

"You know he wouldn't want help from him," Adam says calmly, and while I know he's right, it doesn't take away the fact that it's an option he has.

"You think Danner can actually help?" I quickly change the subject.

"Yeah, she can," he says definitively, and I want to ask more about what he knows about her, since clearly I'm missing something. But before I have the chance, he's leaving the office again and I know that this discussion is over for now.

We're going to make sure to get our girl back. All while somehow managing to keep Caine out of prison. Even though I don't agree with the extreme way that he's handling this, I take a page out of his book and head out into the gym to start hitting the bag as well. Each time my fist hits the leather, the anger and anxiety of the situation increases. Needing her back. Needing her safe. I struggle to admit that I'm probably more like Caine than I want to be at this moment.

※

Soft lips trail along my bare skin. I hum at the feeling, knowing exactly who they belong to without even needing to open my eyes. The tip of her tongue peeks out between those pouty lips as she kisses, licks, and sucks the skin of my torso leading down to my waistband.

Then, another pair of lips join in on her exploration. These lips have more pressure, and are less full. I know whose they are, just like I know hers. His licks and sucks are more vicious, not caring if he leaves a mark. The contrast of his brutality and her softness is what I crave. It's the perfect combination, and it's already got me dying for more from both of them.

The weight of Max's body lays over mine, her mouth just barely moving over mine, taunting me. "How do you want us?"

"However you want, just someone touch my cock. *Fuck*." I push my hips up, to emphasize my point.

Adam is still kissing and biting along my abs, but then I feel a hand cup my rock hard erection. I know it's Max with the way her small hand has a tentative grip on my dick, subtly running her fingers along the rungs of my ladder like she loves to do.

"Like this?" she asks.

"I think he means more like this," Adam's deep voice says right before the waistband of my boxers is pulled down and a hot mouth is enveloping my dick.

"Yes, just like that," I moan, thrusting up into his mouth.

I want to kiss Max, but she stays just out of reach. I try to grab her hair so I can yank her down to me, but I can't. She's right there, but I'm unable to grab her.

"Get over here," I tell her.

She shakes her head. "Make me."

I try again, but again she's out of my grasp. How is she so out of reach when she's right here? I can hardly enjoy the feeling of Adam sucking my dick because she's getting further and further away from me.

"Max," I call out.

"Come and get me."

I wake up. Alone. And with her voice still ringing in my ears, my anger bubbles to the surface. I realize it's not even from the lack of getting off. It's because I miss her. I just miss having her around, the fire she brings in any room she walks in. How she forces the three of us to get along. How we all came together for her in the first place.

How she just *is*. Fuck, I miss her and not knowing if she's hurt or what's going on with her is going to drive me insane. The pang in my chest at the unknown is making me feel like I may have given her more of myself than I realized. We need her back and as soon as we do I'm not letting her go.

Nothing will ever tear us apart again.

Pushing myself out of bed, I act on pure instinct as I drive over to Adam's house. Not thinking about anything else other than how pissed I am and how I just want it to go away. I just want to lose myself like we did before.

He opens the door and I don't let him say anything before I'm pushing my way inside, slamming the door shut before crashing our mouths together. I move him backward as I try to get lost in the kiss with my mouth on his, but he stops me with a firm shove to my shoulder.

"What're you doing?" he asks, the gruff edge to his voice gives away that he's already turned on. That and the fact that I can see his dick tenting his boxers.

"Don't ask." I go to grab him again by the back of his head, but he stops me with a hand on my chest.

"You needing something? You show up here in the middle of the night and think you're going to demand something from me? No, get on your fucking knees. If you want to be desperate for my cock, then I'll make you beg for it."

I grit my teeth. I may give up control at times, but I still like to maintain some of it. I remember when Max called me a good boy, and that's something I'll never be. Not for Adam and not even for her. Though, right now I'm desperate enough to have her back that maybe I would be. Just once.

"Or you can leave." He folds his arms across his chest.

I keep my eyes locked on his, clenching my jaw as I drop down to my knees in front of him. He smirks and I bite my tongue.

"Take what you want." He nods in my direction and I know this is what I can expect from him.

But it's also exactly what I need to get lost, even if it's only for a minute. Everything is out of my control. I feel on edge and like I want to crawl out of my skin. So I don't let myself think about it too much as I reach for the waistband of his boxers, pulling them down to reveal the rest of his tattooed skin to me.

The muscles on his bare chest bunch as his cock bobs in front of my face, and I run my tongue along my bottom lip. He grabs the hair at the top of my head, tilting it back, making me look up at him first.

"You're going to suck me nice and good while you fuck your fist."

I try to nod, but his grip is so tight my scalp burns and I love the pain.

"Reach into your pants and take out your cock then. I want to see how you're going to touch yourself."

I do what he says without taking my eyes off him. Gripping my cock, I rub the piercings with my palm as I fist myself.

"Be good and put my cock in your mouth," he demands. And even though I want to put up a fight, I want to get lost more. I want to use him and have him use me. I want to just *be* for right now.

"Yes, Coach." Without hesitation, I use my free hand to fist his base and guide his length into my mouth as I squeeze the head of mine, feeling the pleasure shoot down my spine as I suck him into the back of my throat.

Moaning around him, I hollow my cheeks, sucking as I move my fist along my cock, teasing the piercings of my ladder, adding to my own pleasure.

"That's so good, Drew. You take my cock so fucking well," Adam groans. "You know what would make this better?"

"Hm," I hum around him.

"When we get Max back you both can suck my cock, just like the perfect little sluts you are. You want to share my dick with our girl like this?"

I suck harder at the thought, while squeezing my fist around my throbbing dick, thrusting my hips up to meet my strokes at the thought alone.

"Or maybe she could be in your lap with your dick buried in her pussy while I fuck your mouth."

I moan again, pushing him deeper into my throat.

"Caine could watch and see how you both are so good for me," he grits out. "So good at listening to your coach and being used like you both want to be."

I let out a muffled, *"Fuck,"* as I work my hand harder over myself. When Adam's hands grab the back of my head and he starts to fuck into my mouth, I let him, matching his pace with strokes on my dick.

"I'll fill up your mouth and not let you swallow. Then, I'll let you kiss Max so she can taste my cum on your tongue. After that, you both can swallow me." He thrusts harder; I gag around him but he doesn't let up and it only spurs me on to jack myself harder, my orgasm starting while I choke on Adam's cock.

Before I fully register what's happening, Adam yanks me off his dick by my hair, pulling me to stand. He slams our mouths together furiously once again. Licking, sucking, and biting my tongue and lips while he takes both our cocks in his hand, rubbing them together.

I groan into his mouth, thrusting against him. I reach down to squeeze both of us even harder with my hand while he bites down on my lip hard enough to draw blood. I'm about to beg him to fuck me, or let me fuck him. Just something, but I'm so close, too close.

"Fuck, gonna come," he groans, holding the back of my head and his grip on both our dicks tightens almost to the point of pain.

Hot spurts of cum hit my skin, while mine do the same to him as my orgasm takes over. We're both breathing hard against each other's lips while we come down.

We part without saying anything, I look down between us at the cum covering our skin and walk over to the sink to wash off what I can. When I turn around he has his boxers pulled up, but is still missing his shirt, just like when I showed up.

"You want to stay?" he asks and it takes me off guard a bit. We never did sleepovers after messing around. Except with Max.

"Why would I stay?" I snap harsher than I probably should.

"Just offering." He shrugs.

"When we have Max back, I will. Because the only bed I'll share is the one that has her in it," I state firmly. With that, I head home, impatient for the day when that can happen again.

CHAPTER 7
ADAM

So far Danner has only been able to confirm what we already knew. Which is, that Carson took her back to Texas. But I'm trying not to worry too much as it hasn't even been a day since we've asked for her help.

Not many people know she's a private investigator, of sorts, and she likes it that way. I had her try and help me once when I was curious about my parents. She said she found information, but I decided I didn't want to know anymore.

The folder is still buried inside a drawer in my desk and I don't think I'll ever look at it, but it's there if I decide I want to.

I rub my eyes with the palm of my hands, exhausted but unable to sleep. Everything feels like it's falling apart around me and I just want one fucking thing to go right. I hear the sound of the front door of the gym opening and shoot out of my seat because I clearly forgot to lock the door, and no one should be here this late.

"We're closed," I call out to whoever is here.

Standing with his hands on his pudgy waist is none other than Officer Doug—or as some of the people around here call him Doogie—staring at me like I've already done something to piss him off.

"How can I help you, Officer?" I fold my arms across my chest.

He looks at me then glances around the gym like it disgusts him. "Heard there's been some break ins and wanted to check if you knew anything about that?"

"Can't say that I do."

"No? Because I've heard one of the victims was someone that attends this gym."

I immediately go on the defensive. None of us told anyone about Max's house other than Danner. I know for a fact she's not talking to any law enforcement. And obviously Max isn't telling anyone since she's not even here.

"Haven't heard anything. Is this something we should be worried about?" I say, making sure that my tone stays completely even.

"Maybe keep your eyes out," he says, looking around the gym again.

"You seeing something around here that concerns you, Officer?"

"No, I just think it's interesting that whenever there's some sort of crime that pops up around here, it's linked back to this place, is all."

"You got any proof of that?"

He looks me over and stands up taller, like it would actually put him close to my towering height. "You have a good night."

I watch as he leaves through the door, gets in his car, and drives away before moving to lock the front door. The street is dark once his lights are out of view. The only thing running through my mind is how the fuck he could know about any sort of break in. Back in my office, I pull out my phone to text the group chat with Drew and Caine and Max. It doesn't matter that she clearly doesn't have her phone because every message has gone unanswered, none of us message without her.

> Adam: Cops just showed up here asking about the break in.

Caine: The fuck?

Drew: How'd they know?

> Adam: It was Doogie.

Caine: Fucker.

Drew: Think he knows something?

> Adam: Unless either of you told the cops for some reason, then yeah. He might.

I switch over to the text thread I have with just Max to see all my unanswered messages. I don't know why, but it makes me feel like maybe she's just ignoring me instead of something else, unable to get out of a situation that may be dangerous for her.

> Adam: Where are you?

> Adam: Just tell me you're okay.
>
> Adam: If you ran, you know we'll always find you.
>
> Adam: Come back to us.

I toss my phone onto my desk, rubbing my eyes once again. I need to go home. The only reason I close up the gym and jump on my bike, tearing out of the parking lot to the house that no longer feels like home, is to see Athena. It's like even she can tell something is wrong. I want to tell her it's going to be okay, but part of me is worried that maybe it won't be. Maybe it's me being a cynic or maybe it's me just being a realist.

"I'm going to do everything I can to get our girl back," I tell Athena as she slides up the largest stick in her enclosure toward the top of her tank closest to the light. I know she understands what I'm saying.

I end up laying back on the couch, watching her move, and it puts me in a trance. Or it's the lack of sleep ever since Caine showed up at my door, but I drift off to sleep, hoping tomorrow will be the day we get more answers. Or even better, we go and get our girl.

CHAPTER 8
MAX

I've always related to Rapunzel. Locked away in her tower, every day looking the same. Shitty mom, the whole ordeal, really. Well, Rapunzel never had a man that kept claiming to be her fiancé. One that used his fists to keep her in line, or that it was his right to have her body.

I'd rather have her life than mine, considering that my reality comes with the unwanted fiancé. My life had included three men I would have never thought I would want, but right now I would consider all of them my knights in shining armor if I could just talk to them.

Too bad there weren't any princesses with that kind of story. I guess Snow White kind of had seven, right? Well, technically they weren't princes and I guess she did end up with only one of those.

I turn the light on in the bathroom illuminating my ragged appearance, and the bruise forming under my eye. Carson had discovered the marks left on my body from the three men that consume my thoughts. Though, if I'm being honest, I think it might be more than just my thoughts that are preoccupied by them. Because there's a pit in my stomach that grows every day that I'm gone, and this feeling like a part of myself is missing tells me that my heart is also consumed by them, too.

"What the fuck is this?" Carson snarls, ripping the collar of my shirt and revealing more of my skin to him. Even as I try to push him away, he only yanks harder and I stop, not wanting him to pull my shirt off completely.

"None of your business." I fight, yanking my shirt from his grip so I can get away from him.

"Really? Because it looks like you've been marked up like some slut."

"And so what? I don't belong to you and if it bothers you so much, then just let me fucking leave."

Before I'm able to see it coming, there's a sharp pain across my face and my head is forced to the side. My jaw drops open, though it shouldn't surprise me. It's not the first time he's hit me, but I wasn't even able to defend myself and I hate that it makes me feel worse.

I've been working on getting stronger. To learn to fight and defend myself, and I'm unable to even do that right now. That hit hurts more than the physical one Carson just threw my way.

"I'll never let you leave. You're not getting away from me again." His smile is sadistic as I cradle my cheek.

"Then I'm going to make you wish you were dead," I threaten.

His laugh follows him out the door as he leaves me standing there, alone once again.

Carson doesn't have the same deal as the Barclay household and the bedrooms do have locks on them. Which is why I'm locked in one of the guest rooms while I assess the damage. Luckily it's not too bad, but mentally it's a lot worse.

I'm going to fucking kill him, even if it's the last thing I do.

※

THERE'S a banging on the door, and it yanks me out of the sleep I somehow fell into at some point.

"Maxine, open the door!"

"Fuck off!" I scream back, burying my face into a pillow.

"Open the fucking door or I'm going to kick it down."

I know I shouldn't taunt him, I know I should make things easier on myself right now instead of worse, but I'm sick and tired of playing nice and being the good little Maxine for everyone. My men back in Seaside helped me discover who I really am and that I'm stronger than I realize.

"I'd like to see you try," I call out.

There's a loud bang from what I assume is either his foot or his body hitting the wood. I know how thick these doors are and it's going to take some serious effort if he really thinks he's going to break it down. Meanwhile, I'll be ready to fight back if he does.

I've been going over all the training in my mind. Attempting to practice alone isn't the easiest thing to do, but I'm going to get myself out of here and I'm going to get back to my real home. But in order to do that, I know it's going to include getting rid of Carson.

Another bang, this one louder and with an accompanied growl. The noise makes me chuckle because it reminds me of Caine's growling, but with him it's sexy and I know that I'm going to be pissed off, but it's going to lead to a fun time. And at least an orgasm or two.

With Carson it sounds like he's trying—and failing—to be tough. Another bang bounces off the door before I hear the sound of his footsteps retreating, knowing he's not giving up. So I wait. When he comes back his voice is lower, darker, and sends a chill down my spine.

"Open the door, Maxine. You're coming out here or I can make a call about one of your boyfriends. Who should I deal with first?"

I shoot up, staring at the door. I want to fight against the way he's using them to get to me, but he already knows that I'll do what I can to spare them. I don't want to find out what exactly he would actually do.

"I'm thinking Adam? He has the most to lose, doesn't he? That shithole of a gym is his entire life, isn't it?"

My mouth gapes; how did he learn about any of them? I think about the ways he could have and come up short. Even if he knew where I was this whole time, there's no way he knows who I was with, or anything about them.

"Yeah, I'll just make a call…" His voice gets quieter and I race to the door, opening it, but I stay standing my ground.

He smiles, tucking his phone away when he sees me, and I watch the movement, raising my chin. "Where's my phone?" I ask because I've been wondering, though I doubt he'll give it back.

"You don't need it."

"I want it."

"Come with me," he demands, avoiding the conversation altogether. It takes every ounce of me not to punch him in the back of the head as he walks ahead of me into the living room.

I hate walking through this house. It's haunted all my nightmares. Walking through the halls unlocks every memory that I've wanted to suppress since leaving, and being back here has me neck deep into the hell I thought I escaped.

We get to the large open space and I anticipate what he's going to ask of me before he can even open his mouth. My suspicions are confirmed when he sits in the chair he always did.

"Dance for me, wifey, it's been too long."

I fold my arms across my chest. "Fuck no."

"You came back feisty, Maxine. I think I like it."

"You shouldn't."

"Come on, you used to love to dance and I've missed watching you, it's one of the only things you were good at." He takes a sip from the glass of brown liquid I just noticed he has and I can smell it from here. I know it'll only get worse if he gets drunk. Everything was always worse after he's been drinking. Especially when he came home from whatever "business meeting" he was just at.

"Things change." I watch his throat bob as he swallows the liquid, my strength retreating every second I stay standing here. The weight of my past consumes me once again.

"They sure do." He looks me over and I fight the urge to cower. "In fact, I think I'd like to see *all* the ways you've changed in these last couple months."

I take a step back, away from him. "You have already."

"No, I want to see *all* the ways you've changed. Strip."

My breath hitches. I shake my head, taking another step back.

"Strip or dance." He takes another sip. "Preferably both."

I steel my spine, gathering every single ounce of the strength I've built to get through the inevitable torture. It's about trading one thing for another with him. If I do this, maybe he'll leave me alone for now. I hope at least that as long as I play nice he'll leave Caine, Adam, and Drew alone.

If I have to suffer for the time being, it will be worth it to know that they're safe. Because no matter what, I won't risk their lives being ruined simply because they wanted to get involved with me.

Even if I tried to stop them. Especially with Caine, but that ship has sailed because we are all in the deep end now and there's no going back.

"Fine. I'll dance," I agree, reluctantly. "But I need the music on my phone."

He barks out a laugh. "You've always been a shit negotiator, wifey." Shaking his head, he pulls out my phone from his pocket, and I think about lunging toward him to grab it, but he doesn't even look up when he says, "Don't even think about it."

I grit my teeth, wanting to go against everything that he's saying. Every fiber of my being wants to fight to get out of here right now, but I have to be smart about this. I have to play the long game, which includes getting Carson to somewhat trust me again. I have to get through this.

He starts playing some music from my phone, turning the volume up as he holds onto it while it plays. "I should take a video to send in the little group chat you have that keeps blowing up."

My heart lurches; I know exactly what group chat he's talking about. "You're reading my texts?"

"Of course. I need to know what my fiancé has been up to and who she's been talking to while she was on her little adventure. Dance and maybe I'll read you some of the ones you've missed."

I don't want to do this. Almost as much as I don't want to hear the words meant to be coming from them pass through Carson's lips. But I start to move, closing my eyes, and let the music flow through me. It takes me back to how it used to be. This isn't like the dancing I did back in Seaside where I was finding my love for it again. This is the dancing I was trained to do.

Each move was beat into me by my ballet teachers. I was forced to repeat them over and over until I'd perfected it. The music is ingrained in my bones, but the way my body is moving is rehearsed and fluid.

Carson's voice breaks through my haze, making me stumble as I listen to what he says, "Adam asked 'where are you?'"

I stumble slightly, but refuse to open my eyes. I don't want him to see my raw reaction. Especially as he continues.

"Adam says to tell him you're okay. I should show him what you look like right now so he knows how okay you are. Or maybe I'll send him a video of me fucking you later, then he can see how *okay* you are."

I turn, attempting to hide my flinch. I may play nice, but I will not let him fucking touch me ever again.

"He says, 'if you ran, you know we'll always find you.' And 'come back to us.' Aw, how should we break it to him that you'll never be coming back?"

I continue moving my body, not feeding into what he's saying. He can't know how badly this is hurting me.

"Caine calls you 'killer' a lot. He says he's going to find you and when he does you're going to pay for leaving them. Sounds like quite the threat. Guess I'm keeping you safe away from these maniacs after all, aren't I?"

"You're the maniac," I murmur, just quiet enough that he can't hear me.

"Hm, Drew just said for you to say something, anything. And he misses you," he scoffs.

I bite my tongue to keep from saying anything that I'm going to regret. I taste copper as I make myself bleed from how hard I'm having to bite down. Luckily, the song ends, and I stop moving as soon as the last notes ring out.

"Fuck, I've missed you." Carson's voice is gravely and I open my eyes to see that he's finished the glass of alcohol. I recognize that tone, and the look in his eyes. The one that tells me he thinks he's going to do whatever he wants with me.

"I haven't."

He laughs, throwing his head back and I know he's buzzed from that action alone. "Guess I should remind you how badly you've missed me."

"If you so much as touch me, I *will* kill you," I threaten seriously because I will. Either he's going to die or I will before any part of him touches any part of me.

He stands up, stepping toward me, and I stand up straighter, ready for whatever confrontation is about to happen. I don't cower this time. I don't step back, even when he closes in, only inches between our chests.

"You're going to beg me to touch you again, wifey. But right now I don't want to fuck other men's whore. You still have their teeth marks on your fucking skin, but don't worry I'll get you all fixed up and ready for our marriage."

"Go to hell."

"See you there."

CHAPTER 9
CAINE

Danner has information for us. It better be good because I'm losing my patience. Some would say I haven't had any for awhile—or ever—which might be true, but it's really gone now. I pull up to Adam's house and know that Drew is already here, based on the fact that there are already two bikes outside.

I go in and it looks like they're talking in the kitchen. Truly, I don't care what it's about, unless it has to do with Max.

"Either of you heard from her?" I ask, even though I already know the answer.

It's confirmed when they both shake their heads. I want to be even more pissed, but at this point I don't even think that's possible.

"When's Danner supposed to be here?"

"Any minute," Adam answers easily, just as there's a sound of a car pulling up outside.

He lets Danner in and she's carrying a folder that doesn't look as full as I would like it to be. She sets it down on the counter, and I want to snatch it from her to look through it but I clench my fist instead.

"What did you find?" I demand.

"Hi Caine, I'm doing great, thank you. I'm really wanting to find my friend, but would enjoy small talk with you even more."

"He doesn't know how to socialize, sorry," Drew teases and I glare at him.

"I'm used to it." She shrugs, opening up the folder. "Okay, where do you want me to start?"

"Start with where she is and the quickest way to get there."

"Caine," Adam scolds and I roll my eyes feeling like a child, and I hate it.

"It's fine," Danner waves him off, pulling out some of the papers and they look like face sheets or something. "So, we can start with her ex fiancé, Carson, since he was the one in the video."

Every muscle in my body tightens at the mention of that asshole.

"He works for his dad, and they run several businesses and own a few houses, but I'm pretty sure the one Carson lives in this one in Piney Point Village, which is just outside of Houston."

"Great, let's go," I announce.

"Hold on." Adam holds up his hand, and gestures for Danner to continue.

"I'm also pretty sure this isn't just some house you can walk up to. From what I could find out, it's gated and guarded. He's serious that no one should come in or out of there."

"What about her parents?" Drew asks.

Danner sighs. "They're harder to track down. They have several houses in several different states, with multiple properties in Texas. So I don't know which is their primary residence, but I also don't think she's there."

"Why not?" I question.

"Because I'm good at what I do. The other thing that's interesting, is how their businesses don't make a whole lot of sense. They consistently run in the red, which isn't totally unusual for all these super rich assholes because they write off everything. But this is not that…it's not just write offs. They actually make no money."

I really want to say I don't care because none of this really concerns me, but I hold back if only for the fact that the information could actually prove to be useful later.

"This is just my guess, because this isn't in writing anywhere I've found yet, but I think there's some sort of deal between Max's family and Carson's. The marriage seems to be more of a contracted agreement than anything else… An arrangement, but I don't know what each family would get out of it exactly."

"Great, so you have nothing other than Carson's shady, which we knew. His house is impossible to get into, and they all suck?" I snap.

"I didn't say that."

"Caine can leave if you need him to," Adam tells her, and I want to drive my fist right through his face for it.

"I'm not going anywhere."

"It's fine," Danner tells him. "I found the details of what would have been their wedding day easily, from when Max left before. I think they're going to try and rush the marriage this time so she doesn't have the opportunity to get away again. I have a connection with the wedding planner they used the first time, and they more than likely will choose to work with her again."

I perk up at the one piece of good news she's shared since she walked in here. "So you know when that asshole is going to try and have another wedding?"

"Not yet, but I will. The last one was supposed to be big but I don't think this one is going to be, but they're going to want people to know it's happening. There's a reason it's happening in the first place, so these people will want everyone to know about it."

"We just sit around and wait for news then? Because I'm sick of waiting."

"If you want, I'll give you all the addresses of her parent's houses and Carson's. You can go off and show up there, half-cocked, and see how far you get." Danner puts her hands on her hips.

"I never go anywhere half-cocked. I'll take the addresses and come back with my girl."

"That's a terrible idea." Drew shakes his head.

"Well, then what the fuck are we even doing here?" I throw my arms up.

"Look, she's strong, okay? She got out all on her own the first time, and I think she'll do it again. But now, she has help and believe it or not I'm going to help you. It's just going to take a little more time, got it?" Danner maintains solid eye contact with me, which is impressive since a lot of grown ass men won't even do that, because supposedly I intimidate them. It actually makes me respect the fuck out of the woman standing in front of me.

Even if I don't like what she's telling me.

"Thank you for helping," Adam tells her, and I recognize the dismissal. So does she, which I think she's thankful for anyway.

"Like I said before, she's my friend, and I want her back too. Plus, everything I've been able to find about this Carson guy isn't good. The last thing I want is her to be stuck with him any longer than she already has."

Yet another thing I don't like her telling me, but I hold back my explosion.

After she leaves, we're all quiet, clearly unsure of what to say. Unsure of what to do without Max here. We aren't best friends, but we aren't enemies. We just are. I know we need to work together on this, and that once we get her back she doesn't want to choose. But we first have to get her back.

"Well, at least we have some answers," Drew breaks the silence.

"Not enough." I shake my head.

"You need a distraction? How about we figure out why the cops knew about the break in at her house when none of us told anyone," Adam says.

"I don't think that's going to distract me as much as you think it will," I tell him, deadpan.

"I think this Carson guy has someone here that's helping him," Drew announces suddenly.

Adam and I both look at him, both clearly wondering where the fuck that came from.

"It all just seemed too easy for him, right? Maybe he's the one that broke into her place, reported back and then Carson strolled into town and just waited until she was alone again to take advantage," he continues.

"And how would the cops know? You think they're working with him or some shit?" I scoff.

Adam's brow furrows. "Wait, you may be onto something with that."

"The fuckwad working with the cops?" I wonder.

"Yeah, it's Officer Doogie. We all know that he's a sketchy

fucker at best. What if Carson paid him off or something?" Adam reasons.

I think about that, and I have to admit that it does sound plausible. Which only adds another person to my list that I'm going to need to murder.

"I guess we'll have to talk to him." I nod. Even though we all know I don't mean just talking to him. Because if we're right about this, I think we all might be on board with killing him.

CHAPTER 10
ADAM

Caine fell asleep on my couch, and I think it's for the best because I don't think he's actually slept since he found out Max is gone. Not that I've gotten much, and I doubt Drew has either, but the lack of rest wasn't helping his already erratic moods.

"What do you think?" Drew asks suddenly.

"About what?"

"This Officer Doogie shit. You think he'll actually admit to working with Carson if he is?"

"Probably not, but I also don't think Caine will give him a choice."

"You're going to let him beat the fuck out of the guy? That's...unusual."

I shrug. "I'm not going to encourage it, but I'm not going to stop him either."

"You good?"

"No. I'm not." I shake my head, answering honestly. "I want her back."

"I do too. I hate not knowing what that asshole is doing to her."

"She's tough. She can handle herself. All three of us have taught her well."

"She is. It'll be fine, right?" he asks, and the glimpse at his vulnerability isn't usual for Drew. He doesn't like to show any sort of weakness. But I can see it in his eyes right now. He misses her. We all do.

I think it's also pretty obvious to all of us that whatever this is has gotten more serious. She's not just someone we're having fun with. We miss her, we want her in our lives. The way I'm feeling is something foreign to me, this pain in my chest a constant ache without her here.

Once she comes back, she's going to know just exactly how much she means to us. At least to me, because I'm not going to let her go again and she's going to understand why.

※

"Let's go, son," *the cop tells me in the middle of the night. I grab my ripped backpack, the only thing I have that's actually mine, and put a change of clothes in it just in case the next place doesn't have any for me.*

Sometimes I get lucky and the foster home is actually decent, but most of the time that hasn't been the case. Especially as I've gotten older. It's like one day I turned thirteen and suddenly no one gave a fuck anymore. I'm just supposed to figure it out on my own.

I follow the cop and the social worker out of the house into the unmarked car. At least it doesn't look like I'm being arrested this time.

"Why am I moving?" I ask, but the cop doesn't say anything and I roll my eyes. It's not like I'm oblivious to the place I was living, I'm fifteen and see a lot more than they think I do. I'm told a lot more than they think too, I just keep my mouth shut about it.

If I had to guess, this was about the bottle incident where my foster dad threw a full bottle of wine at Jeremy, another kid that's been living here. I don't know what caused it, but I know he ducked just in time and then there was red wine everywhere. I thought it was blood at first, but the color is deeper and not as thick.

The social worker turns toward me. "Hey Adam, are you okay?"

I shrug.

"We're going to take you somewhere safe, okay?"

I roll my eyes. I've been told that before and yet, here I am being moved once again.

"Do you need anything?" she asks.

I shake my head, not looking at her.

The next place they take me is the same story, different day. Everything is okay for a couple weeks, until something goes wrong and I'm forced to move again. Rinse and repeat. As I get older, I become more difficult and soon, I'm the only reason I'm being moved. Cops bringing me back home right before they remove me again. I don't trust a single one of them. I don't trust anyone who thinks they have any authority over me.

The only person who will ever look out for me is myself, and that's especially true the day I turn eighteen and the home I'm staying at kicks me out. No longer in the system, no longer a paycheck to them, no longer their problem.

Still to this day, I hate talking to the cops. They always look at me like I'm the problem, it doesn't matter what I'm doing or even if I was involved or not. Their eyes go directly to me, cut and covered in tattoos, and I'm instantly the one to blame. When Jesse came into my life, I decided to actually change how I was. I tried to stay out of trouble as much as possible.

Right now, I don't give a fuck about that because we need to talk to Officer Doug—Doogie—and I have a feeling that if we are right about him being involved with any of this, it's going to go south very quickly.

Especially with Caine because he insisted on being involved.

Though, at least he got a couple hours of sleep on my couch, so maybe his fuse won't be quite so short.

We're all waiting around Max's house to see if he's going to come by, maybe check on his handiwork. I'll stay camped out here all night, every night, if I have any chance to catch that asshole doing something suspicious. Anything that could lead to getting our girl back.

We're positioned away from each other in different spots. Every time a car shines their lights, driving down the street, I tense. It doesn't happen often, but when it does, it's just a normal car.

After who knows how long another one approaches, slower than the others and I stand up straight, watching, waiting to see what will happen. The car drives past me, which is when I see it's a police patrol car. His lights turn off as he pulls up in front of Max's house.

That's when I decide to emerge from the shadows. Doogie steps out of the car, hunched over slightly and I close the distance, stepping in front of him with my arms folded. I hardly notice Drew and Caine walk up as well.

"Is there a problem, gentlemen?" the so-called Officer asks.

"There's going to be unless you tell us what you know about Max." Caine jumps forward immediately, and I press a hand to his chest to keep him from physically attacking this man right away.

"Max? Who's that? One of the guys at that useless gym?"

I do my best not to react, knowing that's exactly what he wants. It's what they always want. They instigate until someone reacts, then they can say they reacted and weren't the reason for the altercation.

"She's the new girl. The redhead that works at The Tavern," Drew explains, calmly. "This is her house you just parked in front of."

"Not sure who you're talking about." Doogie shakes his head. "I got a call about a disturbance here, I'm checking it out."

"You came to me about a break in, right? We know you know who it was. At this house. But the thing is, no one reported a break in. So how did you know about it?" I ask him, directly.

"Someone must have reported it. Just like someone reported the disturbance here tonight."

"You know a Carson Bradford?" I try another tactic, and I see the flash of recognition on his face before he tries to hide it with a shake of his head.

"Another gym member?" He smirks.

"Listen, you fucking bastard—" Caine lunges toward him again, and I continue to hold him back.

"Just tell us what you know. Did he pay you? We'll find out. Someone broke into her house. They took her, and we know you're involved. So, you might as well tell us what you know, or I won't hold him back anymore," I refer to Caine, whose chest is heaving with heavy breaths.

"You threatening me?" he sneers.

"You take bribes and are an accomplice in a kidnapping. I don't think a little threat is your biggest concern right now," I say dropping my voice low.

"You don't have proof of any of it, and if you let your attack dog loose, I'll have you three arrested."

"Then fucking arrest me." Caine sends a fist flying into his face moving faster than I'm able to stop him, and he doesn't let up. I end up pulling him off while the blood pours from the older man's face.

He fumbles with his handcuffs, his hands shaking and blood pouring from his nose. "You're under arrest." His voice is shaky.

"You'd have to be able to get those on me," Caine taunts.

"We'll find out how you're involved. And you're going to lose your job," Drew threatens.

We end up leaving him coughing and gasping, I'm sure he's going to come after us again, but it doesn't matter because we're going to get our girl back and it'll all be worth it.

CHAPTER 11
MAX

I spend my days working on my strength, building it, and maintaining it. I want to be ready for the day that I'm getting out of here and I know it's not going to happen without a fight. Though, things haven't been as bad as they were before. Carson leaves me alone most of the time until he comes to my room and forces me to dance for him. Every day.

He continues to make shitty comments about my appearance. I force my body to dance under his repulsive stare, and then I'm free to go back to my room. He doesn't try to touch me, but I know it's just a matter of time. Especially because he continues to read the texts I receive from the guys. He can tell how much they miss me; I hide how much I miss them, but I'm sure he knows. Which is why he makes sure to tell me how he will erase them from my memory when he puts his hands on me again. That he'll make sure he's the only man I need.

I want to get a hold of my phone. I need to, so I can tell them where I am and that I want them to come get me. I don't want some grand rescue, but it would be a whole hell of a lot easier if they were here to help me.

Though, at the end of the day, this is my battle to fight and my demon to conquer. It's that thought motivating me to drop down onto the floor and do another set of push ups. All while the vile things Carson has said about my body play on a loop in my mind, encouraging me to work harder, but not for him. For myself.

"You have too much muscle, it's not attractive."

"You used to be pretty. Small and delicate but now your arms look almost as big as mine."

"Did you take steroids or some shit? You look awful."

I've never felt more powerful, stronger, or more like myself. And it's all from my training at Uncaged and the men there—my men—that made it possible. Dancing made me strong and I always had some muscle but the lack of proper nutrition kept me small and "delicate" like Carson said.

Apparently, today my parents are coming over for dinner and to discuss the wedding. Which is another reason I'm working myself out to the point of exhaustion. I'd love nothing more than to be passed out cold when they get here and avoid the entire unnecessary conversation.

All I know is Carson wants the wedding to happen soon, but I know that it's not going to happen at all. I won't let it.

I don't pay attention to the time because I've been so in the zone, and when there's a knock at the bedroom door I scowl at it even though I know he can't see me.

"You better be almost ready in there," Carson threatens.

I roll my eyes, but then I realize something. I've been resistant since he brought me back, and for good reason. What would happen if I pretended to be agreeable. Make him and my parents think I'm going to go along with the wedding happily. It worked before.

"Almost," I call out. My muscles are starting to ache now that they aren't being used and the adrenaline isn't coursing through me as strong as before.

"I want you to be presentable. Actually do your hair and makeup and try to look like a fucking woman for once."

I hear his footsteps retreat and I flip off the door like I've done every day. But maybe I will do what he says this one time. Tap into Maxine, the woman who did what she was told with a fake ass smile on her face.

Except this time, instead of crying behind closed doors, I'm going to stay strong and refuse to lose myself again. I'll never truly go back, but I can pretend in order to get back to my life.

Carson has had some clothes brought to me, along with every makeup and hair item I could ever want, though they've remained unopened and untouched. Until now.

I end up picking out a dress I would've worn before; the cut is conservative so I don't have to deal with any "whore" comments. It's deep purple with long sleeves and a hem that falls just below my knee. The top is fitted, but not too tight and the bottom has a small flare. I curl my hair and put on some makeup, making sure to keep it looking natural. Then, I slip into my single act of rebellion—the four inch black patent leather pumps that Carson's going to hate because he doesn't like when I'm too tall.

It doesn't matter that I'm five foot one on a good day and he's at least five foot ten. I already know he's going to say that these are too tall. I want to stab his eye with the heel for it already.

I leave my prison cell before he comes back to bother me again, finding him sitting in his office that I pass on my way downstairs. I step into the doorframe and wait for him to notice me.

It doesn't take long for him to look up from his computer, sitting back with a smirk on his face as his eyes trail my body, clearly pleased. I fight to keep every ounce of disgust from showing on my face. I also have to fight off the nausea when I fold my hands in front of myself and ask, "How do I look?"

He pushes back from the desk, and turns to approach me. I remain standing in the same spot, although I knot my fingers together as he closes the distance between us.

"Perfect. You look like I have my old Maxine back." He runs his hand along my cheek and I clench my jaw so tight I'm worried my teeth will crack. "Too bad when I look at you, all I can see is a fucking slut."

He removes his hand roughly, and I bite back the urge to plow my fist into his face. I'd break my hand, but it would be the most satisfying pain I would ever feel in my life. He walks past me as I stand there, silently fuming.

I just have to hold it together for a little while longer. This isn't forever. Unlike before, I've seen what freedom is like. I've seen what my life could be.

I've seen what life is like with three certain men, and I will do anything to get all of that back.

※

THIS DINNER IS as awful as I thought it would be.

My parents showed up and were as cold as ever. My mother looked me over, silently scrutinizing, but seemed pleased with what she saw. Though of course she didn't say anything. My dad greeted me with a head nod before turning to Carson and shaking his hand, dismissing me in the process.

I've noticed that Carson's personal chef has been giving me smaller portions, and it's even more obvious tonight when I can see everyone else's plate. I want to talk to them tomorrow and tell them to knock this shit off because they work for me too. Even if the words burn my mouth.

"So, we are thinking two weeks until the wedding," my mother announces.

I choke slightly on the bite of chicken I just took. "That's soon."

"Yes, well, you would already be married if it weren't for your little stunt"—she gives me a pointed look—"We had plans in place. Carson had to change a lot of things around, you know?"

If she's expecting an apology she's not about to get it. Instead, I take another bite of food, chewing slowly.

"Yes, well, two weeks sounds good," my dad agrees. "After the wedding, Carson and I will have a lot of work to do, so your honeymoon will have to wait."

"What work are you going to have to do?" I question, and my mother makes a noise that draws my attention to her.

"Maxine, we don't need to know things like that when it has to do with business."

Right. The role of a woman in this world is to be seen and not heard. Just to exist and not question anything going on around her.

Fuck. That.

That was never going to be me, and the fact that everyone at this table expected that to be my life shows just how much they don't know me.

"You obviously can't wear your dress. Who knows what you did with it, plus…" My mother looks at me with contempt. "It's not like it would fit now."

I don't dare tell her she's more than welcome to dig through the dump in Nevada to try and find it so we can see if it still fits me or not.

"So, we can go dress shopping tomorrow, Maxine. I may be able to talk to Abigail to see if we can get the same venue. If not, I'm sure she'll figure something out. She's the best for a reason."

I know she's talking about the wedding planner. I never had a problem with her in particular, she was always nice to me, but she was doing what my mom wanted for everything. Which I get, since the money is coming from somewhere and it's not me.

"I'm sure I can get the caterers on board again, and our guest list will be smaller since most everyone was present for your little disappearing act and no one was pleased," she continues.

The rest of the dinner is mostly my mother and Carson discussing wedding details with my dad attempting to talk to Carson about stuff I don't understand involving the business.

While they all talk about things I don't care about, I continue to plot my next escape. This one will be my final one. I'll make sure of it.

CHAPTER 12
DREW

It's been a week and all three of us are getting restless. Especially Caine, and I'm about to be right there with him. We've started sparring daily so we can both get our aggression out. Adam and I are still working and teaching classes, but every day that passes, it feels worse and worse knowing we're still here without any answers and not feeling like we are any closer to getting Max back.

Caine and I are gearing up for another fight after the last class leaves for the day. I'm wrapping my hands while he warms himself up. We don't say too much, but in a way this is bonding for us. Neither of us are talkative guys, but doing this feels like a mutual agreement we're using to cope.

Adam hasn't been on my ass about my injury, which has been nice. I think he realizes just how badly I need the outlet. Caine may be unhinged as fuck, but he wouldn't pull any dirty moves to reinjure me.

Even remembering the day I got hurt a few months ago sends a wave of pain directly to my knee. I know it's not something

I'm likely to ever forget, but moving on and fighting again is helping get me through this new pain of missing Max. The helpless feeling that washes over me when I think of her is something I've never experienced before. Not even the day of my injury.

"Keep your head on for this one, I don't trust him," Adam says before the fight. I'm in the zone, working on my pre-fight rituals, warming up and only half listening.

"Yup," I say to placate him.

"Remember his weak spots. Use them to your advantage. It should be an easy win for you."

I nod, again to placate him.

I'm called up, and get into the cage while Adam gives me a couple last minute pointers. It's all things he's told me before and I'm just ready to get this started.

My opponent looks ready to kill, and that look doesn't go away even once the signal goes off to start the fight. We circle each other and he tries to swipe at me, but misses. I take the opportunity to try and go at him, getting a solid choke, but he's able to break out of it with an illegal hit.

I grunt out in pain, waiting for a call that doesn't come. I'm not going to let it throw me off. We continue the round, and into another. That's when everything seems to go south.

I get behind him, getting another choke, but this time I know how he will plan to break out of it and I'm ready.

It's the next move that I don't anticipate. Before I'm able to take him to the ground, his leg rears back and he drives his foot right into my knee, kicking it in. I let go, dropping down in pain with a loud roar.

I can't hear what's going on with the ringing in my ears, but I'm not hit anymore. My knee hurts more than anything I've ever experienced.

There's chaos and commotion all around me. I can't focus on anything other than the pain radiating through my leg.

My vision is filled with white spots; I vaguely realize I'm being taken somewhere. I hear Adam's voice, but can't hear exactly what he's saying. Eventually everything goes dark and when I wake up in the hospital I know before anyone tells me anything that my life is fucked.

"After you two are done fucking around in there, we need to talk," Adam announces before walking back to his office.

Caine and I look at each other, both clearly wondering what that's about.

"If it's something about Max then I want to know now," Caine says, and I nod in agreement.

We end up meeting with Adam in his office instead of sparring. And Adam looks at us, confused.

"I didn't mean right now," he tells us.

"Well, what do you want to talk about?" I question.

"Danner's coming by later. She has more info."

"Why isn't she here now?" Caine demands.

"I don't know her daily life, but I assume she's busy and will come talk to us when she can."

"Come on." I tap Caine's chest with the back of my wrapped hand. "Get your anger out in the cage."

Instead of arguing with me, he does. We both do. And it feels good. My mind is distracted, focusing on the moves. This is why I've always enjoyed BJJ the most. I like to think and strategize rather than just fighting to fight.

Caine is good at all aspects of MMA, there's no doubt about that. His strength is his biggest advantage. He's a big guy, but he also knows how to use it in his favor, which is what makes him a great fighter. He's strategic, strong, and powerful and he pays attention. All important details when it comes to MMA. Too bad he knows how good he is because at some point, that will be his downfall. The man doesn't have a humble bone in his body.

We end up sparring for a few rounds, and it's the perfect distraction. That is until Danner walks into the gym and we both stop immediately. Caine doesn't even bother to wipe the beads of sweat from his face before he's pushing out of the cage and hounding her for updates.

I give her a little bit of space, because I'm sure the last thing she wants is the two of us all over her, asking the same questions while also being assaulted by the smell of our sweat.

Adam comes out, likely hearing Caine and gestures all of us into his office. I'm the last to enter as Danner is laying out the new papers from her folder.

"We have a date for the wedding. It's in a week," she says, getting right to the point.

"That's it, I'm done waiting. I'm going to get her. I don't care if I have to rip the gate to his house off its hinges, I'm getting my girl," Caine insists.

"I really hope that won't be necessary." Danner shakes her head. "I think there will be a way into the wedding so we can get her out."

"We?" I question.

"Yeah, I'm helping. I told you this. You guys didn't think I was just getting this information for you, did you?"

"No offense, but I don't think we should all be showing up and suddenly trying to take off with the would-be bride," I tell her gently.

"Just leave the planning to me, okay? Like I said, I'm good at what I do and a big part of that is remaining undetected. Trust me, you need me."

"We trust you," Adam says, and I grit my teeth because I hate when he speaks for other people. Especially me.

"Good. You should, so let me work out the details, but be ready to go to Texas in a couple days, and we're coming back with my friend."

"Damn right we're bringing *my girl* back." Caine nods.

"Our girl, for fucks sake," I grumble.

"Don't argue like this once we're there. If you guys fuck it up from your massive egos colliding, then I'm going to sell you out to the mob," Danner threatens and I want to ask if she's serious. I don't, but I have a feeling she is.

That probably should worry me, but honestly it makes me glad that Max made friends with her. Because I know that no matter what, she has people looking out for her. Even more than just us.

And I now know that we will be getting her back in just a few short days.

CHAPTER 13
ADAM

I don't exactly know why I'm at Drew's front door, but I feel like we need to talk before we go to bring Max home. Everything has been tense and all our focus has been on Max and what to do. Plus, add in this situation with Doogie and I just feel like we need to clear the air on where we stand.

"Hey," he greets, opening the door for me to come in.

I appreciate the fact that things are never awkward with us. Sure, it's tense at times, but there's never been jealousy or anything that makes me regret the situation we've had together. Now, adding Max in, it's just made things even better and I don't want to lose what we could all have together.

Even with that including Caine.

I walk inside and settle on the couch, taking advantage of the opportunity to rest for a moment when everything has felt so chaotic.

Drew sits on the other side, looking at me expectantly.

"I just want to know where you stand. With everything. Max, us, all of it," I tell him.

"I—I—" He sighs. "I really fucking like her. I liked what we were doing. I like it being all of us and I don't want it to change."

"Me too, but I'm worried she's going to come back and want something different," I admit the one thing I haven't even wanted to think about. It's a fear that's been lingering in the back of my mind.

"If she does, we do what Caine did and show her what she wants," Drew attempts to joke. Though, it may not be a joke.

"We could always chase her through the forest again." I smirk at the memory. The way she felt wrapped around me. Pinned underneath me. Fuck. I want that again and I can't wait for it.

Or maybe have Athena wrapped around her delicate throat while I fuck her. The way she looked so scared and out of breath is the hottest thing I've ever seen in my life.

I bet she would like doing that again but with both Drew and myself fucking her at the same time.

"I think she'll always enjoy us chasing her," Drew agrees.

"What about where we stand?"

"I like what we were doing. Everything together just felt right. You, me, Max, and even Caine I guess. I've always just wanted people around who I like to be with and that's what this has been, right?"

"Right." I nod. "So we're good, no matter what?"

"As long as Max is good, then so am I."

"Then we are on the same page."

"And Caine?"

I chuckle. "Caine is going to do whatever he wants to do, just like he always does. But if he really wants her, then he's going to have to continue to deal with us too."

"It's good for him."

I agree and I just hope that once we have our girl back, she's going to still want us the same way. Or even more, because I'd give her whatever she wanted for the rest of her life.

Even things she doesn't know she wanted. I'll always push her boundaries, expanding them to let her learn more about herself than she ever thought was possible.

She may be stuck with us, but she controls all three of us, whether she knows it or not. Whatever prison she's living in now will be the last one she deals with. Because with us, the last thing she will be is contained.

CHAPTER 14
MAX

Everything about planning this wedding has been worse than last time. Not only because it's so much faster, but because I'm also trying to plan my escape at the same time. Before, I had months to plan, make sure I was hiding my trail and think of all the possibilities to make sure I wasn't caught.

I don't have that luxury and I know it's only a matter of time before I get caught, or worse, my plan fails.

I wish I had help, I wish the guys were here. I wish I was back home. *I wish this just wasn't my fucking life.*

I can't let myself dwell on any of that because the only thing that will do is hold me back, and I have a home to get back to. I can have a breakdown once I'm back home, in my own bed, with the comfort of three large men crowding me and causing me to overheat. I would give anything to have that right now. *Soon. I'll be home soon.*

This time, I know these people won't let me get away easily

again. There's no way anyone will leave me alone like before. No, I'm sure that I'll have eyes on me at all times. That's why I've decided that I need to make my escape the night before.

And I know it's not going to be easy.

I've maintained my workouts daily with what I can do from my room because I need to keep my strength up. Especially because I know I'm not getting out of here without a fight.

A couple of days ago, as I made my way back to my room, I managed to grab a fire poker when Carson had his back turned, grabbing himself another drink after making me dance for him. It's been hidden under my mattress and I have a feeling I'm going to need to use it.

It's been killing me to play nice with him and my parents during all their planning sessions. I've been quiet, agreeable, the way they expect the demure Maxine to behave. I nod along to everything they suggest because I'm not going to be around to see any of it, nor do I want to be.

"Yes, that sounds good."

"Yes, that looks great."

"Yes."

"Yes."

"Yes."

All I want to do is scream how I really feel and I want nothing more than to scream, "No!" just for the freedom to do so. Once I'm out of here I'm going to stand in the middle of the street and scream just because I can.

Tonight's the rehearsal dinner and there was quite the argument on whether or not we should have one this time, since there was one before. My mother wanted it and my father went along with it because he got to invite the business people he wants to look good for.

I'm dreading the fact that I'm going to need to be glued to Carson's side for the entire night. His hands on me and having to pretend like I want them to be there instead of wanting to break every one of his fingers for touching me. I'm sure there will be questions about where I went and I'm going to have to force a smile and avoid answering just like everyone else has been.

Smile. Look pretty. Don't talk.

Be Maxine Barclay.

Soon to be Maxine Bradford.

That's what they all want, and it's what they all expect, but that wasn't ever going to be me.

I manage to get ready before Carson threatens to break down my door again. I descend the stairs and find that he's in the kitchen, not even having had the chance to pour his first glass of the evening. Though, I know there will be plenty of alcohol at the rehearsal.

"Wow wifey, look at you," he greets, his gaze lingering on my chest where the white dress hugs my curves perfectly.

I paste a fake ass smile on my face as I step closer to where he's standing, but still making sure to maintain a significant distance.

"Are you ready for tonight?" he asks, his tone suggestive and it sends a chill down my spine. I worry that I may have been playing too nice with him.

I nod, not trusting my voice not to say something about how disgusting he is.

He closes the distance between us, and I grit my teeth, my molars aching from the force when his hand lands on my hip and I fight the urge to grab it and break all his fingers. "You're going to be a good little wifey for me tonight and tomorrow; we're going to get through our wedding. If you behave, then I'll make sure to give you a reward."

I grimace, especially when he leans closer to continue, his lips grazing the skin of my ear. "I'll fuck you the way you like and treat you like the slut you are."

He pulls away, smirking, and I bite my tongue, keeping my face as passive as possible instead of telling him exactly what I'm going to do if he attempts to lay even one single finger on me.

"I'm going to get changed, you want to help me?"

I put the fake smile back on. "I'll get your drink ready instead."

"That's right, I keep forgetting you were a bartender back in that shit hole." He looks pained admitting it. "Good thing you won't have to worry about doing that again."

Without acknowledging his insult, I go to the bar and prepare his drink. I've done this a handful of times over the last week, especially the past few nights. After I found the redness reducing eye drops in his bathroom while he was at work, I remembered something I'd heard on a true crime podcast.

I know that they lower your blood pressure and decrease your heart rate, so I started slipping them into his drink every opportunity I could. Unfortunately, he doesn't have me get him a drink often enough that I've been able to kill him with them. I don't know how much it would take, and maybe tonight will be my lucky night.

Emptying the bottle into the drink, I hope that this might be what tips him over the edge.

I hand him the drink once he comes back down, after changing into his suit for the night. Watching his throat bob with a large gulp of the liquid, I eye what's left, hoping that he drinks it quickly because maybe it'll work faster and I can avoid the rehearsal dinner altogether.

Then he says something that pulls my attention back up to him, even though I do my best not to react. "Your fan club has been pretty quiet lately. You think they've moved onto some other town whore?"

"Probably," I grit out, the word tasting awful on my tongue. I know it's not true, deep in my gut I know they aren't giving up on me. And on the off chance that they are, I'll turn the tables on them and show how crazy I can be right back. They unlocked something in me that I can't come back from.

Carson pulls out his phone and then downs the rest of the

contents of his glass, setting it down on an end table. "Our car is here. Behave."

"I will," I lie through my fucking teeth.

※

The rehearsal dinner is a lot like our first one. People I hardly know and don't care about telling me how happy they are for me. Except this time it's sprinkled in with questions about where I went, what happened, and other things I avoid answering.

Carson's arm is wrapped around me, gripping my hip in a way that's almost painful, and every time I try to push him away he just pulls me tighter. I want to rip his hand off, and break each finger one by one, but I can't make a scene.

While we're standing talking to some business associate of Carson's that I don't know, I get a flash in the corner of my eye, a familiar face catching my attention, but when I turn it's gone. I'm not even drinking alcohol, but I could have sworn I just saw Drew.

"Isn't that right, wifey?" Carson squeezes my hip again, and I hide my flinch.

"Right," I agree blindly, and since he didn't tighten his hold again, it was clearly the right thing to say.

I try to look around subtly, because there's an edge of awareness that has me on high alert. I swore I saw Drew, and I can feel eyes on me, but not the eyes of strangers.

Just then, I catch the cold glare of a man I'll never forget across the room. Caine's stare is one that has death written all over it as he looks in my direction. But it's Carson that he's focused on. I want to scream and run toward him, but I have to stay rooted where I am with another man's hands on me. They're not the hands of Drew or Adam that I want on me as Caine watches.

A woman comes up to Caine, trying to get his attention. I almost react until I realize that she's also a familiar face. *Danner.* I fight to keep my jaw from dropping right onto the floor at my surprise.

They're here. Wait, why are they here? *How* are they here?

I'm looking around to see if I can find Adam, too, because he has to be here. I know I saw Drew and it wasn't a figment of my imagination. I want to jump for fucking joy right now, but Carson pulls me against his chest, and says something to his colleagues before leaning down to speak only to me. "Keep it up, and you'll get your reward."

I flinch. The only reward I'm going to get tonight is getting the fuck out of here.

CHAPTER 15
CAINE

There she is. I was about to drop everything and run over to her, rip that asshole's hands off her body and take her out of here. Danner could obviously tell I was thinking something like that and she stepped in front of me before I could make my move.

"Play it cool just a little longer," she scolds.

"She's right fucking there," I practically growl.

"We'll get her, but we can't get kicked out of here before that happens."

She shoves the tray I'm supposed to be holding into my chest. We're disguised as caterers, which was what Danner's big plan was, and the stupid outfit we have to wear is driving me insane. The black button up shirt is too tight on my arms, I had to roll the sleeves up to my elbows, and my biceps are straining the fabric. The vest remains unbuttoned because it didn't fit over my chest.

I'm sure I stick out around here, but no one has said anything. They just handed me a tray and said to serve. Adam and Drew are also around here, looking equally out of place, but even if one of us gets kicked out we have the others. Danner's the only one of us who blends in, but I still don't like her telling me what to do.

Keeping my eye on Max across the room, I pretend to work, but really, I ignore anyone who tries to stop me to get anything off the tray I'm carrying.

There's a moment where Max says something to the soon-to-be dead man, and he lets her go. Her eyes find mine briefly, and it's the only signal I need. Dropping the tray onto the nearest table, I follow close behind her, not sure of where she's going.

She goes through a door, and I'm not far behind, locking it behind me as soon as I'm in. I think it's a bathroom, but I don't even look around to confirm, because all I see is Max.

She's looking directly at me, her red hair is curled and looks ready to be wound around my fist. Her hazel eyes are wild as her chest heaves with heavy breaths. Her voice is quiet as she sighs, "You're here."

Closing the distance between us, I grip her throat and push her against the wall, letting my mouth hover over hers. "I'm here."

I crash our lips together roughly, tasting her for the first time in way too long. She opens for me immediately and I tighten my grip on her throat while my tongue plunges into her mouth. She moans and I'm tempted to lift this tight little dress she's wearing and fuck her right here. That way the next time that fucking asshole puts his disgusting hands on her, my cum will be dripping from her pussy.

She breaks our kiss, and I move my hand to the back of her head, grabbing her hair and pulling her head back while I trail my mouth down her neck, biting hard enough to leave a mark.

"Wait, Caine, you're here." She pushes against my chest, and I growl, refusing to let up. "Look at me."

This time I listen, pulling back and resting our foreheads together so I can see her. I've missed getting to look at her, watching her even when she doesn't know it. The way she feels in my arms. I'm never letting her go again.

"We don't have a ton of time, I have to get back. How are you all here?" She grips the vest tightly, keeping me anchored to her like I might float away.

"We're here to bring you back home, and if that guy doesn't stop touching you then we're going to have a problem in front of all these people," I say darkly.

"Don't worry, I'll break his hands before you get the chance." She smirks.

I almost tell her I love her right now. The words are so close to escaping, but I manage to stop myself by taking her mouth again. *Fuck* this woman has been perfect for me all along, but she's even more perfect right now.

She pushes against my chest again and I break away with an annoyed sound.

"I need to go back out there; please tell me you guys are

sticking around?" I hear the pleading tone in her voice, the desperation.

"We aren't going anywhere without you, killer," I tell her honestly.

With another quick press of our lips, she rushes out of the bathroom and I don't wait as long as I probably should before following her out.

Once I'm back out there, I see Adam and approach him. "I talked to Max."

"What did she say?" he questions.

"Not much, her mouth was a little busy."

"Seriously, the first chance you get you have her blow you?"

"No, you asshole." I shake my head. "But that guy that thinks he's engaged to her isn't getting out of here alive. Not when he's put his hands on what's mine."

"For once we agree on something. Stay close, and keep track of Drew and Danner."

"You keep track of them, I'm not taking my eyes off Max."

§

THE NIGHT GOES on and I stay true to my word, keeping my eyes trained on Max throughout the entire night. Everyone sits down for dinner, the alcohol in the glasses on the table being kept full. Including the man who won't leave her side.

I've been keeping track of how many drinks he tosses back and the way he's growing loud and unsteady. It's getting harder and harder to hold back because I want nothing more than to just steal Max away from this place.

I lose track of her for no more than ten seconds, and I'm unable to find her again. I see Drew, Adam, and Danner all looking around as well. I rush toward Danner first. "Where did she go?"

"I don't know." She shakes her head, pulling me into a less crowded area, her head on a swivel.

"Where's that fuckwad?" I snap louder because I can't see him either.

Drew comes over. "Where'd they go?"

Adam joins last. "Did they leave?"

"What the fuck?" I shout louder than I should.

She wasn't supposed to leave. We were going to take her out of here with us, so how the fuck did she get away? I rip off the stupid vest, and loosen the buttons near the collar of the shirt. "We're going to that house; I don't give a fuck."

I'm surprised when no one argues with me. We all storm out of the venue, not caring that we're being yelled at. I just hope that we aren't going to be too late getting to Max and getting her the fuck out of here.

CHAPTER 16
MAX

Carson yanks me out of the venue and I try to get away from him, but the death grip he has on my elbow makes it impossible without screaming for him to get his disgusting hands off me. I do think about doing that, until he says, "Do something stupid, and all your guys are dead."

Since we're in a place surrounded by people he knows and is associated with, I don't put it past him. Especially since he somehow noticed that they're here. But I'll get away from him. I'm leaving tonight, at least back at the house I can put up more of a fight. I can get back to the guys and to Danner.

They're here.

They're all here.

For me.

Carson shoves me in the back of the car before closing us in and the driver takes off.

"Pretty nice of them to show up for our wedding isn't it?" Carson's speech is slow and slightly slurred. Although he unfortunately seems to still be aware of everything going on around us.

"I don't know what you're talking about," I lie.

He chuckles darkly. "Oh wifey, you think I'm so fucking stupid don't you?"

"Of course not," I mumble.

When we get back to the house I'm pulled inside, even as I dig my feet in and try to resist. He doesn't let up and I don't know how he still has this much strength. I attempt to peel his fingers from my wrist, but all it does is piss him off, and his grip tightens even more. I know by the force that his fingers dig into my skin that I will be left with bruises.

He drags me upstairs toward the room that I've been staying in as I continue to try and get away. I'm screaming for him to let me go. As soon as we're in the room, he throws me onto the ground. I try to scramble away, but he pulls me back by my ankles before straddling my hips.

I throw my fists at him wildly. I'm not aiming and or using an ounce of my training, just trying to blindly make contact and hurt him. "Get the fuck off of me!"

He manages to grab my wrists and pins them above my head. I try to buck him off of me now that I don't have use of any of my limbs and I scream.

"Come on, wifey, I've been a patient man, but I'm done. I

think I should record me fucking you and send it to them, what do you think?"

"If I don't kill you first, then they will," I spit into his face, and he uses his free hand to wrap around my throat, but it's not like Caine's grip was earlier. This is intended to hurt, to cut off my air, and that's exactly what he does.

I gasp, trying to suck in as much air as I can while thrashing underneath him. Finally managing to bring my knee up and slamming it into his groin. It's enough to knock him off balance and let up on his grip on me. I suck in a breath while scrambling away from him and heading straight for the weapon I have hidden under my mattress.

Before I can grab it, I'm yanked back once again and I claw at the floor trying to gain leverage. He's unable to pin me down again, and my instructions from all my training finally kick in. I learn very quickly why no one fights while wearing a dress, but I don't care.

I use everything I learned from Adam and fight back. Carson is breathing heavily, his movements lag though, his grip remains strong. I manage to bring him to the ground, and get him into a choke. He attempts to throw me off, but since he doesn't know what he's doing, I'm able to tighten my hold even more. Until he manages to stand, grabbing me and my dress and ripping it further up my body. I kick at him. "Don't you fucking dare." I threaten.

He kneels down in front of me, getting closer when he spits, "Dare what? Fuck my fiancé? Too fucking bad, because that's exactly what's going to happen." He grabs ahold of my underwear, pulling the thin lace so hard that it rips off my body painfully. I rear my foot back to kick him in the face, making contact with his nose and he cries out while I get to my feet.

I know I should run, but if I do he'll just catch up to me, and this fight needs to end. Reaching under the mattress, blindly searching for the fire poker that I stashed there and taking ahold of it right before he grabs me around the waist. I thrash in his arms as he tosses me onto the bed, and as quickly as possible I flip around sending the sharp end of the weapon directly into his chest.

We both freeze and I watch the red bloom on his chest, the contrast stark against his white shirt. I let go of the stick, backing up quickly. He inches closer, shock and anger written all over his face as he grips the base, pulling it out, only succeeding in sending more blood to escape his body. I feel the warmth of it hit my skin, but I'm frozen.

"What the fuck did you do?" he croaks, looking down, blood dripping from his mouth as well as his chest.

"What I should've done a long fucking time ago," I tell him honestly, not a single ounce of remorse coloring my words.

Not even as I watch the life drain from his eyes right in front of me.

There's no fear, no regret. Only relief.

CHAPTER 17
DREW

We don't waste any time getting out of this stuffy building filled with people who think too highly of themselves, and too little of those who they consider beneath them. The number of times I wanted to lose it on them tonight has to be a new record. If I ever want to make sure I feel like shit about myself, just stick me in a room full of rich people again.

Adam insists on driving after Danner tells him where to go. Caine is like a wild animal pacing along the door to its cage as we drive to the house. I know he got to actually see her, talk to her, and touch her. I don't think I've ever been so jealous, and I can't wait to get my hands on her again. I don't think I'm going to be able to let her go once we have her back. I'm going to be glued to her side for the foreseeable future.

When we get to the house and pull into the driveway I can see that Danner was right about the large gate and guards. I look over at her noticing that she doesn't look panicked at all. "Let me do the talking."

Adam drives up to a speaker, and Danner rolls the back window down to speak from the backseat after they ask who we are.

"We're with the catering team for the wedding. Mr. Bradford and Ms. Barclay requested that we bring samples prior to the wedding tomorrow."

There's a moment of silence and I don't think it's going to work, but then there's a loud beep sounding right before the gate opens.

"That was easy," I mumble as Danner rolls up the window.

"I made sure the security had a heads up before we got here." She shrugs.

"Who *are* you?" I ask her and she just smiles.

We pull up to the front of the house, and as soon as Adam has the car parked, Caine is bursting out and storming up to the front door. The rest of us aren't far behind but he's already banging on it roughly.

"So I guess we're done playing it cool," I comment.

"He has her in there. You think I give a fuck about playing it cool?" Caine snaps.

He bangs on the door again, not giving anyone on the other side enough time to do anything before he's pushing it open. It wasn't even locked, and as soon as we're inside, there's a scream I know immediately is Max.

The four of us race up the stairs toward the noise, needing to get to her as quickly as possible. By the time we clear the landing on the second floor and make it to the door where the screaming was coming from, she's stopped.

Caine bursts through the door, and my eyes immediately find Max, her white dress stained with red, and worry that she's hurt gnaws at my gut. Especially when I note that her dress is shoved above her hips and that she's not wearing any panties.

Then I see the man who was wrapped around her all night, face down hanging off the bed, the blood seeping from him dripping into a puddle on the floor.

Caine's already rushed across the room and pulled Max into his arms, and I breathe out a small sigh of relief. I don't think the blood is coming from her.

"What happened?" Adam asks, surprisingly calm.

"Did he touch you?" I snap.

She shakes her head against where she's pressed to Caine's chest. "He didn't get that far. I learned from the best."

"Damn right you did, killer," Caine tells her, then looks over at the body slumped on the bed. "Always knew you would be one."

I expect her to flinch or have some sort of reaction, but she just smiles up at him. And fuck if that doesn't do something to me. But then I remember the dead man in the room, and it brings me back to the day with my dad.

Except this is worse. Because it's Max's life on the line. She can't get caught for this, she doesn't deserve to be punished for saving her life.

"Are you okay?" I hear Adam ask. I watch as she moves out of Caine's hold into his, wrapping her arms around him and pressing her face into his chest.

I wait to see if he'll move her, but he doesn't. He tenses for a second before wrapping his arms around her as well and holding her against his chest, letting her rest there. I know he doesn't do well with being touched, and the fact that he's allowing her to right now means more than any words ever could.

"Yeah." She rests her chin on his chest.

Adam presses a light kiss to her forehead that has her eyes closing.

She moves from his arms to mine, and I squeeze her tighter than necessary. It doesn't feel real to have her here in my arms again.

"I've missed you so much, little one," I tell her, not wanting to let her go. It doesn't matter that we should get out of here and definitely do something with the dead body. I just want to keep holding her.

"What the fuck are you doing?" Danner snaps right before there's a loud thud.

I look up to see that Caine has pushed the body onto the floor so Carson's blank eyes stare up toward the ceiling. Now, with him laying prone on the floor, I can see that the shirt that used to be white is completely stained red with blood from the wound in his chest. The wound that my woman inflicted.

I grip her face in my hands, angling her face up to look at me, taking in the blood splatter on her clothes and skin, and check her eyes, trying to see how she's feeling. She still looks like Max. Like my feisty, fiery Max.

"Who the fuck cares? He's dead," Caine argues with Danner.

"The cops are going to fucking care." She steps over, looking down at the dead man. "We have to deal with him."

"We will. You take Max home," Adam insists.

"And just how're you going to do that?" Danner scoffs.

"We'll figure it out. But I don't want either of you involved anymore than you already are."

"I have to agree," I chime in.

"I'm the one that killed him. I'd say I'm pretty involved," Max states.

Caine pulls her from my arms, and I scowl. "Yeah, and you've never looked sexier than you do with blood on you, killer."

"Next time it'll be yours," she tells him with a smile.

"Fuck, I've missed your dirty talk."

"Okay, seriously. We need to deal with him," Danner announces. "I know you guys think you're all tough and can do it yourselves, but we have to make sure this can't blow back on Max."

Max steps away from Caine's embrace to face her friend. "Won't I be the top suspect anyway?"

"Probably, but that's why we have to do this right." Danner nods, "Which is why the four of you are going to listen to me, and do exactly what I say."

"And if we don't?" Caine challenges, which has me rolling my eyes.

"Then you can go turn yourself into the cops and take the blame so Max doesn't go to fucking prison."

"Just tell us what you want us to do," I tell her before Caine can piss her off anymore.

CHAPTER 18
ADAM

We don't have much time to execute Danner's plan. It's impressive how quickly she was able to come up with this and we probably should be a bit worried about that. But knowing Max has a friend like her brings an odd sense of comfort.

We have to be careful about how we do this. Danner insists that we don't have to worry about being seen leaving the house. Carson's body, however, we make sure to hide. Which is why he's shoved in the back and covered up. Max still cowers slightly in the back seat as we clear the gates.

We have to get a car from one of Max's parents' houses that they barely use, but Max said it should be pretty easy. Then, we're driving to the middle of nowhere, putting Carson in the front seat and setting it ablaze.

"I want to light the fire," Max states immediately once we've managed to get to the spot Danner picked.

"I think you've had enough fun," Drew tells her.

"I should get to have it all. This has been my battle. I want to finish it off and see it go up in flames."

"If that's what you want, baby girl," I agree easily. I know how important it is to cope, to feel in control of your life and to take it back if necessary. If this is what she needs, then she should get.

"I don't think I've ever found fire sexy, but you're going to turn me into a pyro, killer," Caine tells her.

"Make sure to wipe all the prints off," Danner says seriously.

I'm the one that drove the car here, and I made sure to not touch anything with my bare hands. Still, I wipe everything down anyway. We position Carson in the front seat, slumped over before dousing him and the car in gasoline to make sure it goes up quickly and thoroughly.

Danner has the matches, and she hands them to Max. "We can't stick around for long after you do this." We're in a remote area without anything for miles, so the remains of the car, and the dead man inside shouldn't be found for a while.

Max nods, grabbing the matches, taking in the scene in front of us while myself, Drew, and Caine lean against the fake caterer van.

"You got this," Danner encourages quietly.

I want to tell her the same, I want to hold her, and whisper to her how I'm feeling about everything, but I don't. I know she needs this. She needs to take her power back. She needs to be able to move on from this life once and for all.

While this may not solve everything, it's the first step for her. Knowing this particular demon won't be chasing after her from now on will hopefully bring her a sense of closure. Though, we all have other things to deal with and this won't fix everything, at least we can go home.

Max looks at the matches in her hands, then up at the car, seeming to be lost in her thoughts. We all stay silent, giving her this moment for herself.

After a few minutes, she opens the box, pulling out one of the wooden sticks before closing the box again. She twirls the unlit match between her fingers. She hasn't cleaned up yet, still in her blood-stained white dress, splatters of dried blood marring her perfect skin.

I want it off of her because it's from him. But she didn't want to take it off yet. Caine seems close to losing it, watching her like this. We're all desperate to have her now that she's back, but I don't want it to be too much all at once for her.

She said she's okay and that he didn't touch her, but something happened. Clearly, tonight—and even the past couple of weeks of being back here—have been more than difficult for her.

Max strikes the match against the box, lighting it and looking at the flame as it eats at the wooden stick in her hand before tossing it toward the car.

I've never seen flames erupt so quickly. They consume the car in just a matter of seconds, to a point that even if we wanted to stop it, we couldn't.

I step up behind Max, who's stayed completely still watching the fire grow bigger. I slide my hand onto her hip gently and then move it around to her stomach, pressing her back into me just barely. She moves easily, melting against me. Brushing my lips gently up against her ear I say, "We should go."

She nods, and lets me guide her back to the car. Drew pulls her into the backseat with him, and Caine ends up pushing his way back there as well, leaving Danner in the front seat while I drive us away.

I watch in the rearview mirror as Max rests her head on Drew's shoulder, but her eyes meet mine in the mirror. Now that the adrenaline has worn off, I see the exhaustion in her gaze. It's more than just being tired. It's like a weight she'd been carrying around has finally lifted and she's able to relax.

When we get back home, I want to make sure she's completely taken care of, even if there's more for us to worry about. She's safe and she will always be safe with us. I'm going to make sure of that. I'll spend the rest of my life showing her how loved she is and how safe she is with us if she lets us.

She's it for me. She was it for me the first day she walked into my gym. When her, Drew, and I fucked around at my house. When she trusted me to wrap my snake around her throat and do what I wanted to her body.

She's everything and always will be for me. I don't know how to tell her any of this, but maybe she can see it in my eyes right now because a small smile stretches across her face right before she closes her eyes and I feel like she knows exactly what I'm thinking.

CHAPTER 19
MAX

I want nothing more than to get out of here and never come back. I don't know what's going to happen tomorrow, next week, or even next month. What I do know is right now, I want to be done with this place, the people here, and any and all of the memories associated with it.

I'm sure my parents won't let up easily. I know this isn't over and that there's a very real chance that I could get caught for what I did to Carson. But right now, none of that matters. I only want to get away and go back home and live my life to the fullest until the cops drag me away in handcuffs.

It doesn't matter how much Danner reassures me that that won't happen, I don't fully believe her. I also am just now learning more about her. Like the fact that she's some sort of a private investigator who also has some pretty shady connections.

She also hasn't said it, but I think she may have killed someone before. She said she has help to "clean up" and that was all the information she would give me. We swung by a sketchy pay by the hour motel so I could clean the blood off my body and change.

We get on the first plane out, and as soon as we're seated, I rest my head on Adam's shoulder. Feeling settled and safe, I close my eyes and fall asleep for the entire plane ride.

※

IT TAKES a couple hours after we land to drive home to Seaside, but I fall asleep again in the car. It's like my body knows that I can finally relax and is letting me for the first time in weeks. Months, even, because before Carson kidnapped me, I was always looking over my shoulder. The guys helped me relax when I would fall asleep wrapped around any of them, but even then, the lingering fear was always in the back of my mind.

Right now, any lingering fear regarding Carson finding me and dragging me back to Texas is gone, so I can drift off easily all the way home.

I'm carried inside by a pair of strong arms and I nuzzle into the broad chest more, breathing in his familiar leather and ocean breeze scent. I've missed it so much.

I want to drown in the smell, to be completely consumed by it for the rest of my life. When I lay down, I reach for Drew, not wanting him to let go. "Come back."

He chuckles softly. "Go to sleep, little one. The guys and I are going to talk before coming to bed."

"No. Stay," I mumble, but I can already feel myself fading back into sleep.

He leans down, pressing a soft kiss to my lips. "I'll be here when you wake up." I fight to kiss him harder, but he lays me down, tucking the blankets in around me. "Rest, I'll be back."

I try to reach for him as he walks away, but he just gets further and further away and sleep pulls me under once again.

※

WHEN I WAKE UP, I'm overheated and I quickly realize it's from the bodies pressed against me. The hot, hard bodies that make me feel so many things I can't even put a name to. I sit up slightly, looking down at Adam. He's sleeping so peacefully, one arm folded behind his head while the other is resting on his perfectly sculpted abdomen.

I'm careful not to touch him, just raking my eyes over the tattooed skin, wondering what they mean. The snake on his throat reminds me of when he had Athena wrapped around mine.

I bring my fingers up to the spot where she was coiled around the base of my throat. Remembering the fear and just how turned on I was at the same time as she tightened even more, cutting off my oxygen while Adam played with my body, bringing so much pleasure that I couldn't see straight.

My eyes dip down to where the blanket is pooled around his hips, wanting to tug it down and release his cock so I can bury my face in his lap to wake him up.

Before I'm able to do that, or anything else, a voice snaps my attention up. "What're you doing baby girl?"

I look up to see Adam hasn't moved other than the fact that his eyes are open.

"Just looking at you," I tell him honestly, settling back down, facing him, still not touching, though I want to rest my hand on his chest and trace the muscles and ink.

"You look like you want to do more than just look," he comments.

I shrug, but then get bold when I ask, "Can I?"

He hesitates, and my shoulders drop slightly.

"Why?" My voice is soft.

He looks over my other shoulder at the sleeping Caine, and then to the other side of him to where Drew is sleeping.

"Come with me," he offers and I nod easily.

As carefully as possible, we sneak out of the large bed in Caine's house, and I'm not exactly sure why we ended up here but I'm glad we aren't at my house. I don't know how I'll feel stepping foot in there again, though I know I need to.

Adam leads us outside to the backyard, and I didn't notice the blanket he must have grabbed along the way until I sit on the bench, pulling my legs up to my chest, trying to stay warm from the chill in the air.

He wraps the soft fabric around my shoulders and I send up a thankful look to him when he sits down next to me. Neither of us say anything right away, but he does take my hand in his, wrapping our fingers together while I lean into him. I love how each of these men make me feel, and Adam is an expert at making me feel at peace.

"I struggle with being touched," he states, and I just listen, not wanting him to tell me more than he's comfortable with. But he continues. "I never knew my parents. I was raised in foster homes until I aged out."

I squeeze his hand tightly, silently encouraging him, but not wanting to ruin the moment.

"I don't think I was hugged until I was an adult." He pauses. "Even then I can count on one hand how many times I have been."

"Me too," I whisper softly, not wanting him to stop, but realizing that we have this messed up thing in common. I may not have grown up in foster homes, and unfortunately, I do know my parents. However, my home still lacked the love and comfort that his did as well.

"I think I just grew used to not being touched. I wanted to be in charge in any intimate situation, and that turned into removing the hands that would try and touch my chest. Tying them up, holding them down, and avoiding eye contact. Sex has always just been sex."

I nod, listening as he continues. "It's not that I don't want you to touch me. I do."

I squeeze his hand tighter. "I understand."

"We can try… We can work on it." He turns to look at me and I see the desperation in his gaze. "I want to be better for you."

My jaw drops slightly at his honesty, not expecting him to be this vulnerable with me.

"You already are," I tell him. "My life before I came here was awful, and you guys have already been better for me than anyone else in my life."

"You've changed our lives too, baby girl, and I don't think you understand just how much."

"Me too." I rest my head against him again, wanting the connection. Wanting to just feel close to him.

"We were never going to give up trying to find you," he whispers.

"I wasn't going to give up trying to get back to you guys either."

CHAPTER 20
CAINE

I wake up and find that Max isn't next to me anymore. I react quickly, jumping out of bed, needing to find her. I immediately worry that she's gone again. That she ran off or was taken. I need to see her. I need to keep my eyes on her at all times.

Racing out of the room, I look around until I see the flash of red hair outside sitting on the bench with Adam. I breathe out a sigh of relief, but also annoyance because she should be in bed with me right now, not outside with him.

I push the sliding glass door open and they both look back at me. The cold air hitting my bare chest doesn't even phase me.

"What're you doing?" I ask her.

"Talking," she answers, simply.

"Well, you should be in bed. With me."

"Come on, it's cold we should go inside anyway," Adam tells

her, standing up and I see their clasped hands as he pulls her up to follow. They walk past me, but I wrap my arm around Max's waist to pull her away from Adam and back into me.

"You've been away from me for too long, killer and I'm going to need a taste of your sweet pussy soon. I've missed it. And I know she's missed me too."

Her sharp intake of breath is all the answer I need, and I surge my hips against her, letting her feel my already hardening cock that's been dying for her.

"You wish," she sasses.

I chuckle darkly. "You can deny it all you want. Your body doesn't lie, but if you don't want to admit it that's fine. I know exactly how to get what I want. And you love it every time."

She turns her head slightly, bringing our faces close together. "And I know how to drive you crazy by fucking Drew or Adam in front of you. Maybe both, and you can't do a damn thing about it."

"Try it, killer. See what happens."

I let her go and she stumbles slightly, walking inside. I follow after her, and when we're back in my bed, I make sure to pull her against me tightly so she knows she's not getting away without me knowing again.

※

ADAM DOESN'T WANT to go to Uncaged in the morning, but Max insists that we all get back to our normal routine assuring us that she's really okay.

"I need to go see if I can get my job back." She sighs, like she just realized that was something she'll have to do.

"We talked to George, he'll take you back no problem," I explain.

"Or, you could come work at Uncaged," Adam offers easily.

"And do what? I'm not a coach."

"No, but you can help with admin tasks, I've needed someone working the front desk," he tells her, though I'm pretty sure it's a lie.

"I don't know, I like working at the bar. It's nice to get away from you guys sometimes." She smirks.

"Excuse me," Drew growls, grabbing her from behind and burying his face into her neck. "You're never getting away from us."

She chuckles, haphazardly trying to push him away.

"Well, you two have fun today. I'll make sure to keep Max entertained." I smirk at her.

"You're not training?" Adam asks in disbelief.

"Not today. I'm going to spend time with my girl and make sure she's doing okay." I look at her and the daggers she's glaring at me.

"Right." Adam looks at her. "Well guess I won't look at any fights for you anytime soon, then."

"Why?"

"If you're not going to train then you're not ready to get in the cage."

"Don't pull that bullshit with me," I snap. "I'm always ready to go and you know that."

"I can stay back today, too," Drew offers.

"No," I snap immediately and he narrows his eyes at me.

"I'm not sticking around just for you all to fight. I'm getting back to my life, and that starts with asking for my job back. So you guys can figure out your shit, on your own." Max waves us off, walking back toward my room. That's soon to be our room because she's not getting any distance from us, no matter what she thinks.

I narrow my eyes at Drew and Adam.

"Someone does need to stay with her," Adam agrees.

"Perfect, it'll be me." I nod.

"No, I think it should be me," Drew volunteers.

"Why?" I snap.

"Because Adam has classes covered, and you need to train." I see the subtle smirk on his face. He knows exactly what he's doing.

"That actually would make the most sense," Adam says easily.

Max comes out from the bedroom, wearing one of my T-shirts and sweatpants that are way too big on her. I'm not even sure how she has them staying up on her hips. But seeing her in my clothes makes me feral. I'm about to take her right here, right now.

"Which one of your motorcycles can I steal?" She smiles widely at me and I shake my head, remembering the night she showed up threatening to do just that. Though, the darkness that lingers over that memory is strong seeing as that was the beginning of the end before she was taken from us.

"You want to go to The Tavern and talk to George?" Drew clarifies.

Max nods in his direction.

"I'll take you. These two have things to do today." He gives me a sideways glance and I clench my fist.

"Sounds good, see you guys later." She walks to the front door, and I don't question the fact that she'll be trying to get her job back wearing clothes that are five times too big for her. If George denies her, it doesn't matter to us.

Drew follows after her without even looking back at us. Once they're outside I turn to Adam. "We will spar one time and if I win then you don't give me shit about skipping training."

He scoffs, "We'll see about that."

ADAM HAS me spar with Cal because I think he's worried about fighting me. It would be embarrassing to lose as the coach. Of course, I win the impromptu fight with Cal easily. Afterwards, I check my phone afterwards to make sure Drew hasn't said anything.

What I find is much worse and makes me feel like I'm going to need to get into the cage again. Or at least hit the bag for a bit.

There's a text from my dad, demanding that I call him. It's the last thing I want to do, but when I also see the one from my brother that has a screenshot of the news reporting Carson's death, I know there's going to be a problem.

I look up the news article myself to make sure Max isn't mentioned. When I see that all it says is that the investigation is ongoing, I breathe out a small sigh of relief. They won't find anything that leads the murder back to her, but unfortunately my family knows something is up.

"Fuck," I mumble to myself.

I dial my dad, pressing the phone to my ear, already irritated.

"Don't say anything other than yes or no," he says immediately and I know what he's asking without him saying it. *Did I do it?*

I don't say anything.

"Goddammit, Caine," he grumbles. "We aren't talking about this on the phone. Come home."

"No," I state firmly.

"If you don't, then I'm coming there."

"Don't bother."

"I'm not getting you out of fucking prison if you end up caught."

"Good." I hang up; I don't want his help anyway. No matter what happens, we're going to figure it out.

CHAPTER 21
MAX

George gave me a funny look, but still let me have my job back without any argument. As soon as we're outside of The Tavern I turn toward Drew. "Which one of you talked to him?"

"Adam," he answers easily.

"I knew it." I shake my head, though I'm secretly happy about it. I look toward the ocean before glancing back at Drew once again. "Can we go to the beach?"

"Of course, little one. We can do whatever you want." He smiles and I can't help but do the same.

We walk to the promenade and down to the sand where I immediately take off my shoes, sinking my feet into the cool, damp ground. The sense of comfort from coming back here is overwhelming as I walk closer to the water.

For the first time, the weight of everything washes over me. Everything I've been through, everything I did and how I ended up back here. I collapse into the sand, hugging my legs to my chest as I look out over the water. I hardly even notice when Drew sits by me because I'm so lost in my own head.

Carson is dead. I'm away from my family, but I know I'm not completely safe. I can still get caught, and can still be sent to prison. I'm sure the only thing that's stopping my parents from turning me in is what that would do to their own image.

I don't even notice the tears streaming down my cheeks until Drew's finger wipes them before pulling me into his lap. "What's wrong?"

I shake my head, not looking at him because I don't like that I'm crying, or that I'm feeling anything other than relief right now.

"Baby, look at me," he encourages and the softness in his voice only makes the tears course down my cheeks even faster. Especially when my eyes meet his. "You're safe now."

I nod, unable to speak because I'm worried if I try, it'll just come out as a sob and I'm already mad at myself for crying.

"We're here for you, no matter what happens. We won't let anything happen to you ever again," he reassures, swiping his thumbs across my cheeks and I melt into him.

"I don't even know why I'm crying." I shake my head, willing the tears to stop.

"It doesn't matter why. It's okay and I'll hold you right here as long as you need."

His words have me burying my face into his neck while the

tears continue to pour down my face, but I don't want him to see. The fact that he's being so sweet to me when I know how savage he *can* be only makes me cry harder. My emotions have been a wreck when it comes to these men anyway and right now it all feels amplified.

Like I'm standing on the edge of a cliff, resisting the urge to dive off head first because of the pain it could cause. But I'm about to be pushed, and there's no going back because they have me and I feel like it's too late.

After the tears finally stop, and I feel like I can look at Drew without crying again, I do just that. "Let's go to Uncaged," I tell him.

"You sure that's what you want to do?" He wipes the remnants of tears from my cheeks as I nod.

"Yeah, I want to kick someone's ass," I attempt to joke.

"How about Caine? I think he deserves it."

I chuckle as we get up and as we walk back to the promenade, I grab his hand, intertwining our fingers like Adam and I did earlier this morning. There's something about having that connection, something as innocent as holding hands that grounds me,. With the way he squeezes my hand back, I feel like he needs it too.

§

WE GET TO THE GYM, and I'm immediately scooped up into Caine's arms. I don't even have time to process what's happening as he holds onto me.

"Knew you couldn't resist being away from me, killer."

"I figured you needed some motivation to train a little harder." I shove at his shoulder as he sets me down.

"You know what really would give me motivation?" He leans down to whisper, "watching you take my dick in your tight little pussy again."

I let out a soft gasp at his words, my thighs clenching together. I can't deny I've missed them. Especially the way they know what my body needs more than I do. I want it again. I feel like it's a piece of normalcy that I'm missing and I want it back.

But I also want them to work for it.

And I want to tease the fuck out of them.

I've lacked control in my own life for so long, and being back with Carson only brought that all back. I just want to feel normal again, and one of the ways I want to do that is to prove to them —and myself—just how in control I am.

And when I *let* them do what they want with me, it'll be because I'm still in control and it's what I want.

Adam comes over and I smile up at him. The feeling of having the three of them all together surrounding me makes me feel so safe, like nothing can ever hurt me again.

"Did you get your job back?" Adam asks.

"Yeah, but I think you had something to do with it." I raise my eyebrow at him.

"I didn't. I told George you'd be back, that's all."

"We always knew you'd be back," Caine says, wrapping an arm around my middle and hugging me from behind.

"Now that I am, who wants to do some training? I think I'm a little out of practice."

They all volunteer easily and I chuckle. Despite the happiness, I hate the feeling that's still lingering at the back of my mind that this is all temporary and that it'll be ripped away from me once again.

※

After training at the gym, I insist that I need to get clothes from my place because I can't keep drowning in theirs.

"You could wear nothing," Caine suggests, and I roll my eyes so hard they may fall out.

"I'll grab your things, and bring them to my house," Adam says.

"I just want to get my own stuff," I practically whine, wanting to get some semblance of independence again.

"We'll go together another time. I just don't want it to be too much for you," Adam comforts and I relax a bit, knowing he's right.

"I'll take you to Adam's," Drew chimes in.

"No, you got to have her all day. I'll take her," Caine insists.

"I'm not being fought over like a fucking toy by you three. I'll go with who I want, where I want, when I want. Got it?" I snap.

They all nod with varying levels of approval at my outburst.

"Great, let's go," I announce, pointing to Caine, "I'll ride with you."

Without waiting for them, I walk outside and directly to Caine's bike, pulling on the helmet while they join me. Once I'm plastered to his back with my arms wrapped around his middle, the ache between my thighs intensifies. Especially when I rub myself against his back.

Even the vibration from the bike has me feeling the wetness starting to dampen my underwear. I know it's not going to be much longer before I'm jumping one of them, or all of them, again.

CHAPTER 22
ADAM

After I grab clothes from Max's house, I head back to my place and find everyone waiting. I'm surprised when I don't see Max when I walk in, but since Caine isn't losing his shit, I figure that she's here somewhere.

"Where is she?" I ask, looking at Drew who's on the couch watching a hockey game and then to Caine who's doing pull ups on one of my door frames.

"Taking a nap, she needs the rest," Drew says easily.

"I tried to take one with her, but she told me no." Caine drops down, stretching out his arms.

"You listened?" I ask, in disbelief.

"Not exactly."

"She managed to get him out of the room and then locked the door." Drew chuckles. I'm just glad he didn't decide to break down my bedroom door.

"Well, I'm going to set this stuff somewhere," I tell them, walking back toward the bedrooms, and I plan to put it in the guest room, but decide to check my room anyway, and find that she unlocked the door. Sneaky girl.

I push inside quietly, locking the door behind me so the other two don't come barging in. Setting her clothes on top of my dresser, I look over at her sleeping form. So perfect, so peaceful. For the first time I understand the appeal to Drew. Why he likes to fuck her while she sleeps. Right now, I'm fighting the urge not to do that myself.

I prefer the chase, I always have. Giving them the opportunity to get away, though it's not what either of us want. The primal need taking over my body as I chase them, hold them down and fuck them.

Especially with Max. It was better than it's ever been with her. The way her body took mine. The way she fully accepted everything that happened in the forest that day. And every time after that. We've all been without her for too long. The longer I stand here staring at her, the more the need to take her consumes me.

But I want her awake for it. I want to look in her eyes as I slide inside her for the first time. I don't hesitate any longer, climbing onto the bed, over her, not being careful as I straddle her hips. She immediately wakes up, thrashing her arms, and I pin them above her head instantly.

Her chest heaves with heavy breaths while she gasps, "What're you doing?"

"I need you, baby girl," I grit out using my free hand to work the oversized sweatpants down her legs.

She lifts up slightly to help me. "You can have me, *daddy*."

"Oh fuck," I groan, my cock already painfully hard and dying to get inside her, especially with her calling me that, which isn't something I've ever been into before now. "You going to keep quiet for me? Or are you going to scream so Drew and Caine can hear how badly you want daddy's dick?"

"*Yes*," she moans, thrusting her hips up slightly, like she's silently begging for me to hurry up.

"Keep your arms up here, got it?"

She nods, but I see the hint of defiance in her eyes. Especially as I climb off her body to stand on the side of the bed, pulling my shirt off first, making sure she keeps her arms above her head where I put them.

Her breath catches when my bare chest is exposed, and I can't help the pull of my lips at her reaction. She squirms slightly, but keeps her arms where they're supposed to be like the good girl I know she can be for me.

I unbutton my pants, but don't pull them off yet, letting them hang on my hips as I peel off Max's clothes so she's completely exposed to me.

"What would you do if I ran?" she asks with a mischievous glint in her eyes.

"Want to find out?"

She shifts slightly and I notice the way her bare thighs press together. How she pushes up her chest, like she wants her perky little nipples touched. And they will be. I want to worship every inch of her body but I don't know how long we have until one of the other guys decides to come looking for us. I assume not long.

"Kinda," she teases.

I raise my eyebrow at her, seeing if she's going to do it. I hope she does, but instead she settles back against the bed, and spreads her thighs for me. I'm greeted by the most beautiful sight as I kneel between them, not moving my eyes from her dripping cunt before me.

Pushing her thighs apart, I make room for myself to settle there, lowering myself onto the bed, bringing my face up close to the only place I want to be for the rest of my fucking life.

"You going to keep your hands up there, while I devour this pretty pussy, baby girl?" I practically growl while my mouth waters, kneading the skin on her thighs.

"Yes," she whimpers.

I blow a breath onto her wet center before dragging my tongue up her entire slit. "Yes what?"

"Yes, daddy," she moans and it's all it takes for me to dive into her, eating her like she's about to be my last meal.

I kiss, lick, and suck every inch of her cunt, gathering as much of her taste on my tongue as I possibly can while holding her down and she cries out in pleasure. I thought she may stay quiet, but I know it's only a matter of time before the guys start pounding on the door because our girl likes to make noise.

I toss her legs over my shoulder, holding her thighs tighter while I bury my tongue into her pussy, lapping up all her sweetness while she writhes and moans.

"Adam, fuck it feels so good. *Please*," she cries and I feel her thighs start to shake as I bring a hand to her center, pressing the tip of my finger into her. She arches against me, and I sink the finger in deeper while I suction my mouth around her clit and suck hard.

Max screams, and that seems to be the final straw for the guys, because a moment later they're pounding on the door.

"What the fuck!" Caine calls out, and I double my efforts to get Max to come on my tongue.

"Give it to be, baby girl. Let them hear how bad you need my mouth on your pussy. Make them wish it was theirs." I press another finger into her while flicking her clit with my tongue before pulling it into my mouth and moaning.

"Adam—*daddy*—fuck!" she cries, dropping her hands to the top of my head and yanking my hair roughly, pulling me harder against her. I fuck her with my fingers while my mouth focuses on her clit and when she tightens around my hand, I know she's almost there.

Especially as her cries get louder, and her grip on my hair gets tighter. Caine and Drew continue to pound on the door, but I don't pay attention to them. All I care about is making her see fucking God.

When she finally tightens around me so hard I almost lose circulation in my fingers, I bury my face against her, willingly suffocating myself as she screams out her release. My mouth is flooded with her sweetness.

I barely give her a chance to recover from her orgasm before I'm lifting her up into my arms, wrapping her legs around my waist and pressing her against the door. On the other side, the other two continue to pound and tell me how pissed they are to be stuck out there.

"I'm going to fuck you against this door so they can hear how badly you want my cock and not be able to do a damn thing about it," I tell her loud enough for them to hear.

"Open the fucking door," Caine calls out.

"After her pussy is filled with my cum," I call back with a smirk on my face.

Max attacks my mouth with her own, moaning and rubbing herself against me. I can't help but give it back to her. Pushing my pants down enough to free my dick, I line up at her entrance and push in without any more teasing because I need to feel her warmth envelop me completely.

We both moan, and I know they hear it.

"This is so fucked up," Drew says from the other side of the door.

"But it feels so…" I pull out to thrust in again. "Fucking." *Thrust.* "Good."

Max moans into my mouth, her tongue tangling with mine as I plunge deeper into her. The sound of our hips slapping together mingles with our moans for them to listen to while I push her against the door.

"Please, more," Max cries, her head thumping back against the wood as she arches against me.

I grip her hips roughly, slamming into her so hard that she's hitting the door with every brutal thrust. And with the way she moans and grips onto me, digging her nails into my skin, I know she loves it.

"You going to come for me again?" I grit against her neck, grazing my teeth over her pulse point there.

"Yes."

"Good. I want them to know what they're missing. They wish it was their cocks buried in your tight little cunt. Filling you with their cum."

"Mm, but it's not them," she taunts. "It's you."

"Yeah, it is me," I accentuate my point with another powerful thrust. "And you're going to scream out *my* name, so they don't forget it."

As I pound into her harder, I can feel her orgasm building again, her inner walls tightening around me as her nails dig into my skin. Her cries of pleasure increase until she's doing what I told her to and screaming my name while she soaks my cock.

I'm not able to hold on any longer, losing my rhythm and fucking into her until my own release consumes me. I grip her hips tight enough to bruise as I hold myself as deep as I can go inside while spurts of my cum coat her insides.

When we come down a voice says, "You better come out here, we aren't done with you."

CHAPTER 23

MAX

"Up to you, baby girl. You want to let them in or torture them a bit more?" Adam smirks, and I smile at the fact that he's giving me the choice.

I wiggle slightly so he sets me down onto my feet. The massive difference in our heights becomes evident as I'm planted back on the ground, looking up at him, "Let's let them have a little fun too."

Turning toward the door, I unlock it slowly before pulling it open, revealing the two very impatient men on the other side. Caine looks like he's about to lose it, the veins popping in his neck while he heaves heavy breaths. Drew doesn't look far off either, his eyes trail down my naked body before flaring with hunger and meeting mine.

"Now you've done it, killer," Caine says ominously before rushing forward, grabbing me with a strong arm around my middle and picking me up, walking back further into the room.

I glance over Caine's shoulder to see Drew storming in after us right before I'm thrown onto the bed. I try to scramble away, but Caine stops me by pinning my wrists down by my head.

I can't see what's happening, but I feel my thighs being pushed apart and a warm breath on my soaked core.

Caine moves to straddle my chest, holding my arms down with his knees, hovering above me. "You thought you could just fuck our coach and get away with it?"

"Yeah, I di—" I'm cut off when a mouth is on my pussy, licking and sucking immediately. Suddenly, I don't even remember what I was going to say.

Caine looks behind him, before back at me. "Seems like Drew couldn't wait to get his mouth on your desperate little cunt again."

"Thank God," I moan, trying to thrust up against Drew's mouth.

"I think your mouth needs something to do, and you're going to take it like the needy little slut you are, aren't you?"

"I don't, I—*ah*, " I moan when Drew spears his tongue, pushing it inside me.

"How's she taste?" I barely register Adam asking.

"Tastes fucking delicious, especially after fucking you."

I notice Caine has moved off me, just enough to shed his pants and climb back over me so I'm face to face with his rock hard erection.

"Open up," he demands, right as Drew does some magic with his tongue that has me crying out and Caine uses it to his advantage to shove his dick in my mouth.

He's not gentle, but with him I don't want it to be. I struggle to take him as he thrusts into my mouth like he would fuck my pussy and it's almost too much, but also not enough at the same time.

The way Drew is eating me out only adds to the moment, and I struggle to breathe around Caine's brutal thrusts. Tears stream down my face, and I don't even notice Adam has come closer until he's speaking right by my ear, "Do you know how beautiful you look with Drew's face buried in your pussy while you choke on Caine's cock?"

I mumble something about Caine, but I know they don't even know what I'm saying because I don't either. I'm lost in the sensations at both ends of my body. I'm being used for Caine's pleasure, but it only adds to my own. I don't even feel like I'm completely present, I'm just feeling.

"That's fucking right, killer, you missed this didn't you?" Caine groans above me, shoving himself deeper into my throat as I gag and struggle, but he doesn't let up.

It's like the harder he fucks my throat the more Drew fucks me with his mouth, and both sensations have me seeing stars.

"Gonna come and you're going to take it all down this pretty throat," Caine growls, grabbing the hair at the top of my head, fisting it roughly while he fucks my face even harder.

I feel my own orgasm approaching and when Drew shoves his fingers inside me, I go off, crying out around Caine at the same time spurts of his cum fill my throat. I feel like I'm having an out of body experience as my orgasm takes over and I try not to choke on Caine's cum as I swallow everything I can.

By the time he pulls himself from my mouth I feel boneless and spent. I try to lift my arms, but they've gone numb, and I don't think I can lift even a finger.

I'm scooped up, and I don't even fight it. Not that I could, even if I wanted to. My head falls onto Adam's bare shoulder and he murmurs, "you did so good for us, baby girl."

Adam sets me on the bathroom counter, carefully cleaning me up, the softness is such a contrast to how he is all other times. The way he takes the warm wet washcloth to my face, wiping the tears, drool, and cum away. Then between my legs, softly cleaning me before carrying me back into the bedroom.

I think I'm asleep before he even lays me onto the bed.

※

My first shift after being back is exactly what I needed. No one, including David or George, have treated me like I'm sensitive or fragile. To them, it's like nothing has changed. And while I'm happy to be back with my guys, I can tell they're all walking on eggshells with me a little more than they used to.

I'm about to tempt them back into the forest just so they can see that I'm fine and chase me down to fuck me again.

The Tavern has a steady crowd tonight and when I notice Danner slide up to an empty seat at the bar, I beeline it over to her, narrowing my eyes when I lean over the bar in front of her.

"You have a lot of explaining to do," I tell her.

She smirks. "I don't know what you're talking about, but I will happily take a dirty Shirley."

"Mhm, you're not getting out of this."

"If you can get away for another slumber party, then maybe I'll give you some answers."

"Will you?" I raise my eyebrow at her.

"Probably not, but you can try to get me drunk and see if that works."

I chuckle, handing over the mixed drink. "I could just do that here."

"No, it won't work here, I'm smart enough to avoid talking about any of *that* in public." She winks.

I'm about to give her more shit about this, because she's been hiding her entire life from me and I'm nosy. I get distracted by someone else flagging me down for another drink and I turn to her with a pointed look. "We aren't done."

Her laughter follows me as I walk away.

As the night goes on, I get more comfortable like everything is completely back to normal. When I see the guys from Uncaged walk in, I scowl in their direction while pouring a beer for someone.

Alexander and Cal slide up to Danner almost immediately

and she brushes them off, finishing her drink, pushing cash onto the bar-top before waving to me.

Caine, Drew, and Adam sit at their usual table on the other end of the room, and are all looking at me. I roll my eyes, trying not to pay too much attention to them. It's hard to avoid the pull they have over me, but I know they aren't here because they wanted to grab some drinks.

They want to keep an eye on me. It may be because they're concerned about my safety. And yes, that could be considered sweet. But I'm fine and I want to move on and for them to believe I'm fine too without hovering over me all the time.

"Want me to help them?" David asks from my side when he notices my scowl at the three large men.

"No, I got it." I shake my head because I know if he tries they'll just send him back over here demanding for me anyway.

I walk up to the table, placing my hands on my hips and looking at each of them. Caine is reclined slightly, his legs spread while he looks at me like he wants to eat me. Drew's smirking while his eyes gaze over my body. Adam is sitting casually, but slightly on guard like he always is. It's a way that I know comes from trauma of never being able to relax.

"You guys realize I'm fine here, right?" I tell them.

"We just want to check in, and get some drinks." Drew smiles.

I roll my eyes. "No you don't."

Adam's eyes move over to the front door and I watch him

steel his spine. It makes me instantly uneasy even without seeing who just walked in. But the voice is somewhat familiar when he speaks.

"You boys causing more trouble tonight?"

I turn to see that officer that seems to have an issue with everyone striding toward their table. Though, he has a healing black eye and a split lip that has me curious who caused it.

"Nope," Adam answers easily.

"Can I get you anything, Officer?" I ask, trying to pull attention away from the guys.

"Can't drink while on duty, miss."

"Oh, well then you'll need to leave. We don't accept loiterers around here."

He looks at the table we're standing in front of. The empty table.

"You kicking these three out too, then?"

"I was in the middle of taking their order when you interrupted."

He grunts, looking at them again, narrowing his eyes before turning to leave.

"I have a feeling there's something I should know," I tell the three of them after he's gone.

Caine smirks. "Don't worry about it too much, killer."

I'm worried about the fact that everyone seems to be hiding something from me when they know everything about me there is to know. Including the darkest secret I now have to keep.

"Well, like I told him, we don't accept loiterers. So either order or get out," I demand, frustrated that everyone in my life seems to have some sort of secret. I'm going to need them all to start spilling because I'm not living in the dark any longer.

CHAPTER 24
CAINE

Max was pissed we showed up to her work, but I don't give a fuck. If she thought I was going to leave her to close this place without us, she's insane. Especially with Officer Doogie still sniffing around.

I don't trust anyone anymore. I hardly did before, and even now Drew and Adam are only somewhat trustworthy to me. If it came down to it, I would throw them in front of traffic to save Max. I would throw myself in front of traffic to save her too.

"You guys have to leave, we're closing," Max tells us with her hands on her hips and daggers in her eyes. She's got that look that makes me hard for her already.

Even though I'm practically always hard for her anyway.

"Yeah, you guys leave," I say without looking at the other two.

"*All of you.*"

I stand up, crowding her, but she doesn't back down and it makes my chest tighten with that same strange feeling again. The one I'm unfamiliar with, but when it comes to her I don't shy away from it. I want to show her how I'm feeling at all times. Too bad I don't know how to do that with words.

"We'll be waiting right outside because we're not leaving you alone and you know it."

She looks around me at the other two. "I want to increase my training so that you guys will eventually be able to trust that I can take care of myself."

"You got it, baby girl." Adam chuckles.

Drew sidles up to her, wrapping an arm around her waist, pulling her into him. He tilts her head up to press his lips against her mouth roughly. I clench my fist fighting the urge to push them apart and the only reason I don't is because I know she wants this.

She wants us to share. She wants all of us, even if it fucking kills me because I want to keep her all to myself.

"We'll be outside waiting for you," Drew says after breaking their mouths apart.

He and Adam walk to the front door, and I grab her for a rough kiss of my own. When she gasps against my mouth, I take advantage of it. Shoving my tongue in, she makes a little squeak that makes me grip her even harder and pull her into me so she can feel the hardness in my pants against her stomach.

She pushes against my chest and I let her break us apart.

Only because the sooner she gets out of here the sooner I can have her underneath me for the night.

While we're standing by our motorcycles waiting for Max to finish up, my phone goes off in my pocket, and I pull it out to see a text from my dad that has me scowling. When I open it, it's even worse.

> Dad: Where are you? I'm at the house I pay for.

He's here? Fuck.

> Caine: Leave.

> Dad: We need to talk first.

> Caine: It's the middle of the night, we aren't talking now.

> Dad: First thing in the morning.

"Fuck," I groan, shoving my phone in my pocket. I wanted Max to come to my house tonight, but that's not going to happen with my dad there. Because of course he probably jumped on a flight to Portland at the end of his work day and drove all the way here just to catch me off guard.

"What?" Adam asks and I just shake my head.

"Something to deal with tomorrow."

The longer I stand here waiting for Max to be done for the night, the more I fume about the texts from my dad. I can't wait for her to be done and come home. I need her now.

"Head back, guys, I got her," I tell them. I'm met with annoyed and skeptical stares. "You don't trust me?"

Still, they stare at me, and I scowl. Adam finally nods. "Fine, we'll wait for you to bring her to my house."

I nod, Drew still hesitates slightly, but finally he relents. "I get to take her home next time."

I don't say anything, and just let him think I agree to that. When they leave, I look back toward The Tavern thinking about getting in, and fucking her over the bar. Or I could try to catch her around the side when she takes the garbage out back. Looking between the buildings there's a tiny alleyway that's barely big enough for one person to walk through at a time that leads to the back where the dumpster is.

Since I know my girl, I know that's the last thing she does before leaving. I head back there, and wait since she should be back here any minute. I wait next to the door, my foot kicked up behind me against the old wooden wall that probably should be replaced. The salty air of the coast is unforgiving on buildings, but gives them all a rustic look.

After only a couple minutes, the door opens, and I grab her quickly, pushing her up against the building as she gasps, dropping the large bag of garbage. I clasp my hand over her mouth to muffle any scream she was going to let out.

Dropping my forehead against hers, keeping my hand against her mouth tightly, I say, "I couldn't wait for you any longer. You going to let me fuck you back here like a good little slut?"

She mumbles something against my hand, and shakes her head.

"What was that, killer? Was that a yes?"

She shakes her head again with another mumble.

"I heard, 'please Caine, my pussy is begging for you already.'" I taunt. "I should find out how true that is." I reach into her pants, and she doesn't try to stop me; instead she raises her hands up to fist the fabric of my shirt because as much as she wants to deny me, she always wants me just as badly as I want her.

As soon as my fingers graze the wet fabric covering her pussy, I let out a guttural groan. "You still going to try to deny me when you're already this wet for me?"

Her eyes widen, but she moans into my hand the second I pull the soaked fabric aside and push a finger into her soaking wet heat. "Yeah, killer, you can't make me believe that you don't want me when you feel like this."

I rub my thumb on her bundle of nerves while pumping my finger slowly. "I'm going to let go of your mouth. You're not going to scream, you're going to jut this little ass out for me so I can bend you over and fill you with my dick. Got it?"

I see the glimmer in her eye that lets me know she's going to fight me, and my cock twitches in my pants even more for it. I want her to hit me, dig her nails into me. Do anything to distract me enough and make sure the only thing I can focus on is her.

Because she's everything to me. She's the one thing in my life aside from fighting that I live for. Even if I had to choose between her and fighting, it would be her. It would always be her.

I remove my hand from her mouth, immediately turning her around and pushing her into the wall. She catches herself quickly so she doesn't face plant into the wood. She resists slightly, a weak attempt to fight me off. I rip her pants and panties down off her ass and she squeaks as the cold air hits her bare skin.

Covering her with my body, I free my dick from the confines of my pants and press against her, but not pushing in yet.

"Tell me you want me to fuck you, killer. Beg for it."

She turns her head slightly, giving me a mischievous grin. "Why would I do that when you fuck me so much harder when I say no."

I groan, knowing she's right. I love proving to her how much she wants me, even when she fights it. Which is why I kick her legs apart as far as they can go while still having her pants around her knees. I press my hand between her shoulder blades pushing her to bend over further as I angle myself at her entrance.

"Last chance to beg," I tell her.

"I'll never beg for you," she sasses, and I huff out a small laugh before grabbing her hips and slamming into her roughly. She cries out, and I hold myself still, buried deep inside her gloriously hot and wet pussy as it constricts around me.

"Fuck, you may not beg me but the way your hot little pussy squeezes me tells me all I need to know. So scream out 'no', tell me to stop, but we both know this is exactly what you want."

Before she's able to say anything else I pull out so just the tip is inside her, then push forward roughly, and she drops her head with a loud moan.

"That's right, fucking take it," I growl against her hair while holding her hips tight enough to bruise and fuck her hard enough she's going to feel me for days.

It doesn't take long until her cries get louder and she starts to pulse around me. I know my girl and what it's like when she's about to come. Just the thought of her reaching her peak has mine approaching right away.

"Come for me, baby," I demand, not sure if she even hears me or if I actually say it out loud, but she does.

Her hands grapple with something to hold onto as she clenches around me, crying out her release. The feeling of her tightening around me has my own orgasm consuming me as I cover her back, pushing in as deep as possible and coming hard enough I swear I black out for a second.

We both come down, and I pull out of her, watching the way my cum seeps from her pussy. I need to claim her in every single way, which is why I swipe it up and push it back into her. She turns her head into her arm and moans.

I pull up her pants and crowd her against the wall. "Finish up, I'm not done with you."

I leave her behind the building, knowing she'll listen because I know how badly she's going to want more. Always so greedy for more. And I'll always give it to her. My perfect girl who was made for me can get anything she wants from me.

After we get to Adam's, I get lost in my woman again, though as the night gets closer to the morning my mind isn't fully able to shake the thoughts of what will be waiting for me when I face my dad.

I get out of bed, kiss Max's forehead, and head out, careful not to wake her so I can deal with my dad and come back. Then I can give her all my attention.

I'm not quiet when I enter my house, not giving a fuck if I wake him up, wherever he decided to sleep. But of course, he's already awake and in one of his suits, sitting at the dining table with his laptop open in front of him.

But that's not all. My brother's here too, and I'm immediately defensive having to deal with both of them.

"What the fuck is going on?" I snap.

"I told you we need to talk and it wasn't going to be over the phone," my dad states.

"So you both decide to just show up here and what? Ask if I murdered that guy?" I come right out with it because that's what this is about and I want to get back to Max.

"Well, did you?" my brother, Bradley, asks with a little too much glee in his tone.

I raise my eyebrow at him, but don't answer.

"Goddammit, Caine, I can only get you out of so much shit. Murder, especially of someone like Carson Bradford, is *not* something I can easily work with."

"Good thing I didn't ask for your help then."

"They want someone in prison for this, and if you didn't do it, do you know who did?" my brother asks.

Again, I just look at him.

"What about your girl?" he goads.

"What about her?" I react, and I see the side of his lip quirk up, enjoying that he finally said something that got a rise out of me.

"She was engaged to him before," my dad states. I don't acknowledge him and remain quiet once again, clenching my fists and stopping myself from punching my brother in the face or throwing him through a wall. We're similar height, but he doesn't work out like I do and he sure as shit doesn't fight.

"It looks suspicious that he is dead right before they were supposed to get married…again," my dad stares at me, and I give nothing away as I look back at him. "Caine, if you know anything that can help us get ahead of this, you need to tell us now."

"Then stay out of it. Unless the cops are sniffing around and think something is up, then there's no point in giving them anything," I say, coldly.

"They've questioned her parents and they're claiming Carson was killed and their daughter was kidnapped," my brother explains. I smirk at that being the story those slimy fuckers are spinning.

Yeah, I would've kidnapped her and held her somewhere

secure so I could make her my personal fuck toy for the rest of our lives, but I like her fight. I like her enjoyment and I like that she wants to be shared which is something I would've never expected.

"Well, she's not kidnapped and she would explain that to anyone who asks." I shrug.

"Yet, there's still a dead man."

"Why the fuck are you here?" I ask again. "It seems like you want for me to have been involved. Maybe then you could have a clean break if I did, right? I go to prison and then I'm not your problem anymore. So fuck off and let me deal with it on my own."

"You sure that's what you want?" My dad closes his laptop, folding his hands on top of it.

"I want to live my life without you constantly on me about everything."

"If that's what you want, then the money stops. No trust fund. No house. Nothing. I'll cut you off and let you figure it out all on your own."

Though I knew it was only a matter of time, it's a little sooner than I was hoping for. Yet the only thing I can think to say is, "Fine."

CHAPTER 25
DREW

When we all woke up Caine was gone and none of us knew where he went. I'm a little surprised that he was willing to leave Max, which makes me believe it was something bad. I don't know what exactly it could be, but the fact that he willingly left her alone, especially with us, is a cause for concern.

Max looked around, and seemed confused as well, but didn't say anything about it.

"I want to train today," she states firmly after a sip of her coffee.

"We can train whenever you want, little one. I'll always work with you." I wink at her.

"I know you all are always willing to give my body a workout, but I want to actually train today."

"If he won't take it seriously, you know I will, baby girl."

She smirks, bringing her mug up to her lips. "Thanks, daddy."

Adam groans. "Well not if you say that. If I'm training you, we're going back to Coach only."

She hums around the drink. "Thanks, *Coach.*"

"Never mind. You aren't allowed to say anything." He shakes his head and Max just laughs.

I slide up next to her, wrapping an arm around her shoulder, pulling her into me. "I think you made daddy upset."

She smiles, looking up at me. "Think I'm going to get in trouble? Coach daddy going to punish me?"

"I think if you keep being a bad girl, he'll have to."

"Well, not all of us can be a good boy like you."

I growl, nuzzling into her neck and sinking my teeth into her skin and she squeals trying to push me away.

"You two are both going to get punished, and I'm not talking about the way you probably want. I'll make your training so miserable you can't do anything fun for a week," Adam threatens, and I don't know why but my dick starts to harden in my shorts at the thought of him punishing us both.

"Call me a good boy again and I'll add to your punishment, little one," I say only to Max, and I see the way her cheeks flush, and she tries to hide the way her thighs clamp together slightly.

She takes another sip from her mug instead of saying anything else.

"If you two are done being brats and actually want to go to the gym today, then get ready and let's go."

"You heard him. Be a *good girl* and go get ready to go," I taunt, and she scowls at me, but takes another gulp from her mug before setting it down and going toward the bedroom.

I can't help but watch her as she goes, loving the way she glides as she walks. I know it's from being a dancer a majority of her life. The natural flow she has in all aspects of her life is so enticing. When she walks, when she trains, when she dances. When she fucks.

She's just perfect and the fact that she's ours is a miracle in itself. We've all done some shitty things in our lives, but somehow still managed to claim her. Even if we don't deserve her, we've stolen her for ourselves and we won't be giving her back.

Though, she's no angel either. That only makes her even more perfect in my eyes.

※

AT THE GYM, we do some warm ups together before running through some of the moves she perfected...*before*. She needs a little help, but she's smart and strong and picks it up again quickly.

I start to teach her a new choke when Caine walks in, somehow looking even more pissed off than usual. He looks around until his eyes land on Max, who's currently on the floor with me. He heads straight toward us, his gaze not straying from her. Not even when he pulls her up from the floor, and despite her protests, slams his mouth onto hers.

She struggles for a second, working hard to push him away before giving in. I just watch the way she melts against him as he invades her mouth. I let it go for several seconds before I get annoyed that he interrupted.

I clear my throat dramatically. "Save some for the rest of us," I joke.

"Fuck off." Caine hardly parts from her lips, but she's pushing him away again.

"You all get to have a turn with me," Max taunts.

"No. I get the whole thing," Caine groans, kissing along her neck, and she slaps at him, though he doesn't move.

"Knock it off," Max demands. "Or I'm going to practice the new choke Drew was teaching me on you."

Caine moans, burying his head against her. "Oh please do that, killer. I'd love nothing more than for you to choke me."

She scoffs, but it turns into a chuckle.

"This doesn't look like training and I know if you're at my gym, then that's what you're doing," Adam's voice calls out, and I smirk without looking back at him.

"You both can get in trouble; I was trying to do what I'm supposed to." I shrug.

"Yeah, because you're a *good boy*." Max looks pointedly at me.

I jump up and grab her out of Caine's arms and prepare for a takedown, but she manages to stop me, and I appreciate her effort. I half expect Caine to interrupt our impromptu sparring, but he doesn't. I move slowly so Max is able to get some practice in, but I don't let her win.

After a couple minutes, I manage to submit her and she lets out a frustrated groan when she taps.

"Not fair," she declares.

"One day you'll beat me, little one."

She scoffs.

"Probably won't ever beat me, killer. But I'll let you take over my body whenever you'd like," Caine teases and she rolls her eyes.

"Who's sticking around for classes?" Adam asks, and I look at the time, noticing the first one is in about fifteen minutes, realizing I truly lost track of time.

"I don't think I have a choice," I shrug.

"I am," Max chimes in.

"I think Alexander wanted to spar with me." Caine shrugs.

"Okay, no fucking around then. We're here to work. Play time can be at home."

I wrap an arm around Max. "I intend to have *lots* of play time with you later."

I feel the way she shivers against me, and I smile.

"Let's go," Adam announces.

Though it's the last thing I want to do, I part from Max and get focused for the remainder of the day. For some reason I can't help but notice something is up with Caine. It feels like more than his usual shit but I know he's not one to talk about it, and I feel like Max senses it too.

If anyone is going to get something out of him, it's going to be her.

CHAPTER 26
MAX

Caine won't admit that there's something wrong, but I can see it. He's not as closed off as he wants to believe he is. I may not be able to read him like a book, but I can see through his bull shit. He wasn't there when I woke up this morning, and Drew and Adam didn't know where he was either.

He showed up at Uncaged tense and kissed me like his life depends on it. Which isn't unusual, but I could see something swimming in his eyes. Almost like worry.

After class, I change into my work clothes at the gym before heading to The Tavern for my shift. As I'm walking in my name is called, and I look up to see that asshole, Officer Doogie. I stop at the door, squaring my shoulders. "Can I help you?"

"Dunno, maybe. Just heard some news about a murder, out east a bit. Where'd you say you're from again?"

"I didn't."

"Well from what I heard you used to know the victim."

"If I did, I don't care to know them now. I left for a reason."

"Hm, heard you were engaged to him."

I don't say anything, just glare at him, waiting for him to continue.

"You don't seem to be concerned about him being the victim of a murder."

"Like I said, I left for a reason. Is there something I can help you with or are you just reporting news to me?"

He narrows his eyes at me. "Just checking in. If you happen to hear anything, you report it to me."

I wait until he's walking away before I mumble, "I won't." Then, heading inside, I let out a breath of relief. I shake the memories of that night from my head when they start to surface. I don't want to remember being in that house. I don't want to remember his hands on me. I don't want to remember what it felt like to shove the sharp end of the iron poker into his body.

I just want to move on and past it so I can live my life without worry. So I square my shoulders and shake all the thoughts of the last couple weeks from my mind as I get ready for work. As soon as The Tavern opens, I lose myself in the drinks and customers. I'm even able to distract myself from the guys for a little while, even though I know they'll be waiting for me as soon as I leave.

ONCE I'M DONE with work, and we all get back to Adam's, I'm a little surprised they don't immediately try to jump my bones. Though, I'm thankful for the slight reprieve because I need to shower the bar stink off of me and they let me go into the bathroom alone.

I'm in the shower and I close my eyes, rinsing the shampoo from my hair. Suddenly, I feel the cool air hit me from the door opening, and I squint to see who it is.

Caine steps in, my eyes dropping down to his cock which is already pointed straight up toward me, but I close my eyes again to stop the burn while I rinse out the rest of the soap.

"What're you doing?" I ask when he hasn't even touched me yet.

"Just looking at you." His deep voice is even deeper than normal, and when I open my eyes again I see the primal heat there as he looks at my naked body. "I loved watching you when you didn't know it. When you'd be sleeping in your bed. When you'd touch yourself."

I let out a small gasp. "You asshole."

He crowds me against the shower wall. "You liked it too. I've been obsessed with you since the moment I first saw you. And you've enjoyed every second of my obsession."

"You're delusional," I argue weakly.

He drags his fingertips up the inside of my thighs, and I find myself parting them slightly. When he reaches my center, I know I'm already wet for him and I bite back a moan.

"Yeah, I'm delusional. But you're already soaked for me, just like you have been every time I touch you."

"Nope," I deny.

He shoves one of his thick fingers into me so hard I gasp. "You're a liar, killer. I've had a shitty fucking day, so I need you to come on my hand to make it better."

I open my mouth to ask why his day was so shitty, but then he pulls his finger out before shoving it in again, rubbing my inner walls while his palm hits my clit. I moan at the sensation, reaching out to latch onto his arms to stop myself from falling as my knees wobble.

"Yeah, dig your nails into me while I make this needy pussy cry for me."

"Shit," I gasp, thrusting my hips harder into his hand.

"That's fucking right, killer. Fuck yourself on my fingers." He pulls out again, shoving two digits back in and white spots dance across my vision at the intrusion. The stretch that feels so good, but also the pain from being sore from all the attention they've been giving me.

"Caine, oh my fuck," I cry, pushing myself harder against him. He pushes me into the wall, never slowing the pace of his hand but the cold tile has me trying to push away from it.

He doesn't let me; his hard, hot body pressing completely against mine while he continues the brutal way his fingers are fucking me.

"You're going to come and then I know how desperate you're going to be for a cock to fill this tight little hole."

I nod, no point in denying how badly I want more.

"And what about this tight little hole too?" he asks, bringing his other hand around to my ass, pressing in between my cheeks and I buck against him. "You want to be completely filled up?"

"Oh God, *yes*," I moan, the thought of taking more than one of them again has my orgasm dancing just out of reach.

They've been mostly delicate with me, taking their turns fucking me, but I want more again. I want to feel so full of them. I want to reach my limit and then beg for even more.

"Fuck, killer, do you know how much you mean to me that I'm willing to share you?" he groans, his hips starting to thrust along with his fingers. "I will give you anything you want even if I would rather cut their hands off then let them touch you. I do it for you."

"Caine, I can't—" I moan, digging my nails into his skin even harder as my orgasm starts to take over.

I scream out as the release consumes me. Caine has to hold up my body so I don't fall onto the hard shower floor. He continues to work me through the ecstasy until I come down, even though I still feel unsteady, and he doesn't let me go.

"So fucking pretty. You see what you do to me?" He grabs my hand, wrapping it around his length. The need between my thighs is back again, despite the Earth shattering orgasm I just had.

I look up to his bright blue eyes that flare with even more heat as I pump my fist over him once, squeezing the head. He groans, closing his hand over mine to stop me from doing it again.

"Keep that up, and I'm not going to be able to make it out there without fucking you. So if you want that, then continue. If you want me to share you then you need to leave the shower."

I smirk, wanting to test and tease him, but I also want to be shared more than I can even express right now. So I remove my hand from around him, turn the water off, and say, "Let's go."

CHAPTER 27
ADAM

Max comes out of my room wearing only a towel, and Caine isn't far behind her, barely covering himself with one of his own. I'm checking on Athena, but quickly get distracted by all the bare wet skin of Max's body I can see. Knowing the only thing that stands between my mouth and her is the towel that would take one tug to get rid of has the need surging through my blood.

I'm not paying attention to Caine, but I can feel him watching me as I approach Max, tracing my finger along the edge of the towel wrapped around her chest without taking it off yet.

"What're you doing, baby girl?"

"I want something," she breathes out.

"What's that?"

"All of you." She looks past me toward Drew who I know is also staring at her, hanging onto her every word. "I want you all to fuck me."

I raise my eyebrow at her, wanting her to say even more.

"Please. Fuck me."

I hope she's saying what I think she is, and I pull at her towel slightly to reveal her completely naked body to all of us. She doesn't move to cover herself. Her pink nipples are hard, making my mouth water. My hands itch to grab her tits and squeeze them, kiss them, lick them. Fuck them.

I'm hesitant to assume that I know what she's fully asking for right now. So I run my fingertips along her cheek, pushing her wet hair back behind her ear, searching her eyes. I want to make sure she's okay after everything that happened before we push her too far.

But the way she's looking at me tells me she's ready. Her green/golden eyes are wide open, and confident. She doesn't need to say anything for me to understand what she wants. That she's ready for more. We sure as shit are going to give it to her.

I lean down, grazing my lips along her neck, and up to her ear. "Take Caine into the bedroom. Straddle his lap and rub your pretty pussy all over him while you wait for us." I take her earlobe into my mouth, nipping it before I continue, "I'm going to feel your ass tonight, baby girl."

Her breath hitches, and I turn her toward Caine. "Go," I tell her, nudging her forward slightly and she goes easily, walking past him toward the bedroom.

Caine follows immediately, just like I figured he would. I turn toward Drew who's been watching from the couch. He stands up with a question in his gaze before he speaks it. "You think this is a good idea?"

"I think she knows what's best for herself and she knows we're able to give it to her."

Drew nods and then follows me as I walk toward my bedroom. The sight that greets me once we're in there is exactly what I wanted. Max's naked body on top of Caine's. His grip tight on her hair, kissing her thoroughly while she grinds her pussy along his cock.

I grip my dick in my pants, adjusting while I watch. Drew lets out a low grunt next to me while I assume he does the same.

"Get undressed," I tell him as I'm already starting to shed my own clothes. Tossing them onto the floor without taking my eyes off what's happening in front of me.

I hear him doing what I said as I step up to the side of the bed. Max looks over at me while Caine continues to kiss down her neck and onto her chest, pulling one of her nipples into his mouth roughly. She lets out a moan while swiveling her hips over him.

"Ride his dick, baby girl."

She lifts up, pressing her hands to his chest, forcing his mouth to part from her nipple, which results in a displeased sound from him. But once she takes him into her hand, and angles her center over him he grabs her hips, trying to thrust up into her already, but she has the control in this position. As much as he wants to have it, it's all hers.

"You're torturing him." I smirk.

"Good, he deserves it." She rubs the head of his cock through her folds and he lets out a pained grunt, thrusting his hips up to try and push his way into her.

She moans as she rubs him over her clit, then moves him back to her entrance, positioning his dick perfectly for her to sink down easily.

They both groan as he enters her, but I can't take my eyes off her face. Watching her reaction as she stretches around him. It's the most beautiful sight I've ever seen. She's absolutely perfect like this and I could watch forever, but my cock is rock hard and dying to feel her ass.

So I don't waste any time climbing onto the bed behind her, pushing between her shoulder blades so her chest is flat against Caine's. I reach into my nightstand to grab the lube that's there. I pour it between her cheeks and when it drips down Caine grunts, thrusting up into her roughly.

"Fuck," he groans.

"You better be able to hang on," I tell him and he glares at me over her shoulder.

"Fuck you," he sneers.

I coat my finger in the lube, teasing and massaging Max's tight hole, ignoring Caine's quip. I push the tip in slightly and she moans, pushing herself further onto Caine, but I continue to rub my palm over her ass cheek, kneading and massaging so she'll relax.

"You wanted this, baby girl. You're going to take it," I tell her, pushing my finger a little deeper into her ass. Just then I feel Drew behind me, wrapping his hand around my cock and I thrust into his hold while continuing to prep Max.

It's all so much. Feeling and connecting, yet not enough as Caine continues his shallow thrusts into her. I push another finger in while Drew pumps his hand over my dick, groaning at the sensation.

I doubt it's been enough prep for her, but I'm going to explode if I don't get inside her soon. I coat myself in more of the lube before handing it back to Drew, locking eyes with him, silently telling him what I want.

I feel him behind me, doing what I did to Max, pouring the lube, and I think he coats himself as I line myself at Max's back entrance. Caine slows his movements as I lean over Max.

"You ready for us both, baby girl?" I ask.

She nods. "Where's Drew?"

"Don't worry about him." I start to push into her slowly, feeling her tighten around me as she tenses. "Relax for me. Once I'm inside your perfect little ass then Drew can fuck *me.*"

She gasps at my comment, just like I thought she would, and she relaxes enough for me to push past that first ring of muscle. She's so tight, and the way she clamps down around me has white spots dancing in my vision and I have to breathe to make sure I don't blow too soon.

"You have to let me in. You're already so tight, but especially with Caine buried in your pussy. I need you to relax."

"It's so much already," she gasps, rocking herself onto Caine. "So full."

"I'm barely in, baby. You have to let me."

She moans as I push in farther, gripping her hips tightly and fighting off the need to come right fucking now. I knead her ass, pushing her harder down onto Caine. When I feel her relax just the slightest bit, I push all the way in so my hips are flush to her ass.

Max cries out, and Caine groans under her, all our sounds of pleasure mixing together while we're encased in warmth and so much tightness it should be impossible. Drew doesn't waste any time behind me, pushing his lube covered tip to my ass and I know he's not going to work to prep me as much as he should, but we're both too eager to care.

I should stop him, but I know how it feels to have his pierced dick pushing into me, and to have that sensation happen while I'm balls deep inside Max's tight ass is going to be the best feeling I've ever experienced in my life, I already know it.

So I don't argue as he starts to push in. Caine starts thrusting up into Max's pussy and I'm barely able to stay still while Drew works himself inside me. I groan, feeling a fraction of what Max is with being so full. She clamps down around my cock and I see stars.

"Oh fuck," I groan, Drew's piercings rubbing me as he pushes in fully.

"Fuck, that feels good," he moans behind me, and I don't even bother to shove his hands off my hips where he's got them anchored. I just focus on everything I'm feeling. Being buried inside Max while I start to thrust in time with Caine so she can feel us both moving.

Drew matches the pace and soon we're all moving as one, and it feels fucking incredible. The room is filled with moans, groans, and curses while we all move and sweat, finding our pleasure within each other.

I've never felt this close to anyone before. The fact that it's with three other people is overwhelming, but in the best way.

"Need to feel you come for me again, killer," Caine grits out, his thrusts becoming harsher and I can feel every move he makes.

I feel the way Max starts to rub herself against him, meeting our thrusts. Her moans get louder as she gets closer, teetering on that edge between pain and pleasure.

"Fuck, so full. I want, *please*. Oh *fuck*," she cries, not making any sense, but honestly I can hardly focus on anything other than holding off my orgasm.

She tightens around me, coming with a scream, and Caine starts to fuck up into her roughly, which makes me hold onto her hips tighter while trying to maintain a steady pace so she can ride out the rest of her orgasm before I blow.

The way Drew's fucking my ass, hitting my prostate, groaning as he fucks me while Max tightens and screams…it's all too much and I'm unable to hold back any longer. Filling her ass with a groan that mixes with Caine's when I think he finds his release as well. We both fill Max completely as she's collapses onto Caine's chest, pinned between us and writhing against the sensations, her fists gripping the sheets.

Drew's hands tighten on my hips and I fight the urge to remove them again. Before I can, he's pushing in completely, dropping his head between my shoulder blades and groaning as he finds his release well.

We're all breathing heavily, and somehow I don't even feel claustrophobic, even though I should being trapped between two bodies. That would have had me pushing away quickly before, but somehow I'm comfortable between them.

Drew separates himself from my body first, and I feel empty without him there. I pull out of Max, as she stays collapsed on Caine, but I can see the cum dripping from both her holes and it has my cock surging with need again.

Max manages to roll off Caine and onto her back on the bed. I know she needs to be cleaned up, aftercare is always important to me, but I can see the look of satisfaction written all over her face and I just want to lay with her.

Suddenly, Drew is handing me a warm wet washcloth, and I look at him as he nods in Max's direction. I'm thankful he understands what she needs. I clean her up, and I feel his tentative touch behind me as he uses another one to wipe away his cum as well.

The moment is almost too much without any of us saying anything, but it also doesn't feel like there's anything that could be said. That stays true even as we all collapse into the bed together. I wouldn't know what to say even if I wanted to. There are too many emotions I've never felt before and they scare me. Somehow there's a sense of comfort as well as I fall into a rare, deep sleep.

CHAPTER 28
MAX

This is the second time I've woken up to Caine not in bed, and it throws me off because he would usually be the last one to leave before. I know something's wrong, and he mentioned how shitty his day was while we were in the shower, but then distracted me so well I wasn't able to follow up with him.

Now that he's not here again, I want to see if he's somewhere else in Adam's house, or if he left again.

I can't deny that if he left I'll be disappointed. Because it doesn't matter that I claim not to like his obsession with me, the reality is that I do. He knows it, and I know it, even though I'll never admit it. I've slowly become obsessed with all three of them.

I leave the bedroom, and don't see Caine when I go out to the living room. The house is silent, I start to think he really did leave until I check the garage and see him punching the heavy bag that Adam has set up.

I lean against the doorframe watching him, waiting for him to notice me. As he continues to throw measured punches, I appreciate the muscles that cover his bare torso. They bulge even more with each hit, and I appreciate the physique of the man in front of me.

"I know you're watching," he says without breaking his pace.

"Do you have a problem with that?"

He finishes his set, using his teeth to undo the Velcro wraps on his hands. I've seen him do it before a couple times at the gym. That, plus him flicking his weight lifting belt off are the hottest things I've ever witnessed.

"No, but you should be sleeping," he says, stepping closer to me.

"So should you."

"I was."

He tosses the wraps to the side, and tries to crowd me, but I don't move. "Something's wrong," I state, because it's not a question with how he's been acting.

He clenches his jaw but doesn't bother denying it.

I place my hand on his chest, feeling him flex under my touch as I trace a path to the defined muscles on his abdomen. "Tell me." He doesn't say anything, and when I look up at him I can see the internal battle. I run my nails along his stomach, stopping at his waistband. "Please?"

He sighs, his eyes not leaving mine. "I don't like talking about this shit."

"I know."

"I'll handle it."

"I know."

"You don't need to worry."

"I know."

He clenches his jaw; I watch the muscles in it tick as he does. With an annoyed sigh, he takes my hand in his, pulling me into the living room and sitting on the couch, pulling me onto his lap so my back is to his chest. He bands his arm around my chest, and I wiggle around, but he tightens his grip.

"Stop moving or I'll fuck you like this instead of telling you anything."

I stop instantly. He grunts like he's displeased, but I want to hear anything he'll tell me about what's going on.

"My dad showed up with my brother." His deep voice is even lower. My jaw drops and I try to turn around.

"Wha—" He grips me harder to cut me off and stop me from moving.

"They heard about your asshole ex, and wondered if I had anything to do with it."

"You didn't," I state firmly. It doesn't matter how involved he, Drew, Adam, and Danner made themselves. Technically if it came down to it, I'm the one that killed him and I would never snitch on any of them.

He huffs before continuing, "They only cared about protecting their precious reputation. It has nothing to do with me and I told him to fuck off. So he cut me off."

"Wait." I fight his hold, really wanting to look back at him, but he keeps me with my back to him. "What do you mean he cut you off?"

He hesitates before continuing again, "I had use of my trust fund before. My parents hated me coming out here and pursuing fighting, but I don't give a fuck. I was never going to become a lawyer like my dad. I was just biding my time until I made it and wouldn't need them anymore."

It's quiet and I'm not really sure what to say. Finally, I decide on, "Are you okay?"

"Yeah, I don't give a shit. I don't need his money."

I nod, understanding in so many ways. I don't need my family's money either. It's never worth it when you're so unhappy. You shouldn't have to have a relationship with your family just because you share blood. If someone makes you miserable then they don't deserve to be in your life.

I understand that more than anyone.

"What are you going to do?" I ask.

"I have to find a cheaper place to live. The house is in his name and I want to get out before he kicks me out."

I bite my bottom lip to stop myself from offering something I probably shouldn't. Not that they've even let me go back to my house, but maybe if Caine was living there it would make them—and me—feel better.

I'm not sure I can even handle living there, but I don't want Carson to ruin yet another thing in my life. I used to love dancing, but he ruined it with the way he demanded it, forced me in more ways than one.

I just want to live with as much freedom as possible, so I open my mouth and say, "You should just move your stuff into my house."

He chuckles. "How'd you know that was my plan all along, killer."

I roll my eyes, even though he can't see it. "Take the cameras out of there first."

"No way, not after what happened."

"Does that mean I can go back?"

"If I'm with you, then yeah. I don't know how Adam or Drew are going to feel about it, but if you want to, then it should be up to you anyway."

I'm a little surprised to hear him say that. Neither of us say anything, and we just sit here with him holding me. Eventually, I sink into his embrace so it's less like I'm being held hostage. He ends up laying us on the couch, keeping his arms around me and I don't even notice when I drift off to sleep again.

Too bad my sleep is anything from peaceful as I'm plagued with the nightmares again. This time it's about the moment I took Carson's life, like it's on repeat over and over in my mind. If Caine's dad heard about it and was sniffing around and that creep Officer Doogie was as well, word is getting out. I'm worried it's only a matter of time before it's tied back to me in some way.

Which is why I need to enjoy the time of freedom I have left.

CHAPTER 29
DREW

"I'm going to sleep over at Danner's house," Max says the next morning after we found her and Caine sleeping on the couch.

"Are you asking for permission, little one?" I tease.

"No, I'm telling you. Because I know you'd all freak out on me if I tried to do it without letting you know," she accompanies her sassy comment with an eye roll.

"Lucky for you, we trust Danner," Adam tells her with a kiss on her cheek.

"Even if you didn't, I'd just tell you too bad." She raises an eyebrow in his direction. I can tell by the look on his face that her defiance makes him want to do something about it. That makes two of us, but we don't have enough time this morning since we have to go to the gym.

"I'm skipping training today. Gotta move my shit into Max's place," Caine announces immediately.

"Hold the fuck on, what?" I shake my head, sure I didn't hear him right.

He just shrugs with a smug look on his face.

"Explain," Adam demands and I see the defiance on Caine's face, knowing he doesn't want to tell us anything.

"I can just ask Max, she'll tell me. Even if she doesn't want to. I can be *very* convincing." I raise an eyebrow in her direction.

"Then ask her, she can tell you that she asked me to move in," Caine says easily.

"Why the fuck would she do that?" I'm taken aback. "You sure you aren't just forcing your way into her place so you have another excuse to stalk her?"

"Ask her," he says again, nodding in her direction before grabbing his shit to leave.

"I plan to," I declare as he is leaving. Then I turn toward her. "You going to explain that?"

She finishes the gulp of the coffee she must have gotten as we argued and just rolls her eyes. "He needs a place, I stupidly offered. Don't make me feel like I made more of a mistake. I'm already second guessing myself."

"Pretty sure he's trying to play you, baby girl," Adam tells her.

"Guess I'll find out. I'm going to go to the beach before heading to Danners."

"Alone?" I question.

"Yes, *alone*. I'll be okay. I have good trainers." She winks.

"You have the best, and I want to up your training," Adam states.

"Yes, *daddy*." She rolls her eyes. It shouldn't get my dick hard to hear her call him that, but it does and I think about hearing her scream it while he fucked her on the other side of the door from where Caine and I were standing.

"Careful," he warns and the deep timbre of his voice has me adjusting my half mast cock at their interaction.

She blows a kiss in our direction and I watch her hips sway as she leaves the house. I turn toward Adam, "We're just trusting her going alone?"

I'm still hesitant for her to be without any of us. Carson may be dead but her parents aren't and Officer Doogie seems to have his sights set on her. Until we can take care of him for good I don't trust her being alone.

"No, Danner will keep an eye on her." He pulls his phone out, I'm sure he's about to text her. I don't need to question it because after what she already did with us I know we can trust her with our girl. "Let's go."

I shake my head at his bossiness. One of these days I'll push him on it, but that will only be when Max is with us and can be a part of whatever punishment he wants to dole out. I know one day we will push him far enough to make it happen.

THE CLASS I'm teaching is going well, though I wish Max was here for it. Especially when Karissa calls my name and I inwardly groan before turning to face her, keeping my face blank while she pushes her tits out.

"I need your help," she whines.

"That's what your sparring partner is for," I say blankly, referring to the skinny guy she paired up with and I know he's practiced with Max before.

"But I don't know if I'm doing it right." The way her tone makes her sound like she's throwing a fit has me wanting to go shove my head through a wall having to listen to her.

"Then show me," I gesture. She takes a step toward me and I hold my hand up stopping her. "On your partner."

"I want to try it with someone who knows what they're doing," she pouts. She's actually pouting, and I don't know why she thinks any of this is attractive, but it isn't at all. Even before Max came into our lives, I was never interested in her despite all her attempts.

Even now it shows how desperate she is.

"I'm coaching, and I'm telling you to show me. With your partner. Who knows what she's doing." I fold my arms across my chest just waiting.

She makes a scoffing noise before turning toward her partner and gives a very half assed attempt at the choke they're supposed to be practicing. Once her partner taps, I shake my head.

"Maybe if you actually put some effort in instead of trying to get my attention, you'd be better. Keep trying."

I move onto another pair in the room without giving Karissa another ounce of attention and count the minutes for this class to be over.

I half expect Karissa to try and talk to me after class, but she doesn't. Instead, she seeks out Adam who just came out of his office, and I watch the way she tries to catch his attention with whatever she's saying. Especially with her hip cocked and looking up at him.

I can only see his face, and he looks completely unfazed and just as annoyed as me. He ends up saying something short, but she doesn't walk away yet. He shakes his head, and looks even more annoyed when I turn to clean up the mats to prepare for the next class.

After I turn back around she's gone and I walk over to Adam. "She decide to try and coax you for some extra training?"

He grunts. "Yeah. Said she wasn't really doing well in the group setting."

"Bet she's not," I scoff. "Have you heard anything from Danner?"

"Yeah, she's with Max. She's okay."

The relief that comes over me is instant, and even though I didn't feel it, the tension in my shoulders lessens. Though now I know she's going to be with Danner all night I'm irrationally annoyed. I want her in bed with me—with us—and with my cock buried deep inside her all night.

Preferably while she's sleeping. I know she liked when I did that before. I think about sinking into her warmth while she's sleeping, and just staying there. Letting her tight wet heat hug my dick in her body while we both sleep.

Fuck, that thought has me even harder than I was this morning before we came here. Now I'm expected to go without her for a night. I might be tempted to just show up to Danner's anyway.

Before, I would have probably tried getting into her house and taking what I want from my girl. But now knowing that Danner is involved in some shit that none of us really even know about? I'm sure her place is like a fortress, and I don't really want to deal with pissing her off.

Once Max is back home, she's going to regret leaving us alone for the night, because I know we're going to be showing her exactly what happens when we're desperate for her. Again.

CHAPTER 30
MAX

Danner found me at the beach and I know the guys sent her. It makes me want to show up at Uncaged and scream at them for being so overbearing. There's also a part of me that enjoys how protective they are because it's different than anything I've ever experienced before.

Them being protective isn't about control. It's genuinely because they care and just have a unique way of showing it. I don't argue with Danner, when she claims she didn't know I was here.

We end up back at her house, and after ordering pizza, I decide to bother her for some answers.

"So, are you going to tell me what you do and why you're so mysterious?" I raise an eyebrow at her. "Who are you? *What* are you?"

She chuckles, grabbing another piece of pizza, sitting on the couch next to me and kicking her feet up.

"I wouldn't say I'm mysterious. I just don't put my business out there."

"Me either, and yet you were able to find out a lot of things in order to find me." I give her a pointed look.

"I wouldn't say I'm a private investigator per se, but technically I guess that's what you could call me," she takes another bite of her pizza.

"And the whole hiding a body thing…"

"You're too curious." She smiles.

"I thought we were friends."

"We are. If we weren't, you wouldn't be here. I don't let anyone into my house."

"Oh, so have Alexander and Cal been here?" I ask, knowing her reaction every time they come up.

"Don't start with me," she deadpans. I can't help but laugh. "Especially when you have Caine, Drew, and Adam literally ripping apart everything they come across for you. You should've seen them when you were gone."

I don't know why her saying that makes my heart swoop in my chest. It probably shouldn't. I should probably be worried that I left one prison just to find another one, but I know I didn't. Rationally, I know that's not how this is. But knowing how badly they wanted me to come back here, to come home makes me melt.

It also makes me wish I was with them tonight, but I shake

that away because I'm here with my friend. While I'm still learning how to be a friend, I don't want to fuck it up by ditching her to go be with my boyfriend...s?

Are they my boyfriends?

Before I'm able to spiral anymore, I distract myself by trying to pry into Danner's life a little more.

"Then you should know I won't judge if you tell me the truth about you three."

"Good thing there's nothing to tell." She finishes the slice of pizza and I continue to keep my eyes narrowed at her, knowing she's in denial. I've seen how they are around her. I have also seen her not give them the time of day, but that doesn't mean anything.

I mean look at me. I didn't want anything to do with Caine, Drew, or Adam, yet they've forced their way into my life and I can't go back. Not that I want to.

"Let's watch a shitty cheesy movie," she announces. I know it's a diversion tactic, but I go along with it anyway.

I haven't seen many movies in my life, so I give in because I'm curious what shitty, cheesy one she wants to watch and what it's like.

After she picks something with a badly photoshopped cover on it from a streaming service, my phone goes off. I keep forgetting that I have one again. The only people who have the number are the guys and Danner, so I rarely need it since one of them is usually around.

I take a peek at the text I just got and shake my head, fighting the smile that wants to appear.

> Caine: All moved into our place, killer. The only thing missing here is you sitting on my dick.

Instead of replying, I put my phone away to focus on the movie. Though, it's really obvious only five minutes in that she wasn't kidding about how cheesy it is. Or awful. Still, I find myself laughing right along with her at the ridiculousness of it all.

My phone goes off again and I expect it to be Caine saying something else about how he wants to fuck me. I'm not surprised that's almost exactly what I see, but it's not from Caine.

> Drew: You should be here. Sleeping in my bed so I could slide inside your perfect little pussy while you're passed out and make you come for me while you're still dreaming.

I squeeze my thighs together thinking about the scenario he's described. The way these men have showed me that my dark fantasies were what I've always needed is something I can never come back from. Being chased in the forest, the primal need coming out for all of us. The way it feels to wake up with a cock already inside me and fucking me. The way I can fight, and say no, but we all know I really want it.

It's everything I've always needed. I just needed it from them.

I should put my phone away and focus on the movie, but it's so ridiculous and they've already created this ache between my thighs just from two messages, so I decide to have a little fun.

I open the group chat and text all three of them.

> Max: Sounds like you guys miss me. Too bad I'm having a great time without you. Might need to be away from you all more.

Caine: Don't you dare, killer, or I won't let you leave the house.

Adam: None of us would hold you captive, but you know you miss us too.

Drew: Was it my text that gave it away? I'll admit it, yeah I want you here, little one.

Caine: If you're going to Drew, you're coming home first.

Adam: Ignore them and enjoy your night with your friend, baby girl.

> Max: Yes, daddy *wink emoji*

Because I really want to fuck with them, I turn my phone off as soon as my text sends and I enjoy the movie.

※

I WAKE up the next morning feeling like I got punched in the gut and I already know why before I open my eyes. Crawling off the couch I make my way into the bathroom, immediately searching for a tampon, and luckily I find one. The worst part about getting my period right now isn't even that these underwear are now ruined. It's that I can't have the sexy fun time with my guys I was hoping for after I get off work later.

Now I realize that I'm going to have to work while I'm this miserable, and I let out a groan. My cramps are always the worst for the first two days and I know I'm about to suffer in silence. I can't afford to call out since I need the money, badly. I want to just be miserable in bed with a heating pad and some shitty food.

Danner is in the kitchen and I try to hide the way I'm hunching over after I exit the bathroom. Though, I clearly don't do a very good job because the second she sees me the smile she had on her face drops.

"What's wrong?"

I wave her off, taking a seat, and wincing slightly as the change in position sends a sharp cramp through my belly.

"Are you good?" she asks.

"Oh yeah, I'm fine." I wince again when another sharp pain shoots through me and she clearly notices. "I started my period, that's all."

"Oh shit. Do you need anything?"

"I already stole a tampon, but I think I'm going to head home and curl up with a heating pad until I have to go to work tonight."

"Let me know if you need me to bring you anything," she offers while I'm struggling to stand up again as the pain migrates more into my lower back.

"I think I'll be okay," I tell her, trying to convince myself more than her.

I try not to think about it too much as I drive back to the house I haven't stepped foot in since I've been back. I don't want to text the guys and interrupt whatever they have going on today. They've put their lives on hold enough for me.

When I pull up to my house, I see Caine's bike outside and realize I almost forgot that he's staying here now. It's weird when I walk in seeing him shirtless and cooking breakfast in my kitchen, only wearing sweatpants that hang low on his hips. His large sculpted body is on full display and right now, he doesn't look like the giant intimidating fighter I've come to know.

Right now he just looks like a normal guy. A really hot, normal guy.

He notices me enter and gives me a smirk. "Hey killer, welcome home."

I break our eye contact because this all feels so domestic and weird to have him here like this. When I turn, I notice that my entire place is cleaned up. There isn't broken furniture everywhere, and it doesn't even look like anything ever happened here. It all just looks *normal*.

When I look back at Caine, he's just leaning against the counter with his arms folded as he stares at me. I open my mouth to say something, but I'm unable to make the words come out. My jaw snaps shut and I shake my head instead.

"I'm going to lay down." I keep my eyes down as I walk to my bedroom, and even in here, it's clean other than the bed that was clearly slept in.

I don't have the energy to question it when I should have expected it anyway. Once I'm laying down, I'm annoyed with myself because I didn't grab the damn heating pad. In fact, I don't even know where it is.

It's fine, I don't need it. Turning over, I shut my eyes to try and go to sleep. I'm almost there when the ache in my lower stomach shoots through me and I have to bite back a groan at the pain my body is putting me through.

I feel the bed dip behind me and I don't question it, but when I feel the heat of the warm body behind me I subtly scoot toward it, wanting more. Especially when he places his hand on my lower stomach. I melt into his touch, and it may not be a heating pad, but it's close enough.

The warmth surrounding me is almost enough to have me falling asleep, until I feel his hand start to move lower and he dips into my waistband. My eyes shoot open as I snatch his wrist, stopping him.

"What're you doing?" I squeeze his wrist tightly to make sure he doesn't continue.

"Touching my girl because she decided to keep her pussy away from me all night," he practically growls.

"Yeah, well said pussy is out of commission so remove your hand before I break it."

He doesn't move his hand, and thrusts his hips against my ass, and I can already feel how hard he is behind me. "You know what threatening does to me, killer."

"Then you might want to take care of it yourself because I'm in too much pain to deal with you."

Clearly, that was the wrong thing to say because immediately he's rolling me onto my back, and hovering over my body. "Why are you in pain?"

"Take one guess."

He looks genuinely confused and I want to laugh, until he asks, "Did someone hurt you?" I realize he really doesn't understand what's going on. This psychotic man of mine isn't familiar with a woman on her period, and it makes me want to laugh even harder.

"No, no one hurt me but myself. I'm on my period, Caine." I roll my eyes.

Understanding dawns on him, and instead of him getting off of me and acting disgusted, he drops his hips against mine and I squeak at the sudden pressure that doesn't make my pain any worse, but creates a different ache and has me spreading my legs slightly for him to settle in between.

"You think I don't want to touch you while you're on your period? That I'm afraid of a little blood?" he taunts.

"You probably should be."

"Well, I'm not. Do you know how hard I was seeing you with blood on you after you killed that piece of shit?" His voice is low and I suck in a gasp as he mentions my crime. The ache intensifies though and I may be more fucked up that I thought. "I'd love nothing more than to see my dick covered in your blood after I fuck you good enough that you come so hard it makes your cramps go away."

I suck my bottom lip between my teeth because I've heard

orgasms help, but it's not like Carson was ever able to give me one, and he wouldn't have even thought about touching me while I was on my period. Though it's not like I ever wanted him to anyway.

"That's…gross," I breathe out, not really believing it myself because the more I think about it, the more appeal the idea has. The sick part of me is coming out to play, just like that day in the woods.

Or the way my orgasm crashed through me when I opened my eyes to find Drew fucking me while I was asleep.

Or when Athena was wrapped around my neck and my pussy flooded for Adam.

"You like it," Caine growls. "You want it too, don't you? Want to claim me for yourself. Claim me, killer, I want it."

"I've never—" I shake my head, unable to finish my sentence. It seems ridiculous to say, and really there's no point. I can deny that I want this all day, but it's a lie and we both know it. Plus, it doesn't matter if I say no, because he prefers if I do.

"Never had this pretty little pussy fucked while on your period? Never claimed a man with your blood covering his dick?" He scoots down my body, pulling my pants as he goes, and I don't even try to stop him. "Good. I want to be the first. The only. Just like you were my first and will be my only kiss."

That comment has me shooting to my elbows to look down at him. "What?"

"Mhmm," he hums, pulling my pants off completely, bringing him face to face with the new underwear I had to pull on before I left. "You heard me, killer. Never kissed anyone before you, and never will."

My mouth gapes as I stare at him, laying between my legs, all the pain forgotten. Everything else around me is gone. His confession tilts me on my axis for some reason, and all the emotions that I've been trying to suppress…about him, this situation, Drew and Adam as well, it all floods in.

I have nothing to say. Nothing can even come close to describe the rush I'm feeling throughout my entire body. So, instead of attempting to say anything I reach for him, grabbing his face in my hands and pulling him up to crash our mouths together.

His first kiss.

His only kiss.

Me.

Our lips move together as he takes and I give. This time, instead of him forcing it from me, I give willingly. I give myself to him with the way our tongues tangle. I don't think I could speak right now but even if I could, the way he's kissing me is stealing all the words from my mouth.

His hand snakes down between my legs and I cringe when he moves my underwear to the side and pulls at the string, removing my tampon. I let out a sound of protest against his mouth that has him separating our lips for a moment, but he speaks against them. "Don't even try to tell me no. You know I'll just take what I want anyway."

I jut my chin up toward him, our lips barely grazing his. "Then take it."

A sinister smile spreads across his lips right before he moves down my body so quickly I hardly understand what's happening. He pulls my underwear off, with the tampon wrapped inside and I want to protest, but it's cut off when he's back on top of me again, his tongue invading my mouth roughly while his fingers are pushing into my pussy.

The first touch against my clit has stars shooting behind my closed eyelids, and when he bites down on my bottom lip, shoving two thick fingers inside me as his palm rubs my clit, I swear I'm already about to combust.

I always get hornier on my period, but I've never really done anything about it except becoming very familiar with the shower head. This is an all new experience. A whole other level sexually. It feels like he's touching live nerve endings and the sensitivity dial is cranked up to a million.

His lips on mine, tongue massaging my own while his fingers rub my inner walls. I'm moaning and gasping, clawing at his back as I buck up against his hand, wanting more. Needing more.

It doesn't take long before I'm unable to hold back the orgasm any longer and I come with a scream into his mouth as he groans, working me through it. I hardly notice when his mouth parts from mine and he's sucking a nipple into his mouth until the bite of pain from his teeth shock my system at the tail end of my release.

He moves to the other one, licking, sucking and then biting the same way, and I writhe underneath him. The one earth shattering release suddenly not enough for me. I need more. Caine smirks up at me, pulling his hand from between my thighs and I cringe at the tinge of blood on them.

Instead of him reacting with disgust, his eyes flare with heat and I don't get a chance to ask what he's doing before he swipes the finger between my chest, down my stomach, smearing the blood down my stomach.

"What're you doing?" I question.

"I want to fill up your pussy with my cum, and then see how it looks mixed with your blood on your perfect body."

"Wha—" I don't get to finish before he's pushing inside me roughly and I cry out at the sudden intrusion. The stretch while I'm so sensitive has a mixture of pain and pleasure racking through me.

"Stop asking so many questions," he grinds out, thrusting in as deep as he can go.

My eyes roll back at the feeling of being so full, and yet I know what true fullness feels like, and I wish Drew and Adam were here with us.

As if Caine can read my thoughts, he pulls out, almost completely, his grip on my hips hard enough he may leave bruises as he sits back on his heels, pulling me onto his lap, my back still on the mattress so I'm at a different angle. This one making him go even deeper when he pushes in fully once again.

I'm clawing at the sheets beneath me as he fucks me so hard my tits bounce roughly. I reach up, cupping them and pinching my nipples and Caine groans above me.

"Fuck, killer, you look so fucking good playing with your tits like that while I fill this cunt."

I moan, attempting to meet his thrusts with my own, the punishing pace he's set has me struggling to keep up. I feel like all I can do is hang on and enjoy the ride, hoping like hell that when the second orgasm hits me it doesn't kill me.

"You feel so fucking good. You don't even understand what you do to me, do you?" he grinds out, and I feel like I need to hold on as the orgasm starts to crest once again.

My eyes roll, the sensation building low in my stomach and I worry I'm going to pass out once it finally hits. I grapple, trying to find purchase on something as I feel the freight train of ecstasy barreling toward me.

"Caine! I can't, I'm gonna, I need you to, *please*." I don't even think I'm saying real words at this point, just sounds, but he doesn't let up.

"You can, killer. Come all over me. And I want to hear you scream for me while you do it." He pounds into me harder and all I can do is try to hang on. Especially as the pleasure racks through me and I come, screaming, as he drops my hips, moving his body over mine as he fucks me even harder.

The move prolongs my release for what feels like forever and I don't know if I want it to ever end. I don't know if it's possible for it to ever end.

"That's it, killer. So fucking pretty for me," he groans, right before I feel the flood of his cum filling me. It triggers an aftershock of my own orgasm at the possessiveness and feeling so full of him.

Once he comes down, he pulls back before removing himself from my body. I watch his face as his eyes remain locked on where we were just joined. I whimper at the loss of him, but then watch as his hand moves to his dick and I watch him slide his fist along his length using my blood as lubricant.

I'm transfixed on the movement, unable to take my eyes off the way he works himself. Though he never seemed to have softened, he's hard once again as he fucks his fist.

"I love the sight of your blood on me, killer," he groans.

"That's—" I stop, unsure of what I want to say. *Gross, disgusting, wrong.* But none of this feels that way. It all feels right and perfect in its own way.

It feels like us.

He reaches between my legs, his fingers swiping through the wetness there before pushing back in. "I want you to keep all my cum inside this pretty little cunt. Then, I'm going to cover your stomach with more of it so I can mix it with your blood on your perfect skin."

A chill runs through me, especially after he pulls his hand from my pussy and then switches to use the one that now has the mixture he just talked about to pump his cock. He moves to his knees between my legs, and all I can do is watch as he finds another release, shooting ropes of hot cum onto my stomach.

I moan at the feeling as it covers me, and he reaches his hand down to rub it into my skin. I should be grossed out by this. It should disturb me in more ways than one.

But it doesn't.

Even after Caine settles next to me in bed, my heart doesn't slow down in my chest. The flood of emotion is back, and suddenly, I'm worried about how strong my feelings for this man are.

I've never felt this way before and despite everything I've been through, my feelings for the man wrapped around me is the scariest thing I've felt.

The fact that I also feel them for two other men only adds to that fear.

Because what if this isn't real.

What if it's all stolen away from me because I don't deserve to have good things in my life? I never have, so I don't know why I feel worthy of them now.

That's why I refuse to voice how I'm feeling. Because once I do, it'll be so much easier to snatch it away from me.

CHAPTER 31
CAINE

"You ready for another fight?" Adam asks as I finish up my warm up set. Although I should be tired from fucking Max earlier, we took a short nap and I woke up ready to train.

I wanted her to come with me to the gym, but she insisted that she needed to work. She claimed to not be in as much pain, which I take full credit for, but I still tried to convince her to stay home, or at least come with me.

It didn't work and now here I am, focusing on training until I can't anymore. Then waiting for her to get off work for the night so I can steal her away again.

Though, I'm sure Adam and Drew will insist on joining. I want to fight it, but I can't deny that I like seeing how happy she is with all of us.

"I'm always ready for a fight. Where?"

"Los Angeles."

I huff in agreement. I'll take any fight I can get, especially now that my dad cut me off. Plus, it feels like a piece of normalcy since we got Max back and it's something we all need. There's a darkness that lingers all around us, like we're waiting for the other shoe to drop and I know we're all feeling it. Despite Danner reassuring us that it'll be fine, I know that the visit from my dad has set me slightly on edge, though I won't show it.

"When?"

"Next weekend."

"Max is coming."

"Already got her a ticket."

I don't have anything else to say about it, nodding and grabbing my hand wraps to get started on my training for the day, especially since I now have a fight. I won't say it, but I'm glad he already had the forethought to bring Max. It makes me glad that it's these two fuckers she decided she wanted.

If I can't have her all to myself, I at least want to share her with decent guys. That's the nicest thought I'll ever have about them, though.

Before I get into the cage to spar with Cal, I send Max a text to check in. She hasn't been at the bar long, and I'm just hoping she's not miserable.

> Caine: You okay killer, or do I need to come rescue you?

> Max: We both know I can rescue myself. I'm fine.

"What're you doing?" Drew asks. I toss my phone down onto my bag and shrug.

"Just checking on Max."

"I was going to head to the bar after I'm done cleaning up here." I scowl at him. I'm going to insist on joining, but stop myself. I need to train and it's okay if he goes to see her. It's okay if he comes home with her, or if she goes home with him. I'll still join, but it's okay.

I'm trying to learn to accept this.

For Max.

I nod, entering the cage where Cal's already waiting for me as he bounces on his feet, and stretches out his arms.

"You're going to be rusty, bro, it's been a bit for you," he taunts.

I give him a deadpan look. "It hasn't been a week and I don't get rusty."

"We'll see about that." He smirks and the little shit thinks he's actually getting to me.

"You going to just keep talking or actually fight me?"

He chuckles, and we circle each other for a little longer before he comes after me first. I easily dodge him and huff out a breath.

"You're too predictable," I tell him, annoyed that we have this same scenario every time we spar.

That gets him to take a different tactic and I bite back a smile. He thinks he's challenging me. But at least this time it's different. I play with him a bit, not giving my full effort until I get bored and take him down until he taps.

Once I let up I see Adam standing just outside the cage. "Glad you're giving Cal some competition, but you need some yourself."

"Yeah, well, unless you want to get in here and fight with me then that won't really happen."

He leans back slightly, seeming to debate it.

"Come on, old man," I taunt, seeing the flare in his eyes that he wants to meet the challenge.

"Nice try. Not tonight." He shakes his head, "You need to be fully ready and not just coming down from another fight."

"That was hardly a fight," I scoff.

He keeps walking away and I look around for Drew, but he must have already left to go to The Tavern and see Max.

Alexander is around shooting the shit with Cal, but I know they're about the same level and I don't feel like babysitting another fighter right now.

Instead, I hit the bag until sweat beads across my brow. When everything floods in about my life now that I'm cut off, I just go harder. I still have access to my cards, at least I did when I checked earlier, but I'm not going to use them.

My dad didn't lock me out of the house, but I wasn't going to give him the chance to do it.

Then, there's the whole talking to Max thing that night when she found me. For the first time, I talked about the shit going on and she just understood. I've never experienced that before. There's so much with her that I've never experienced before, and it's making it harder not to pin her down and say the words I've never said before while I force her to listen and not talk.

Maybe I'll stuff her mouth full of her cum covered panties so she can't say anything and just lets me speak.

Then she can't try to reject what I tell her with weak protests that I won't accept anyway. I can make her bend to my every will and she does it willingly. I can even make her love me if I need to.

CHAPTER 32
MAX

Drew showed up at the bar and hasn't left the entirety of my shift. Luckily, I'm able to function, my cramps having subsided slightly, probably thanks to the orgasms. Or the medication I took, but I'd like to give credit to the orgasms.

"Time to go," I tell him sternly, a little surprised Caine and Adam didn't join him. Or maybe they're taking shifts being on "Max duty."

He stands up, towering over me, and apparently the orgasms earlier weren't enough because his large looming body makes my thighs clench as he smirks, leaning down to graze his lips against mine. "I'll be outside."

I try to chase his lips with mine, but he evades me and I scowl at his back. He walks out the door, but runs into someone walking in.

"Place is closed," he tells whoever it is. I join him and see that it's Officer Doogie and roll my eyes.

"Can I help you with anything, Officer?" I ask, trying to be friendly.

"Just wanted to come by to see if any of you have heard anything else about that murder. I got Feds starting to sniff around asking questions."

"Can't say we have," Drew answers for us, folding his arms across his chest. "And I don't know why you think we would."

The officer looks past him to me. "Your girlfriend here would."

I shake my head. "No, I don't and I need you to leave so I can close up."

"I'm sure I'll be seeing you again soon, then." He looks directly at me as Drew guides him out the door, using a little more force than he probably should.

"I'll be outside," he tells me quietly.

Nodding, I lock the door behind him and quickly clean up the bar so I can go home. The warning of the Officer's parting words replaying in my mind. *Seeing you again soon.* I want to believe everything will be okay, that whatever Danner did was enough that no one would suspect me. Though, with the FBI supposedly asking questions I feel like I may be working with borrowed time.

༄

"WE'RE TAKING A TRIP NEXT WEEKEND," Adam says shortly after

he gets to my house. Drew took me home, and Caine was already there waiting for me of course.

"What do you mean a trip?" I shake my head. "I have a job and I can't just leave whenever I want. I need money."

"Don't worry about it, George is cool with you having a weekend off," Drew says easily, draping an arm across my shoulder.

I narrow my eyes up at him. "You guys need to stop talking to my boss on my behalf. Wait." I look back at Adam. "Where are we even going and why?"

"I have another fight in LA and you're coming with," Caine explains.

The thought of going to another fight is exciting, so I choose not to argue about this and actually start to get a little excited. Though, I'm aware how I need to shower, and my exhaustion is hitting me along with the pain in my lower back starting to creep up again.

So I shake off all the offers to join me. I just want to have an effective shower and crawl into bed. As the hot water hits my skin, I feel myself get more and more exhausted. My eyelids feel heavy even before I turn the water off, and hardly keep them open as I throw on a T-shirt that I'm pretty sure is Caine's before I crawl into bed.

※

THE NEXT WEEK we get to California the day before Caine's fight and check into the hotel which is another large suite. I shake my head turning toward Adam. "You don't need to get such a nice room, you know?"

He shrugs. "I know, but there's a lot of us, it's easier."

I just turn away, taking in the room that he probably paid way too much for and I hope it's not because he thinks I need stuff like this considering who my family is. I really don't.

"Caine, we have to get you registered," Adam announces and Caine grunts in response.

"Want to go with?" Drew asks me.

"Sure." I shrug. I'm curious about the process; I've seen the fights and I'm excited to see more. I'm glad they wanted me to come with, even if it is because they refuse to leave me alone.

We get to the venue and Drew hangs back with me while Adam and Caine do whatever they need to in order to get him registered. I'm looking around and seeing all the fighters, coaches and people with them.

It's not like the last time I went to a fight with them where I was looking over my shoulder worried about being seen. Right now, my uneasiness feels different. Especially when my eyes catch on someone across the room staring at me. He's big, probably around the same size as Caine. He has light hair that hangs over his forehead. I can't tell what color his eyes are from here, but they're intense as they bore into me.

When his lips spread into a smile, a chill runs down my spine and I feel Drew wrap his arm around my stomach, pulling me back into his chest. I don't look away from the man across the room, but his smile fades as he sees the way Drew is touching me.

"You're drawing attention from other fighters, little one. You're going to give Caine more motivation for his fight tomorrow."

I smirk, turning my head slightly. "A little jealousy is good for him."

"The only people you're allowed to make him jealous with are coach and me." He nips my chin and I giggle, pushing him away before looking back at the other man who's still staring at me.

He winks in my direction and when I turn away I notice Caine has been watching the entire interaction and looks ready to kill the man. I don't know what it says about me, but the thought gets me even more excited to see what's going to happen tomorrow.

"Let's get you out of here before you cause an unsanctioned fight," Drew jokes, guiding me out. I chuckle, but then realize I don't actually think he's kidding.

CHAPTER 33
DREW

I wake up with my chest pressed against Max's back while she's facing Caine on the other side of her. Adam is sleeping on the other side of me, but he's on his back with his hands on his chest like he always sleeps. Not touching anyone and no one touching him.

I groan quietly, sliding my hand over Max's hip and to her stomach to pull her back against me so I can feel more of her.

She lets out a sleepy moan when my already hard dick pokes her and I know I need to do something about it. I think about sinking into her, about fucking her while she sleeps, but then I may end up needing to share. I want to be selfish with her right now. I want a piece of her all to myself.

My hand dips lower between her thighs and she sighs as I graze her center, rubbing her clit lightly to get her wet. She wiggles against me, moaning quietly, and I move her leg carefully, lifting slightly so I can angle my dick at her entrance.

I rub the tip through her wetness, coating myself before I press against her and start pushing in slowly. I bury my face against her shoulder to muffle the groan as the tightest, wettest, hottest cunt sucks me in, welcoming me into her body so perfectly.

She feels so fucking good.

She lets out a little sound of pleasure and I pause, not wanting to wake her up. I just want to feel her. Be surrounded by her. Just *be* with her. She settles back again and I continue to push the rest of the way in.

"Fuck," I groan once I'm fully seated inside her. Completely encased in her pretty little pussy that was clearly dying for me with the way it pulled me in and how she clamps around me keeping me there.

I don't even want to move. I just want to stay here all night just like this. Banding my arm even tighter around her middle, I bring the rest of our bodies even closer until we're as close as two people can possibly be.

I settle against her, my eyelids feel heavy and I give in, letting sleep pull me under with my cock buried deep inside her and it's the best sleep I've ever had.

When I wake up, it's to my girl's ass pressed completely against me and it registers that I'm still inside her. She moans a little louder than her sleepy moans sounded like last night, and I know she's awake. I don't think I can handle not fucking her right now.

Clamping a hand on her hip, I thrust roughly and she gasps loud enough I know that she's awake for sure.

"What're you doing, killer?" I hear Caine ask on the other side of her.

"Mmm, nothing," she answers and when I thrust into her even harder she cries out.

Caine pops his head up, looking at me, clearly catching on. He stares daggers at me, but turns toward Max shoving his hand in her hair, gripping it tightly. "You lying to me about Drew's cock being buried inside this sweet little cunt?"

She shakes her head and he grips her hair even tighter while I fuck into her even harder, digging my fingers into her hips and I'm not able to stop. I need to keep going.

Caine grabs one of her hands, and brings it below the blanket, I think to wrap around his cock by the way he groans. I'm a little surprised Adam hasn't woken up, but then I feel him shift behind me, and I know he is now.

I glance at him over my shoulder, locking eyes while he looks down at where Max and I are connected, then back up at me. I move my hand between Max and I to gather the wetness from us and coat my hand before reaching behind me for Adam blindly, wrapping my fist around his cock, covering him as I pump.

He grunts and I continue to jack him off at the same pace that I'm fucking Max.

"I fucking love waking up with my cock buried inside your pussy," I tell her.

She moans, "Me too."

"Keep strangling my dick, killer, fuck you're perfect," Caine grits out while I assume she's jacking him like I'm doing the same to Adam.

We're all moans and movement. Just primal need.

"Come for me, little one, I need to see how tightly you squeeze my cock. Force the cum out to fill you up, baby," I groan.

She cries out and I think Caine's hand has moved close to where her and I are connected as he starts to rub her clit. Max starts to writhe against me, and I want to pin her down to really fuck into her, but I like having Adam and Caine involved like this too and I know doing that would break the connection.

Though when she detonates, coming all around me, I don't care anymore, moving quickly, shoving her face down into the mattress while I cover her back and fuck her hard and fast. It doesn't take long to find my own release, filling her with a groan.

I pull out of her as Caine shoves me slightly and forces Max's mouth onto his dick. He thrusts his hips up into her throat, not even giving her a chance to adjust, but the way she moans and rubs herself against the mattress I know she fucking loves it.

I'm so busy watching I hardly notice when Adam leans down, running his tongue along my length, tasting Max and my cum together. I groan, fighting the urge to shove his face against me, and take my already hardening dick down his throat.

He sits up, takes my hand and puts it back on his cock, squeezing the way I know he likes, growling, "We don't have time for me to fuck you like I should for pulling this shit. But you're going to get me off just like this and then later you both will get punished for think you can fuck while we were sleeping."

I smirk, hoping he follows through on the threat because it's what I've wanted since this all began. I tighten my fist around him watching Caine fuck Max's throat roughly and I try to match his pace with my hand around him.

Caine groans, holding Max's head against him, as he comes down her throat. It's one of the hottest things I've ever seen. When he lets her up, she wipes her mouth, eyes locking in on where I'm touching Adam.

Max crawls over, and wraps her hand around mine, looking up at me with a smirk while we both move around Adam. He groans loudly, throwing his head back as we both fuck him with our hands.

"Just like that, you two, fuck that's so good. You're both so fucking good," he groans.

I squeeze even tighter for the good comment, but all it does is cause him to swell in our hands, groaning as he shoots ropes of cum onto our hands as we work him through his orgasm.

We're all sated, breathing heavily and Max has the prettiest flush of her skin when Caine speaks up.

"I can't think of a better way to wake up before a fight." He grabs Max by the back of her head, dragging her to him, crashing their mouths together in a rough kiss before pulling back to say, "If I win tonight, that's going to have to be my ritual from now on, killer."

"I won't argue with that," she replies easily. And I think I speak for all of us with my silent agreement.

CHAPTER 34
MAX

At the fight later, Drew's with me in the audience while Adam and Caine prepare. Just like last time, we watch the fights before his and I get lost in all of it. The more I watch, the more I enjoy what I see. It's nice to not have the looming worry this time around, with the crowd of people, wondering what eyes are on me.

I know it can't be Carson.

It can never be him again.

After one of the fights ends, they announce that Caine is up next and we watch him get into the cage. It's the same routine as last time with Adam talking to him, while Caine doesn't even look like he's paying attention. My eyes drift over to his opponent on the other side and I immediately recognize him as the guy from yesterday that was staring at me.

He looks even more intimidating today, shirtless with various tattoos decorating his skin, and the look in his eyes seems like he's ready for murder. Suddenly I'm uneasy because this guy looks like he could and would actually kill Caine.

I know he can handle himself, but something about the man makes me worried. Though, when I look at my man inside the cage I can see that he recognizes his opponent too because that look of murder in his eyes is there as well.

I know this is going to be a blood bath.

That's exactly what happens as soon as the timer starts. It's blow after blow. Blood spraying. Moments pass by where I'm worried that Caine is going to lose because it looks like he's not going to have any choice but to submit, though he always ends up getting out of it.

Other moments, I think he's going to completely cut the oxygen from the other man, but he escapes. The rounds seem to go on forever, both seeming to get tired, weaker with every second that passes.

That is until Caine delivers the winning blow, resulting in a knockout.

The breath I didn't realize I was holding is let out as I scream in celebration at his win.

"That was a good one," Drew says next to me, and I nod in agreement, my eyes not leaving Caine.

The moment he sees me, a bloody smile spreads across his face. He mouths something, but it's hard to tell what exactly he says because there's no way it's what it looks like. There's no way he just said "Fucking love you," to me across an arena packed with feral MMA fans. I refuse to believe it, and yet I know Drew saw it too when he says, "Did he just say that?"

I shake my head. "I don't think so."

Even though I kind of hope he really did because that means the emotions that have been burning in my chest for all three of them may be reciprocated. Unless they admit it to me first, I don't think I'll ever be able to tell them.

Yet, that may be exactly what just happened.

§

EVERYTHING FEELS different after we get back from California. It's like there's more between us than there has been. Nothing outwardly has changed, they're still over protective and insisting on my extra training and not letting me leave work alone.

Luckily, I'm able to start my shift alone while they are all at Uncaged still. It's been several days since we've been home and tonight is really slow at work, which I'm partly thankful for. The lack of tips won't be great for my wallet, but the break from the mental load will be nice.

I'm just finishing restocking some of the more popular beers in the fridge behind the bar when the front door opens and I prepare to serve whoever it is that just walked in.

What I don't expect is to see my extremely put together parents walk into a place that they'd view as being beneath them. I swear I'm hallucinating. There's no way they're here. They don't know where I am or where I work. I know they would never actually come into a place like this willingly, either.

My mother wraps her coat around herself tighter like it will protect her from the germs in the air as she looks around with a disgusted look on her face. I hope they enjoy their shoes being sticky forever from all the spilled liquid covering these floors.

I'm still convinced that I'm hallucinating until they're directly in front of me, the wood of the bar the only thing separating us.

"Maxine," my mother says, her venom laced tone slices through me and confirms that this is, in fact, my reality.

"What the fuck are you doing here?" I snap.

"We've come to take you home. For the final time," my father says seriously.

"No."

"Enough of this, Maxine, we've been more than accommodating with your little outbursts, but it's over. You're coming home. You're marrying who we say you are so that you can fulfill your duty to this family," my mother declares.

"No."

"You could have just followed through and married Carson. Everything would have been fine, but look what happened. Speaking of which…" My father stands up straighter, training his eyes on mine. He's never spoken much to me, I've mostly been my mothers problem to deal with, but I know now with Carson out of the picture he's probably even more sick of me than my mother is. "Do you want to tell us what happened to your fiancé?"

I shrug. "I think you'd know more than I do," I say easily, sticking to the plan Danner had to frame them for the murder.

"Why would we know anything?" my mother gasps.

I just shrug again. "Why would I?"

"Probably because it was the felons you've decided to associate yourself with. Don't think we don't know what you've been up to here. We aren't idiots, Maxine. You're a Barclay, and you're coming home for the last fucking time," my father spits.

"They're not felons, you don't know anything about them."

"What do you know? Hm? Do you know that the Aldridge boy practically threatened his own father's life? You think he wouldn't do the same to you? He's a fighter, he will always be one," my mother explains.

I scoff. "You think Carson wasn't? The problem was he only fought me and that was because I wouldn't fight back. I was never going to marry him. And I will never go back with you."

"You will, or we will go to the police and explain to them how your little *friends* killed your fiancé so they could steal you away from us," my mother spits.

"You have no proof."

"Want to see if that's true?" she challenges.

I raise my chin, most likely regretting what I'm about to say, but I'm confident in Danner and the plan she set in place. "You can try."

"Fine, if that's what you want to do then you can come crying to us when you've lost your little pack of...whatever they are." She grimaces.

I fold my arms across my chest, because I'm slightly worried what her threat will do. I don't dare show it to her, not even as she raises her chin, meeting my gaze.

"We will have someone lined up for you within the month, and I will force you down the aisle this time, no matter what it takes," she threatens.

When I don't say anything, they walk out and I breathe out a sigh of relief as soon as they're gone, but the heaviness weighs on me from what just went down. They are going to try and frame my guys for a murder I committed.

Immediately, I reach for my phone and text Danner.

> Max: We have a problem.

> Danner: I'll come over after you're off work.

CHAPTER 35
ADAM

I'm waiting for Max outside The Tavern. When she comes out, she doesn't look at me right away, and I know something is wrong. She turns to lock the door, and keeps her eyes on the ground as she approaches, taking the helmet from my hand and getting on my bike without a word.

Instead of trying to talk to her right now, I accept her silence, getting on the bike in front of her, but before I drive off I grab behind her knees and pull her into me tightly. She doesn't fight the move and wraps her arms around my middle, the layer of clothing helping me accept her touch like this.

I want to take her to my house, maybe have Athena wrap around her throat again while I tie her to the bed and eat her out until she screams my name, but she said we all have to talk to Danner at her house.

That text she sent about needing to talk, plus the way she's acting right now, have me going to her house to get whatever this is sorted out before anything else.

Danner's already at Max's house by the time we arrive, and so are Caine and Drew. I'm sure they're both dying to know what's going on. We all are, really.

Again, Max doesn't say anything as she gets off, setting the helmet on the handlebar before walking ahead of me inside. I'm not far behind, and it's no surprise that Caine is the first to grab her, kissing her fiercely as if he's staking a useless claim on her in front of us.

He also doesn't seem as tense when Drew does the same, kissing her softer in greeting. I try not to get distracted at the sight of her with them, even if I wish Danner wasn't here so we could be doing something else.

"Alright you lover boys, there's a reason I'm here and Max needs her mouth free to tell me what it is." Danner sighs.

Max and Drew break apart, and she looks up at him with a lightness that wasn't there when I picked her up. Maybe I should have pushed a little bit to try and help her to feel better about whatever's going on, but I'm not them.

Max looks between all of us before saying, "my parents showed up at work tonight."

"What?" Caine practically yells. "How did they do that and why the fuck did none of us know about it?"

"You need to stay calm and let her talk," I instruct sternly.

"Look, I don't know anything because they shouldn't even know I'm here. Unless Carson told them before…" Her voice trails off and we all know what she's talking about without her needing to say it. "Doesn't matter, they said I need to come home or they'll frame you guys for it."

"This is your home," Caine insists. "You're not going anywhere."

"I know." She nods. "I know, but I'm also not letting you guys get dragged into this mess more than you already are."

"No one is getting dragged into anything," Danner interjects. "We're all already dragged, technically anyway. But they wouldn't be able to put it on any of you unless they pay off the cops."

Max gives her an incredulous look. "You don't think they would be willing to do that?"

"You're right," she agrees. "So we have to get ahead of it, clearly the cops aren't catching onto what we planted so I'll have to figure some stuff out."

"What exactly can you figure out that can frame people for *murder?*" Max questions.

"If anyone questions any of you, say nothing," Danner says, ignoring Max's question.

"You," she points to Max who has her eyes narrowed at her friend, "do not worry too much about them and their threat. This is all going to work out, got it?"

"I'd just like more reassurance than 'trust me.'"

"You'll get it, but right now that's about all I got."

"I know it's hard, baby girl, but I trust her," I tell her honestly.

"What if you go to jail? What about the gym? Everyone who goes there, I'm not going to ruin your lives because mine is fucked," Max yells.

I take her face in my hands, forcing her to look up at me. "Nothing is going to happen, I'm not going anywhere. None of us are, got it?"

She swallows roughly, eyes shining as she looks up at me. I see the tears she's refusing to let fall, but she gives a hesitant nod.

"Like I said," Danner starts. "If anyone questions you guys, say nothing."

Max tries to drop her eyes from mine again, but I don't let her, keeping them locked on mine as I answer for all of us. "We won't."

"I'll check in later." Danner heads out leaving us all with so many questions, none that can be answered right now.

Max holds my hands that are still on her face, and pulls them off carefully. She sniffs, working to keep the tears at bay. Her voice is hollow when she says, "I'm going to shower." I let her go because I know that she likes to get cleaned up after work.

Usually we allow her the alone time, but I think we can all see how much this is eating her up, and that's why Drew and I don't protest when Caine follows her. At least he'll make sure she's safe and isn't alone if she's about to have a giant meltdown.

Once they're in the other room, Drew leans against the counter with his arms folded across his chest, looking at me.

"What?" I ask, realizing he's not just looking. He's doing that thing he does where he's not quite glaring, but definitely not happy about something.

"It just seems like you're really passive about all this shit, even though you should be demanding for it to be fixed like you do for everything else all the time."

"The fuck does that mean?"

"You want to be in charge of everything and everyone all the time. And yet, the one time you should be doing that? Directing everyone around and getting shit done you're just… not."

I'm confused and getting more pissed off each second he's speaking because I'm anything but calm about this. I just want it to be taken care of. I want us all to be left alone. I want Max to not be scared that something's lurking around every corner.

"You don't know what's going on in my head. So don't you dare try to tell me how I'm being."

"No, I don't know a damn thing with you, ever. No one does, Adam, because you don't say anything, *ever*."

"Why do I need to say anything? Words don't mean shit, actions do, but both yours right now are being pretty damn annoying." I clench my fist, not sure why he's picking a fight like this right now.

"How about this? Do you even want to be with Max? With

me? What is it you want because you don't say shit about that either."

I rear back, even more confused where this is coming from.

"What the fuck are you even talking about? You need reassurance or some shit about this situation?"

"You can't even say relationship. This is exactly my point," he scoffs. "And no, I don't need the reassurance. But maybe Max does. Maybe she wants to know exactly where we all stand with her."

"She knows."

"Does she? Because Caine is the only fucking one of us that may have said he loves her. But I know damn well he's not the only one feeling like that. And maybe she should know it. Especially with the entire future up in the air for all four of us."

"You don't fucking know anything about the future. Why don't you say something to her, instead of getting on my ass to—"

"What's going on?" Max's voice is a lot sharper than it was before and I notice how close Drew and I are. Our argument has turned into getting into each other's face and I didn't even realize.

"Just having a chat, little one," he answers easily, neither of us backing away from each other.

"Sounded a lot like you were fighting. But it looks like something else."

I turn toward her, the question in my eyes. That's when I really notice how close our bodies are, chests are barely an inch from touching.

"Seems like to me, you two need to kiss and makeup."

I look over at our girl and see the smirk on her face. I also see she's alone, and wonder where Caine is since he's usually her shadow.

"That an order, little one? You want to tell us what to do?" Drew teases, looking at me, knowing I don't want to let anyone else have control. She had a piece of it once, but it's hard for me.

She leans against the wall, kicking her foot up on it. "Yes. Kiss."

I clench my jaw, and Drew's eyes lock with mine, meeting the challenge. "What do you say, Coach?"

CHAPTER 36
MAX

Holy shit. I heard the yelling and got out of the shower quicker than I intended while Caine hung back, probably hoping I would join him again. But I'm not going anywhere, not with this sight in front of me.

Adam and Drew are in each other's faces, clearly irritated with one another and just like before, I feel like they need to fuck it out. It seems to be their go to and today shouldn't be any different. One of these days, they're going to have to talk about their feelings, even if I have to pry it out of them. Until then, this is what they need, so I say it again.

"Kiss."

Drew challenges Adam and he meets it with fervor, grabbing the back of Drew's head and slamming their mouths together. Their kisses are always aggressive, rough, and possessive, full of so much need that I can feel it between my thighs.

I'm taken back to the night I directed them with each other

and want that again. I want to see them touch each other. To watch them fuck each other. I want to see it all.

"Strip," I demand roughly, squeezing my thighs together to try and relieve the ache from watching them.

They do as I say, grabbing each other's shirts and pulling them off, their mouths only parting to do so. They both attempt to shed the other of their pants, fumbling slightly in their haste.

I didn't even put on panties, just a T-shirt like I normally sleep in, and I can't help but slide my hand up my inner thigh at the sight in front of me. Especially when they're both naked, still kissing like their lives depend on it, their rock hard cocks rubbing between their bodies. The silver of Drew's piercings shine in the low light and I want to feel them again. On my tongue. In my pussy.

I want to touch them while I watch Adam fuck him. I let out a groan at the thought and the way my finger grazes against my clit, feeling how wet I am already.

"Sounds like she likes what she sees," Drew taunts.

Adam reaches between them, gripping their cocks together, and they both groan. My own sound mixes with theirs as I swipe my clit again, lightly, but enough to send a shot of pleasure down my legs.

"That true, baby girl? You're liking what you see?"

"I'd like to see a bit more," I sigh.

"What're you wanting to see, killer?" Caine's voice cuts through the moment, and I expect it to be ruined, for the two men to break apart and for this to all be over before it really even started.

But they don't. They stay standing exactly how they were before, unmoving.

Caine comes up to my side, his chest grazing my arm as he looks down to where my hand is snaked under my shirt. "Oh, look at you. You like watching them, don't you?"

I suck my bottom lip into my mouth and nod slowly.

"Then, you may want to tell them to keep going. Tell them what you want to see."

My mouth suddenly feels dry; I don't know if I can even get the words out, but the three of them seem to be waiting on me.

I open my mouth to say something, but nothing comes out. I close it before trying again.

"I want…" I pause again, forgetting every single word in the English language because all my attention is on the incessant need in my throbbing core that's dying to be filled. All worries from earlier are gone because in this moment all I care about is how turned on I am and how I need these three to help me take care of that. "I never get to see you fuck each other. I want to watch."

Adam reaches between them, gripping their dicks roughly. "You want to see us fuck, baby girl? We'll give you whatever you want. Won't we?"

Drew grunts as he nods. "Anything."

I look at where they're standing and then over at the kitchen island, nodding toward it. "There."

"Be more specific, little one. Tell us exactly what you want to see."

I look between them. "I want coach to fuck you while I watch." I finally find my words.

"Thatta girl," Adam praises, moving them over to the island.

Caine crowds me against the wall while my eyes remain locked on the other two men. "Does watching them fuck turn you on, killer?"

I nod.

"You're running the show, what do you want me to do?"

I continue to watch Adam grab some coconut oil from a nearby cabinet while Drew leans over the counter. As Adam begins to prep him, I want to touch myself. I want Caine to touch me. I want to be in the middle of them. I want to keep watching, but also be involved. My skin feels like it's on fire while I wait for whatever is going to happen next and it's already driving me insane.

"You can touch me," I breathe out, thinking that he's going to do just that. But the bastard only teases me.

His fingers slide up the inside of my thigh, slowly, painfully slowly while his calluses scrape against my skin. Even that sensation has me ready to lose my mind at how good it feels.

I feel Caine's giant body closing in on my space while he

continues his teasing touch and I don't look away from Drew and Adam. Drew's groans start to fill the air and my own join his as Caine continues to move, and touch, but never where I want him to.

"You want to watch, killer? Let's go watch," Caine says, removing his hand from my skin and I whine in protest until he drags me over to the island where Drew and Adam are.

Caine brings me to the other side, so I'm facing them, and he shoves me down roughly, my chest hitting the cool stone, the thin shirt does nothing to lessen the sensation against my skin. Especially since it's already burning up from the anticipation.

"Looks like you get a front row seat, baby girl." Adam shifts and I think he's positioning himself against Drew.

Caine leans down, pressing me harder against the counter, "You're going to keep your eyes on them while I do whatever I want to you. And you're going to take it."

I squeak out a sound of agreement. Or arousal. I don't know anymore, but I want whatever it is he's going to do to me. I will do it without taking my eyes off the men directly in front of me. I'm distracted by them, completely entranced by how they're together. They can say their attraction is purely sexual all they want. That every time they do this it means nothing. I see the truth. The way I feel more for all of these men, I know they feel something for each other too.

Even if they refuse to admit it.

"Such a perfect girl for us," Caine praises and I'm taken off guard at the softness of his voice. It quickly changes when he's ripping the shirt off my body and pushing my bare chest against the counter. My already hard nipples turn even harder at the coldness underneath me. I gasp at the sensation and at that same moment Drew lets out a primal groan while Adam thrusts forward.

"Oh my God," I breathe out, watching both of their faces while Adam pushes inside Drew.

I hardly get a chance to appreciate the sight in front of me before Caine is distracting me by shoving two fingers inside my soaking core and groans.

"So fucking wet, killer. You do really like watching them, don't you?"

"Yes," I moan, trying to push back against him to get him to move his hand even harder.

Drew drops his head, but Adam's quick to grab a fistful of his hair, lifting it up so he's looking directly at me again.

"Don't take your eyes off her. Our girl wants to watch, she's going to get to watch," Adam insists and I see the smirk lift on Drew's face.

Caine pulls his hand out before pushing in again roughly, this time not letting up as he fucks into me. "You're already so wet and ready, killer. You want to take my cock while you watch them?"

I think about fighting him or saying no like I used to. Partly because I know he loves the fight, but also I don't have it in me to fight him right now. I just want to feel, to watch and to succumb to all the sensations my body is going through.

Caine removes his hand and I protest at the loss, but he's quick to position the head of his cock at my entrance. I'm trying to push back against him, to force him inside my body, but he holds me still with a strong hand on the middle of my back.

"Look how desperate she is for it," Caine says, to the other two men. "Watching you guys has turned her into a needy little slut, trying to fuck herself onto my cock."

"You're going to look so pretty taking him, little one," Drew groans.

"Do it. Fuck yourself on him, baby girl. I want to see your face when you take him inside you."

I moan, "Yes, Daddy."

Caine grabs a fistful of my hair from behind, yanking me up roughly, and I have to catch myself with my hand on the counter.

"The only name on this pretty mouth is going to be mine as I fill you. You can watch them, you can want them. But when I'm inside you, the only one you're calling out for is *me*," Caine practically growls and I nod against his hold in my hair.

Then he pushes me down again as he thrusts forward, filling me to the hilt and I cry out at the invasion. The initial stretch is as painful as it is pleasurable. I feel a hand grab mine, and I look up to see it's Drew, clasping our hands together, eyes locked on mine while the men behind us move, fucking us into the hard cool stone. The way we're connected feels like it's more than our hands.

The entire moment is heated. It's raw and feels like so much more is happening here than before. We're all together even if we're a few feet away. It's intimate in a way I didn't think was possible. The worries from earlier, every other thought about what's going on in our lives, fades in this moment because the only thing that matters is us. Here. The way it feels and I never want it to end.

Caine angles himself behind me before thrusting in again so hard I cry out, loud enough I'm sure the neighbors can hear me.

"Drew, why don't you stuff our girl's mouth so she can't make so much noise. I'd rather see her make a big mess because she can't scream," Adam instructs while delivering his own punishing thrust into Drew causing him to groan.

Drew's lips quirk as he moves his hand up to my mouth, shoving his fingers in, and I suck them in greedily, giving him a grin around the digits before I bite down. He groans, and I somehow have enough brain power to come up with an idea that the dirty part of me revels in.

Reaching down, I swipe my hand where Caine and I are connected, gathering the wetness seeping from my body. Then, lifting my hand up to Drew's mouth, I swipe it along his bottom lip.

"One of these nights I'm going to bury my face in your sweet little cunt while you're sleeping and see how long it takes before you wake up with my tongue buried in your pussy," Drew says with a feral growl, using his free hand to grab my wrist, running his tongue along my soaked fingers before sucking them into his mouth.

"How does she taste?" Adam asks, while tightening his grip on Drew's shoulder while he pounds into him.

Drew sucks my fingers so hard it's almost painful before popping them from his mouth, moaning. "Like the best and worst thing to happen to me." His eyes lock on mine. "You could ruin my entire life and I would beg you to do it again, little one."

I gasp around his fingers in my mouth and Caine leans over sinking his teeth into my shoulder while his rhythm intensifies. He snakes a hand between my body and the counter and starts to play with my clit. The shot of pleasure runs through me as my orgasm gets closer and closer with every thrust, every moment that I watch Drew and Adam, feeling connected to all of them like this.

The emotions swirling though me are almost too much. I mumble around Drew's fingers something I know they can't hear, and I don't think I want them to yet. I don't get a chance to think about it because my release is barreling through me with enough force that I know if Caine wasn't holding me up, I would collapse onto the floor.

"Fuck yes, squeeze my fucking dick, killer. Let me fill up this pussy so I can watch it drip down your thigh," Caine groans behind me, slamming into me so hard that I know my hips are going to be bruised from the way the counter is digging into me.

I'm panting as Drew removes his hand from my mouth, gripping the counter as he groans loudly, Adam's pace punishing and I think he's close to finding his release.

I manage to speak, though it's breathy and probably sounds more like a squeak. "Drew, be a good boy and don't come yet. I want you to come down my throat."

"Fuck," Drew grinds out.

"Shit baby, you can't say things like that, I'm already close," Adam groans behind him.

Caine grabs a fistful of my hair, yanking me up so my back is completely plastered to his front, and he slams into me to the hilt, reaching the furthest point inside me that has me screaming.

He doesn't let up, fucking up into me until he's moaning his own release, burying his face into my hair. "Fucking love the way your pussy takes me."

It reminds me of what I think he mouthed to me after his fight that neither of us has mentioned. I don't know if I want to, though I feel like I should.

Before Caine is even finished, Drew is calling out my name with a pained voice, "Max, you better get your perfect fucking ass over here and swallow my cock if you're wanting me to fill that little throat of yours."

Caine holds me tightly while his cum coats my pussy, but then surprisingly, guides me over to Drew, keeping our bodies together while he shuffles us to the other side of the counter. Adam says, "Get on your knees like the good little whore you are and suck the cum from this desperate slut."

"Yes, Daddy," I moan. Caine pushes me onto my knees in front of Drew and I don't waste any time sucking him into my mouth.

Adam fucks him, pushing Drew deeper into my throat. It doesn't take long before Drew reaches down, holding my head against him with a primal growl and the warm salty taste of him fills my mouth. I swallow quickly around him, trying to get it all.

He lets me pull off him, and before I have any time to adjust, I'm being pushed onto the floor, Adam descending on me, demanding, "push your tits together."

I do what he says without a second thought. He's shoving his cock between them roughly, fucking between them in a way that shouldn't be as hot as it is, and within seconds he's shooting cum onto my chest and chin as he finds his own release.

I feel like a complete mess. I'm sweaty and covered in cum, both mine and theirs. And yet I don't think I've ever felt better. Especially when I'm lifted in a strong pair of arms, I come close to voicing how I feel. It's on the tip of my tongue, I'm about to say the words I said earlier that were muffled by Drew's fingers.

But I can't tell them I love them, because if I do, then I know it'll only be a matter of time before it all gets ruined.

CHAPTER 37
CAINE

Max is in her BJJ class while Adam coaches, and Drew acts like he's assistant coaching, when really I know he's just keeping an eye on Max. He's probably watching her ass the whole time.

Which I'm doing too, but from a distance while I work out. And not as obvious as him. Even if my eyes are glued to her more than what I'm doing. I don't give a fuck, she's my girl and I can stare at her all I want. Especially when she's in class, having to practice with some other guy who has to touch her.

The only reason I don't demand to be her sparring partner instead is because I can see how scared the guy is anyway. He's skinny, barely talking and the hesitant way he grips Max shows he's not at risk of hurting her or touching anywhere he shouldn't.

She's doing well, growing more confident and after this class she has a private one-on-one with Adam, which I know will turn into one with all of us because I don't always agree with the way he coaches her. He can coach the guys how he wants, but when it comes to our girl, there are things she should know how to do that aren't in Adam's technical rule book.

Like delivering a proper punch without hand wraps or gloves. And how to give a solid kick in the nuts. Despite how hard she tried to do that to me when I was first…interested in her. She wasn't good at it, and she should know just in case someone actually tries to attack her. Again.

I keep myself distracted until the class is over and everyone leaves. Which is when I finally allow myself to go up to her, taking the wrap I just undid and wrapping it around her throat from behind, pulling her body against mine.

"It's torture to watch you move without being able to touch," I tell her and she bites back one of those sweet little moans. "You can make it up to me later, though. Your pole hasn't gotten much use lately."

I feel a shiver run down her spine, and I hope that means she wants it too. I've missed the music she would play, the way she would move when she didn't think anyone was watching. One of my favorite things from when she didn't know how deep my obsession for her ran.

"It may never get any use again," she says darkly; the comment has me spinning her around in my arms.

"Why not?"

She hesitates, biting back her response, but I grip her chin and force her to look at me. She's not going to hide anything from me. Not anymore. "What's that, killer? You loved to dance. Especially for us."

"Did. I did love to dance."

I see it. The flash of pain and some of the darkness she tries to conceal. "What did he do?" Because I know it has to do with the man whose body was burnt to a crisp. With every new bit of information that we learn about him, I find myself wishing that I could kill him over and over again.

"Nothing," she tries to deny, but I don't let her. We both know it's a lie, and that shit won't fly with me.

"If you don't tell me, I'll find out and you won't like how I plan to get the information out of you."

She sighs. "He used to make me dance for him. And when I was back there…he did the same."

"Did he fucking touch you?" Every muscle in my body tenses.

"No," she insists firmly. "He just made me dance for him."

I start to ask for more information, but then the front door opens and I look up to see who's there. All the annoyance in my body that was directed at a dead guy is now directed at the very alive man that just walked in here.

"You here to sign up for a class, Officer?" Drew asks sarcastically.

"I've been told to bring you four in for questioning," he responds, way too smug for his own good. My knuckles ache to crash into his face again and I know that the feeling would be so satisfying.

"We're not going anywhere, and especially not with you," I yell across the room, tightening my hold on Max.

Adam steps out from behind the front desk. "Are any of us under arrest?"

"You could be if you don't come with me."

"That's not how the fucking law works you mother fu—" Max slaps her hand over my mouth, cutting me off and I bite her palm in retaliation.

"Pissing him off isn't going to help us," she says through her teeth.

I bite down harder on her flesh and she winces, but she doesn't move her hand, just narrows her eyes at me. I shouldn't be turned on right now, but she does it for me even in the worst situations. I wonder how fucked up it would be if I just took her how I want. Right here, right now.

"Either you all come with me, or I come back with the Feds that are down at the station asking for you." He sounds way too pleased with himself sharing that information.

Panic flares in Max's eyes, but not mine. I'm not worried about Officer Doogie, the Feds, or any of this bullshit. I am, however, sick of the interruptions that keep coming and of how they keep affecting my girl.

"We'll go, but we can leave whenever we want," Adam states and I glare at him. He gives a single nod in our direction.

I clench my jaw, wanting to argue more, but Max rests her

hand on my chest and it grounds me in a way that's so unfamiliar I can only lean into it. Lean into her.

"If you don't, then you're coming with me in handcuffs," Doogie threatens and I scowl at him as he walks out to his car.

"We aren't seriously going down there are we?" Drew questions.

"Yeah, we are." Adam nods. "Just do what Danner said, don't answer. They can't force us to talk. We have rights."

Good thing I'm a professional at not talking. They can enjoy trying to get me to say something because I'm a stone wall. They're going to learn that the hard way.

"You're coming with me." I pull Max into my side because we're going to walk in there together and we're going to walk out of there together. Without saying a fucking word.

⸙

THEY SPLIT US UP IMMEDIATELY. The Seaside police station isn't very big, but they have two interrogation rooms and some offices, so they stick us all somewhere and I'm one of the lucky ones in an interrogation room. I'm chomping at the bit to get to Max.

I tried to demand they keep us together, but it didn't work. It was either going to be me getting arrested or us getting through this separately. I hate being away from her again. My skin is itchy and I want to crawl out of it to get to her. It reminds me too much of those weeks she was gone.

I need her next to me. I need to know she's safe and okay at all times or it drives me insane.

Some guy in a suit walks in and I can't help but demand, "I need to see my girlfriend. I need to know she's okay."

"She's fine, you'll see her soon. We just have some questions."

I fold my arms across my chest and lean back in the chair, glaring at him as he sits down across from me. I'm not saying a fucking word, especially not without getting to see Max.

"Do you know a Carson Bradford?" he asks immediately.

I keep my face completely neutral, and just shake my head.

"Are you familiar with your girlfriend's ties to him?"

I narrow my eyes and say nothing.

"Listen, Mr. Aldridge. You're not in any trouble right now, we just want to find out what happened." The man tries to act calm, but I can see right through it.

I also want to punch him in the face for calling me Mr. Aldridge.

"You're on your way to being a professional fighter, aren't you? Going to get sponsors, move up to the UFC?" He tries to act like we're buddies just chatting. "Pretty sure spending some time in a jail cell may fuck that up for you, don't you think?"

Again, I say nothing, keeping my face completely blank.

"We know you were in Texas when Ms. Barclay was set to marry Mr. Bradford. And now somehow she's back here, and Mr. Bradford is dead."

I stay silent.

"Seems like convenient timing is all. Don't you think?"

"Do you know who my father is?" I ask. I hate to pull this card, but I want to get out of here and back to Max as soon as possible. They don't have any evidence, if they did we would have been arrested and not just questioned. Plus, I know Danner has a plan and whatever it is must be a good one.

"Yes, I'm familiar."

"Great, then you should know that unless you have evidence of anything you're accusing us of, we don't have to stay here. If I need to, I'll call him and he can get it straightened out."

I won't call him. He cut me off and wouldn't come help me even if I asked, but this fucker doesn't need to know that.

He narrows his eyes at me, clearly trying to get a read, but I won't give him anything. He can try, but he won't notice anything from me.

"Is there anything you want to share with me that may help? I just want to get justice for the victim."

I want to say the real victim got her justice, but my girl isn't a victim. My girl is a survivor and she did what the fuck she needed to do, and I'll support her for it forever.

"I don't know anything, so I doubt there's anything I could

share that would help," I tell him seriously. He watches me a little while longer. I don't move and finally he nods.

"Alright, you can go."

I've never raced out of somewhere faster, determined to get my hands on my girl again.

CHAPTER 38
MAX

They separated us as soon as we got here, and I was stuck in an office instead of an interrogation room. I think their plan is to drive me insane in here though, all alone and wanting to leave. I checked the door and they locked it.

Which is probably illegal.

Finally, someone walks in and it's a woman in a pantsuit, looking very official. I know right away she isn't with the Seaside police and my hackles rise because that means she's FBI. Though the smile she sends my way shows that she's playing good cop with me.

"Hello Maxine, it's nice to meet you, sorry it had to be like this. I'm Camilla."

"It's Max," I snap probably more harshly than I should.

"Sorry about that, Max." She sounds sincere and I have to

give it to her, she's a decent actress. "I think by now you're well aware of what happened to your fiancé, Carson Bradford."

I bite my tongue to prevent myself from screaming that he's not my fiancé and how much I hate him because I know that won't help establish my innocence.

So instead, I nod.

"I'm very sorry about your loss. We're working to find out what happened and make sure whoever is responsible is caught. That's why I wanted to talk to you. Do you have any idea who could have done this to him?"

"Nope."

"Not a single idea? No one threatening him or any enemies that may have wanted to hurt him?"

Yeah, you're looking at her. And if I didn't, the three men you also have here would've done it for me.

"I wasn't involved much with the people he associated with." I know I shouldn't answer, but I can't help it, putting on my best act as the old Maxine. The innocent, quiet, uninvolved, unassuming Maxine Barclay.

Camilla looks skeptical for the first time since she came in here. "How'd you end up here in Seaside, Max? It's a little far from Texas isn't it?"

"Yes it is."

"So, how did you decide to come here?" she asks again.

I should stop talking, I know I should. But I also want to end this once and for all and knowing I might regret it, I give a part of the truth. "My parents...I just—" I shake my head, trying to will tears to appear in my eyes. "I needed to get away from them. They aren't good people, and I was scared." My voice turns into a whisper and I think I've got a tear welling in my eye, so I look at the ground trying to see if that'll help it fall.

"What about Carson?"

I shake my head, still looking at the floor and I think this is working to get me to cry. "He didn't want to come."

"Did you want him to?"

I should've listened to Danner and said nothing. I either act like I loved him and he was my fiancé, love of my life and I'm distraught, or I say no.

I shake my head.

"Why not?" she asks softly, and again I really try to play up the tears before I look up at her.

"Because I just—" I sigh, forcing my voice to crack. "I just really needed to find myself."

She nods, seemingly understanding and now I'm impressed by my own acting skills. I guess I had to act for a majority of my life so playing some innocent fiancé of a murder victim comes a little too easily.

"Max," she takes one of my hands in hers and I think it's supposed to be comforting, but all I want to do is snatch it back, "I need you to tell me if you know *anything* that can help us."

I should say more about my parents. Or I should say nothing. I feel like I'm already too far down this path to stop now. That's especially true when she mentions my guys.

"Could any of the men you came in here with have had something to do with it?"

I shake my head adamantly. "No. If it was anyone I would question my parents."

"Why do you say that?"

"I don't trust them."

"Have they ever threatened him?"

I'm not sure what to say, and luckily I'm saved from having to say more when I hear Caine losing his mind calling out my name. I suppress the smile that wants to break free because he may be a bit of an unhinged psycho, but the fact that he's *my* unhinged psycho does something to me.

"What's going on?" Camilla shoots up and storms out of the room. I follow after her, and as soon as Caine sees me he rushes toward me, cupping my face, slamming our mouths together in a kiss that's definitely not appropriate for public, but I don't even care.

"Are you okay?" he pants against my lips.

I nod easily, and he tucks me into his side. "We're leaving. Adam and Drew are coming too. We aren't under arrest and you guys have had enough time."

Camilla looks at me and I think she's measuring my reaction, so I hide my smile. "Are we done? I'd really like to go home." I ask her.

She hesitates, but nods. "We'll be in touch if we have any more questions."

"You won't," Caine responds. "Where are Drew and Adam?"

Camilla looks at him with narrowed eyes, then back at me. "I'll get them."

When she walks away, Caine leans down to whisper to me, "Are you really okay?"

And I realize he can probably see the evidence of my fake tears, so I look up at him with a subtle wink. "Yeah, I'm fine."

He kisses me again. "This is why you're perfect for me, killer."

With the way I'm feeling, this is why I know all three of them are perfect for me.

CHAPTER 39
DREW

The past week has been training, classes, and nights with Max where we all find a distraction with our bodies and refuse to talk about the fact that the FBI is lurking around every corner and keeping their eyes on us. Even from a distance.

Danner has said to not worry about it. That they're just trying to get one of us to break, or catch even the smallest thing.

We've all been on our best behavior. Which isn't the easiest thing, especially for Caine. Though, I see the fire blazing in Max's eyes every time Karissa is in a class and tries to hit on any of us. My girl is possessive, and I like it. Everything has shifted with us, everything is stronger now, though none of us can seem to admit it out loud.

I want to. I want to tell her everything, every single thing she does to me. I just don't know how to put it into words, but I want her to know.

"Danner's coming by. Says she has news," Adam announces at the end of class once everyone has left.

"Good or bad?" I question.

"Didn't say, just news."

I huff out an annoyed breath. Something is better than nothing I guess, I just want this all to be behind us.

Max drops down on the floor to start stretching, and it makes me want to stretch her out in other ways. I'm addicted to her, and there's no use in denying it. I join her on the floor under the guise of helping. She gives me a smirk over her shoulder as I drop down behind her as she sits with her legs spread. I cage hers in with mine, pushing on her back to help her go lower into her stretch.

She turns her head to the side. "This would be a lot more fun naked."

I chuckle. "It's like you took the thought right out of my head, little one."

I'm about to see if I can dip my hands into her tight pants she's wearing to feel her cunt to see if she's already wet, but that plan is interrupted when Danner walks into the gym. I inwardly groan, especially when Max removes her body from mine and I fall backwards on the mat dramatically.

She stands above me with her hand outstretched. "C'mon, big guy, we can have fun time later."

I take her hand in mine, letting her help pull me up to

standing where I'm able to tower over her. I want to close the distance between our mouths. I want to take her right here on the mat. I want to do so many things with her but she turns away from me, walking toward her friend and I know we need to get this out of the way.

Instead of the folder Danner usually has when she brings us information, she has a tablet.

"What've you got for us today, boss?" I tease.

She glares at me. "Not your boss."

"You're right. We all know who the real boss is." I direct my gaze to Max.

Max just shakes her head with a smirk.

"Okay, who wants to know how much of a piece of shit Carson was?" Danner announces.

"Pretty sure we're all caught up on that," Caine grumbles.

"Yeah, I had a front row seat to his asshole tendencies, I don't know what else you could tell me at this point," Max adds.

"Do you know how he found you here?" Danner asks with a raised eyebrow and Max freezes.

"No, actually."

"What about his actual involvement with your parents and the reason they were so desperate for you to marry him?"

I tense at the mention of the would be marriage, and I swear I feel the anger radiating off Caine from the mention of it as well. Adam keeps his cool, remaining still as stone, just staring and waiting for whatever Danner is going to tell us.

"I just assumed it had to do with money or something." Max shrugs.

"Or something," Danner agrees, pulling something up on the tablet. "So, I was able to get into Carson's computer and phone, it all took some digging though which is why it's taken me so long. Plus it wasn't at the top of my list, but keeping all of us out of prison is."

"Hold on." Max holds up her hand. "You hacked into his stuff? Who the fuck are you?"

"Shh, sweetie, we've been over this." Danner smiles and I really would like the answer to the same question. I've also overheard Cal and Alexander talk about her, but they couldn't handle her, especially with all this mystery. I'm sure they'll figure it out eventually. '

Danner continues, "First of all, I had to sort through a lot of porn, like *a lot*."

"Not surprised." Max rolls her eyes.

"I was finally able to find a contract and it was between the Bradfords and your parents." Danner nods toward Max. "It was worded very carefully, but essentially they were selling you to the Bradfords. Your parents finances are not doing well at all."

"Okay, but Carson didn't even really want me, so what the

fuck did he get out of this deal other than his parents shelling out a bunch of money?"

"Carson got to become the CEO. Essentially a win-win to everyone. Your parents get paid, Carson runs their businesses, and in turn it would be partnered up with the Bradford's company as well."

"A win for everyone but me." Max shakes her head. "So, how did he find me?"

"That was pretty easy to figure out, he's not great at deleting his communications. He made a connection here and I'll give you one guess as to who that is." Danner looks at all of us, waiting.

"Doogie," I say immediately.

"Bingo." Danner points to me.

"Hold on." Max holds up a hand, seeming to process what we're being told. "That doesn't explain how he knew I was here."

"It does, though," Danner disagrees. "All it takes is looking you up to find your family and Carson. He just needed your name, got a hold of Carson and kept an eye on you for him until Carson was ready to come here himself."

"That mother fucker is dead," Caine growls, seeming like he's about to go commit the murder right now.

"We'll deal with him, but chill for a second," Danner tells him calmly, though I have to agree with him and Doogie's days are numbered.

"So, he kept tabs on me or something? All while Carson was just biding his time until he came and kidnapped me?"

"Pretty much. Doogie's the one that broke into your house too," Danner adds.

"Oh, we knew that already," I add.

"You did?" Max swings her narrowed gaze onto me.

I give her a small smile. "Yeah, doesn't matter now. We're going to handle him for good this time."

"I'm not covering up another murder. I know you guys have your revenge you want to take out on him and that's fine, but one at a time is enough for me," Danner says, deadpan to all of us.

"At a time?" Max gasps.

"Where do we stand with the investigation?" Adam chimes in, attempting to get everyone back on track like he does.

"They're looking into Max's parents. Of course they lawyered up immediately, but I have info being fed to the detectives to help move the investigation in our favor."

"What do you mean?" I ask.

"The contract, some of the communication doesn't look the best. Add in the guards I planted at his house while we went in who can give a story about both of them showing up." Danner shrugs like it's simple. "Plus, we all have alibis."

"We do?" Max asks.

"Yeah, don't question me so much. I'm starting to think you don't trust me," Danner says, acting offended and Max just scoffs. "Look, it's a simple story, they just have to believe it. Then your parents will get to spend the rest of their days in prison."

"What's the story then?"

"You ran away from an arranged marriage twice and they got mad at Carson for letting it happen again. They weren't going to get their ass saved by you. They got desperate and pissed, so they killed him."

"You think that's going to work?" Adam asks.

Caine has been noticeably quiet, so I look over at him to see he's still fuming and definitely fighting the urge to rush out of here to find Doogie. He finally says something and I can see the anger in his eyes with his question. "Who's their lawyer?"

Danner looks at him, swiping through her tablet a little bit before letting out a humorless chuckle. "Aldridge." She looks back up at him. "Your dad and brother."

"Of fucking course," he grumbles.

"It's fine. You all really need to work on trusting me. I've done nothing but help you." Danner shakes her head.

"We do, we're just on edge I think," I add.

"Should be almost over, Even though I told you not to say anything," she directs her comment to Max, her eyes narrowed. "It seems like it got the FBI off your back a bit."

"See, I know what I'm doing," Max announces proudly.

I pull her into my side, kissing the side of her head and chuckling. "Good job, little one."

CHAPTER 40
MAX

I insist on riding with Caine back home, because I know if he's left alone, he's going to go after Doogie and will kill him. There's no doubt in my mind he would drive his fist into that man's face and not let up until he stops breathing.

He would take out all the pent up rage he had against Carson, and now Doogie out on the one man. One that certainly deserves it, but I don't want to lose him when it looks like we may get away with what I did to Carson.

After Caine climbs on the bike in front of me, I wrap my arms around his middle, pressing myself against his back tightly. I swear I feel the tenseness in his body soften at my touch, but I also may just be imagining it.

We end up getting to my house at the same time as Drew and Adam. There's a tension around all of us, and I feel like it's because of everything we just learned. They're pissed, and so am I but I know right now we just have to trust Danner and the process.

We need to distract ourselves, especially Caine because he reminds me of a caged beast who's been throwing themselves at the bars and the enclosure is seconds away from breaking. I keep myself plastered to his side as we walk inside, trying to ground him.

Once we are inside I feel like it's safe to put a tiny bit of distance between us without him immediately bolting from the house. Of course when I try, he yanks me right back against him, growling in my ear, "Where do you think you're going?"

I look up at him, the anger and some other emotion swimming in his bright blue eyes, I blurt before I can think about what I'm doing, "We all need to talk."

"That doesn't sound good," Drew comments.

I shake my head. "No, not like that, I just, *fuck*."

I feel like this isn't how I should start this, but I can't go on any longer without getting this confession off my chest. It may be ridiculous, and maybe I'm reading too much into everything. I've never experienced real love and attention, but right now I know that if I don't say something soon it's going to burst out of me at the worst time.

I know I should trust Danner, and I do. I also know, there's always an opportunity for everything to get derailed and if I never get to tell them it'll be the biggest regret of my life.

"Sit on the couch," I tell them all, reminiscent of another time we did this.

I've never been good with words, I've always had to express my feelings in other ways. Dancing used to be my biggest outlet. The one way I could get out everything, and actually *feel* freely.

This may not be the most conventional way to express my feelings, but it's mine. They've accepted me fully and wholly up until this point, and I can only hope they'll accept me like this as well.

None of them argue as they sit on the couch, facing the pole that's still up, though I probably should have taken it down. I'm glad I haven't. While the thought of dancing has repulsed me since I got back, I want to now. I want to feel how I used to feel.

I want to take my power back.

Because it's mine.

Their eyes are glued on me as I stand there, not doing anything, just looking at them. I quickly steel my spine and plaster a smile on my face.

"I want you all to tell me something. For everything you tell me, I'll take something off."

Caine doesn't move, Drew tilts his head slightly, and Adam adjusts his position to sit up a bit straighter before asking, "Tell you what, baby girl?"

I toy with the hem of my shirt, the loose fabric hanging on my body and covering my sports bra underneath. I tease them, lifting it just slightly. "Tell me how you feel about..." My voice gets quieter, insecurity taking over with what I'm asking.

"About what?" Adam's deep gravelly voice asks.

"About me," I practically whisper.

"What do you want to know, killer? I tell you every fucking thing. The way I'm completely obsessed with you, that you changed my life the second you walked into it. The way I've never wanted anyone the way I want you. The fact that I fucking love you," Caine confesses almost too easily.

I practically lose my footing at his words. Hearing them, watching him say them. I thought I saw him mouth them after the end of his fight, but convinced myself that I hallucinated. There's no denying right now that this is real and that those words just came out of his mouth.

"Your turn." Caine gestures to my body. "Take it off."

Because I can't speak, I do just that. Removing the loose fitting shirt and dropping it on the ground at my feet. I step toward the men on the couch, kicking the fabric aside, stepping up to Caine and straddling him.

"Keep your hands to yourself. You're not allowed to touch the dancers," I tell him with a smirk. "And if you don't, I'll have to tie them up."

"I may love you, killer, but I'll break free of any restraint you try to put me in."

I roll my hips against him, already feeling his hardness underneath his sweats and I groan. I'm very aware of the other pairs of eyes watching us, and that I want them to touch me too. I want all of them in a way I've never had them before. I want to be completely consumed.

I dip down, barely grazing my lips over Caine's trying not to second guess what I'm about to say, not overthinking any of it. I just let the words roll off my tongue. "I fucking love you too."

He tenses and I know he's about to grab me, but I remove myself from his lap. He looks like he wants to come after me, but I hold my hand up. "If you ruin the game then you don't get the prize."

My eyes fix on Drew, moving closer to him, but back up near the pole. Once it's at my back, I swing around it once with the back of my knee hooked around it. "Your turn," I tell him.

"Fuck, little one. You don't know what you do to all of us, do you? How you have me so fucked up, wanting things I've never wanted. Feeling things I've never felt. When you were gone and I thought I wouldn't see you again, I didn't know what to do with myself. You balance me. You fill all my missing pieces and if that's not love I don't know what the fuck else it could be."

Hooking my thumbs in the waistband of my pants, I start to push them down, my heart racing at this entire game while keeping my gaze focused on Drew as I drop another piece of clothing onto the floor.

Repeating the same move I did with Caine, resting my knees on either side of his hips, resting my hands on his shoulders, I lean down to bite the lobe of his ear and whisper, "Remember the rules?"

"No touching this perfect body."

I breathe out, "You're such a good boy."

He growls, his body tensing and I chuckle, letting my breath fan the side of his neck. But amazingly, he doesn't grab me even though I know he wants to. I want to rile them all up. I know exactly what buttons to push. How to distract them, and get them to bend to my will.

Because I'm the one in control and we all know it.

Trailing my lips down his neck, I move to the other side, repeating the motion, working up the nerve to say the words again. The ones I'm feeling just as strongly for this man as the other two are sitting on the couch. I didn't think it was possible to love one person, let alone three.

That's why I'm able to whisper, "If that's what it's like, then I must love you too."

He turns his head, capturing my lips with his, and I melt against him for a moment before pulling back and giving him a glare as I get off his lap. "That's breaking the rules."

"I think it's a technicality," he teases.

"Or maybe the good boy wants to be punished," I taunt right back and he narrows his eyes at me. But I don't miss the way he adjusts himself in his loose pants that are suddenly tented. He can deny that he's a good boy, but he likes it just as much as I do.

"Keep it up, baby girl, you're going to unleash two monsters if you aren't careful," Adam growls.

I turn my attention toward him this time. "Only two?"

He nods slowly. "I'm able to control my monster."

I raise my eyebrow. "You think so?"

He nods again.

"Good thing it's your turn then. Prove it."

He shifts again, taking his time as his eyes rake over me. I'm only in a sports bra and a thong. He takes in every inch of my exposed skin. I watch as the snake tattooed on his throat bobs with a rough swallow, the only tell he has that there's any sort of reaction to me.

I shift my own weight on my feet, trying not to feel uncomfortable by his staring. Though, I know it's not uncomfortable. I like him staring. I like how they all look at me. I knew he would be the one that struggles the most with telling me how he feels.

I'm aware he may not, and that this could all blow up in my face. Even if I say something first, and with the way he's looking at me, I just might. It's like he's willing the words from my mouth. Like he can force me to say them before he does. His brown eyes lock on mine and I open my mouth, but no words come out.

"Do you want to know how I feel, baby girl?" he asks finally. I snap my mouth shut and nod.

He nods toward the pole behind me. "You going to use that while I do?"

"If that's what it takes," I offer easily. It's not like when Carson would make me dance for him. Right now I want to, if it'll get him to say things he would never normally say. If it'll keep him looking at me the way he is right now, I'll do anything that needs to be done.

"Go on." He nods toward it again, and I listen.

Holding onto the cool metal, I swing myself around slowly, my movements controlled and unpracticed while I get used to the feeling. There's no music, but when he starts to speak, I don't even need music. His voice and the words he's saying are better than any song I could start playing.

"You're the perfect woman, baby girl. Perfect for us. Perfect in every way. And you don't even know it. You not only complete each of us individually, but as a whole. You bring us together. You're the glue. You're the only person who could ever get me to say so much at once. You're the only one who could get me to admit how much I love you."

My breath catches, for some reason hearing him say those words holds more weight. Knowing his history and the fact that he's never known love just like me. This man who doesn't handle some levels of physical intimacy well due to his past is able to let himself be emotionally intimate. With me.

Not only that, really it's an emotionally intimate moment with us all together because they were able to tell me this in front of each other. This makes me feel like we're all closer than ever. Another level to this relationship because it proves to us all that this is it. We're all in it.

Together.

Even if it didn't start that way, considering Caine forced his way into my life. Then, they all did in their own way. It's all I've ever wanted but didn't know I could have.

"Get over here, baby girl," Adam demands and I realize I've stopped moving around the pole.

Stepping toward him, he stops me with the simple raise of his hand, and I listen, easily like my body is programmed to listen to him even if it's nonverbal.

"Take something off," he reminds me, and I've been so distracted I forgot that was even something I'm supposed to do.

I pull my sports bra off, tossing it somewhere in the room and I don't know if I'll find it again. Then, he drops his hand and I climb onto his lap, the same way I did to the other two, careful not to touch him in a way that will have me ruining the moment.

"Thank you," I say softly. "Thank you for telling me; I know it's hard for you. I know all of this is new for all of us. But this is why I love you. Because you trust me, and treat me better than anyone ever has in my life. You see me for who I really am, and have helped me discover who that really is."

Adam shakes his head, cupping the side of my face. "No, baby. You discovered yourself all by yourself. That was all you, and always will be."

I crash my mouth onto his to stop the sob that wants to come out, I didn't realize how desperately I needed these words from all of them. It means more than I can even express. We're all so imperfect, but together it doesn't matter. We get to be imperfect together which is what I think makes us even better for each other.

He pulls me back, and I didn't even scold him for touching me, which I'm sure is pissing off the other two a bit, especially Caine. It doesn't matter because this is about us coming together. Right now, I want that in a whole other level. Which I'm going to get.

"Turn on some music, baby girl, and finish up your little show for us," he tells me, and again it doesn't feel like it did with Carson. I don't feel forced. My body buzzes with the thought of dancing for them. I want to do this. I want them to watch me.

"Yes, Daddy." I slide off his lap and see the flare in his eyes at my words because, just like the other two I want them unhinged as soon as I say. Because what I'm going to ask for is going to push all of our limits.

Yet, it only makes me even more excited for what's about to come.

CHAPTER 41
MAX

I turn on the music, a sensual song with a good beat, which is always my favorite. It's easy to feel the melody as it plays. The lyrics start and I close my eyes letting it flow through me. I can feel their eyes on me as I move, swinging around the pole. The music grounds me because I feel unpracticed and unsure in a lot of my moves, but I don't care.

Because the music makes it better.

Along with their eyes on me. The way they want me.

The way they love me.

Despite everything. Through everything. They love me.

I fucking love them. It may be new to all of us and we may not know exactly what we're doing. I'm sure we'll fuck this up more than we'll get it right, but that doesn't matter because we're together to deal with it.

I remove the last piece of clothing, tossing it to the side, my back to the pole and I slide down, opening my thighs as I drop down to a squat. I open my eyes as the song starts to come to an end. They all are staring at me, the feral look in their eyes shows how hard they're holding themselves back from completely mauling me.

That solidifies what a good decision this was, just to prove the control I have. It'll never be like my old life, they would never do anything to take away my power. They just want to give it to me.

Which is why I'm going to give them this.

The next song starts, and it has a quicker beat, but the blood rushes through my ears, and the only thing I can focus on is the way they're watching me. Especially as I slide my fingers up the inside of my thighs. They're all locked on the movement as I ascend up to my core.

I take my time, but once my fingers make contact with the wetness that's pooled there, I'm unable to continue to tease myself. I'm so worked up from the dancing, their eyes on me and feeling their hardness already when I sat on their laps.

I rub my fingertips over my clit, pulling a moan from my throat, and I drop my head back against the pole behind me.

"You need to quit teasing us, baby girl, I don't know how much more we can take."

I slide my finger down pressing into my entrance moaning again at the sensation. But also at the fact that it isn't enough. My moan turns more into a whimper as I try to grind down against my hand.

"Looks like you need a bit more, killer."

"Hmm," I hum, not wanting to end this yet, even if I am borderline desperate to get their hands on me. I don't want to have to ask. I want them to take. I want to be held down and forced to take all of them. I want it raw, rough, and dirty with them.

"You're killing us, little one."

I push another finger in, gasping while pumping them, trying to convince myself it's enough. It doesn't work because I know, and they know it's not.

"Fuck, please," I cry out, frustrated that I'm not feeling the sting of stretch of them, or the press of their fingers digging into my skin. The bite of teeth, the brutal way they fuck me.

"Please what, baby girl?" Adam grits, and I can tell he's on the edge as well. I can practically feel the way they're all vibrating, dying to get over to me, to give me what I want, but don't want to voice.

"I need more," I finally cry out, accepting that I can't do this myself any longer. I do need more. I need *them*.

They don't waste any time shooting up, and coming toward me. My face is grabbed in a strong hand, and lips crash onto mine. I know it's Caine immediately with the way his tongue invades my mouth, taking just like he always does the way I'll always want from him.

Adam comes up behind me, moving my hair from my shoulder, running his lips up my neck before saying, "You ready to take us all into this perfect body? You going to be able to take it?"

A shiver runs down my spine, but it's exactly what I wanted for tonight, though the thought still terrifies me. It's exactly what I wanted. Yet, with the way Caine is kissing me, all I'm able to do is nod.

Caine growls against my mouth before pulling back, and I want to chase after him, but I don't because he's looking toward the other guys, like they have some plan they're plotting non verbally. I want to ask what's happening but everyone is moving again. Clothes are being shed and I'm not able to form a single thought, let alone words as the glorious expanse of skin, muscle, and dicks are exposed to my greedy gaze.

Caine looks like he was carved from stone with the way his smooth tan skin shows his defined muscles that cover every inch of him. His bright blue eyes don't leave mine; he's so intense. So perfect in a way I never knew I needed.

Drew is no different, the way his toned body shows the life he's lived, he has scars all over, even though some are somewhat covered by the ink that spreads down both arms and onto his chest. But every single inch of him makes him who he is and I wouldn't change a thing.

Adam's muscles are covered with all the art decorating his skin, but the definition of his strength is still obvious. Especially since I can see the way his veins run down his arms as he pushes down his pants. "Caine," he snaps, pulling my attention up. "Grab some lube."

I half expect Caine to argue with the demand, but he doesn't.

Instead, he goes somewhere I can't see because suddenly, I'm too focused on Drew's thick, pierced cock. My mouth waters and I want him in my mouth. He must notice because he hooks a finger under my chin, tilting up. "You look like you want something, little one."

I lick my lips and nod in response.

Caine returns, and I feel him at my back, pulling my back against his front, dipping his hand down between my thighs. "You're already so wet for us, killer."

"Always," I breathe out, dropping my head back against his shoulder. Though, I keep my eyes locked on Drew, and now Adam's cocks that are rock hard in front of me, all while Caine dips lower, shoving two of his thick fingers into my pussy. I cry out, already pent up from my own touch, but his is so much better.

"We have to get you ready for all of us, baby girl, come over here and get our dicks nice and wet with that needy mouth," Adam demands smoothly, and I clench around Caine's fingers.

He growls behind me, nipping my neck. "You fucking love the thought of that, don't you, killer?"

I nod furiously, gasping when he pushes his fingers in rougher, and I try to grind against his hand.

"Go ahead, then, get them ready while I get *you* ready." He nudges me forward, and I crawl the short distance over to the two men towering over me. The hard floor is tough on my knees, but I hardly notice, completely focused on getting my mouth on both of them.

I kneel in front of them, looking up through my lashes, so

turned on, so full of emotion it's impossible to think of anything other than the way they're going to feel in my mouth. But before I touch them I have one demand of my own.

"Kiss," I rasp. "I want to watch you while I swallow both your cocks."

They groan, and Adam immediately grabs the back of Drew's neck, slamming their mouths together in that way that's unique to them. The rough passion of thrashing tongues and biting teeth. I can't help but think that even though we all have established their feelings toward me, there may be more between them that they refuse to admit. Now is not the time to think about that because as soon as Drew groans, thrusting forward trying to find friction against Adam, I snap.

Leaning forward, I wrap a fist around Adam's dick, and another around Drew's, licking the precum already leaking from his tip before running my tongue along the piercings, toying with each rung on the ladder.

I try to keep my eyes upward, continuing to watch the way they kiss each other and shift, pressing my thighs together to try and relieve the ache it's causing while pumping my fist around Adam and sucking Drew's length into my mouth.

Drew groans above me, a hand drops to the top of my head, tangling in my hair while his other remains on the back of Adam's head. I hollow my cheeks, sucking him as deep as I can go, gagging slightly when he reaches the back of my throat.

I pull back, quickly moving to Adam's doing the same to him while continuing to pump Drew's cock in my fist, using my thumb to toy with the piercings. He thrusts into my hand while Adam thrusts into my mouth as I suck him deeper.

I remove my mouth, continuing to use my hand on both of them. I look up, fixated on the fact that they're still kissing and wanting to be in the middle of it, of them. I want to be crushed by them and the strength they both have.

"Get closer," I instruct, guiding them with my grips on their dicks so they rub together between my hands. They're completely pressed together, and I open my mouth wide, attempting to take them both in it.

Caine comes up behind me. "You trying to fit them both in this desperate little mouth of yours?"

I nod around the two men while Caine starts to knead and spread my ass. I shift forward slightly for him, and moan. Especially when he presses a lube covered finger against my hole.

"Fuck, little one," Drew groans against Adam's mouth as I attempt to take them both into my mouth, but hardly even get past the tip.

Instead, I rub them against each other between my hands, running my tongue along both of them, going between the two, tasting and savoring everything. The unique taste of them, the sounds they make and the feeling of Caine prepping my ass for his abnormally large dick. It doesn't matter that I've felt him there before I don't think I'll ever fully be prepared for him, or any of them. Yet, the stretch and pain is what I crave. I crave their sweetness as much as their brutality and I know that's exactly what I'm going to get.

Especially when both Adam and Drew's hands tangle in my hair, together, pushing and pulling me, as I work both of them at the same time, moaning when Caine pushes his finger into me, and I clench immediately at the familiar foreign feeling.

"You gotta let me in, killer. You want all of us, let me into your tight little ass so we can fill you up."

I moan, sinking slightly as my legs grow weaker with need. I relax slightly, letting him push past the ring of muscle and pumping his finger in.

"We're going to stuff you full, baby girl. You think you can handle it?" Adam rasps against Drew's mouth.

I nod. "I can take it."

"I know you can, killer. You were fucking made for us."

I moan, feeling the added pressure of another finger and I lean forward trying to take both Adam and Drew into my mouth again. They groan above me, and I hear the sounds of them starting to make out again.

A large hand comes down, wrapping around mine, tightening my grip around them. It's Adam's as he helps me fuck both of them with both my mouth and hands.

"Fuck, you're so desperate for us, aren't you?" Caine grits out behind me and that's when I notice I'm starting to fuck back against his hand. Seeking more, needing more.

"Mhmm," I mumble around the two men, dipping down to run my tongue along Drew's piercings again because I love the sounds he makes when I do that. The pained pleasure that makes me practically feral for him.

Caine pushes another finger in and I cry out, struggling as he fucks them into me, groaning behind me and I squeeze my hands tighter around Drew and Adam who both grunt in response.

"Shit, killer, I need to get inside you. You're so fucking ready for us," Caine growls and I nod furiously, wanting that too. Wanting all of them inside me. I know it'll hurt. I know it's going to push me to my absolute limits and yet, I'm craving it.

"Please. I want all of you. Use me because I'm yours," I say, looking at each of them, and it was the last thread they needed because in an instant they're on me and I can barely register as I'm grabbed, pulled down onto Caine who lays on the floor. My back against his front as he positions his cock at my back entrance.

"No going back, killer. You're ours." He starts pushing in and I grapple for anything to grab which only results in me digging my nails into the skin of his forearm that's banded around me.

It doesn't matter how prepped I am, or how much lube covers his dick, it's so much pressure. I gasp as he pushes in deeper and I take it because it's what I want. I already want more, my pussy clenches around nothing, dying to be filled.

Caine pushes the rest of the way in and I cry as my ass makes contact with his groin. He's fully seated, groaning behind me.

"You two better hurry because she's already squeezing my dick like a fucking vice," he groans.

Adam kneels in front of me and there's a sheen of sweat already covering his skin, making the tattoos even more prominent, darker, and I want to lick every inch of him.

"You already look so pretty with Caine's cock buried in your ass. But you're going to be even prettier once Drew and I are also filling up this little pussy." Adam smirks, looking down at me.

I gasp. "What?"

"You said you can handle us, baby, time to prove it." He squeezes my thighs, pushing them further apart and my muscles burn slightly, but as scary as the thought is, I want it.

Especially when he presses his tip to my soaked entrance. His brown eyes look up from the spot where he's about to push inside, watching my face while he does. My jaw drops as he fills me along with Caine who has just been barely thrusting, just enough to drive me insane.

Adam pushes all the way in, and I moan at the additional sensation. He reaches down, rubbing my clit as he works the rest of his length into me, holding my thighs open with his other hand as I try to slam them shut.

With a final rough thrust he fills me completely and I cry out. Caine thrusts up roughly into me once. "I didn't think you could get tighter, killer but *fuck.*"

Adam continues to rub my clit, with shallow thrusts timed with Caine, and I quickly start to lose my mind. My orgasm has been dancing on the edge for what feels like forever.

"You're going to come for us, we need this cunt soaking wet and then Drew is going to push inside along with mine," Adam explains, and I yelp as he pinches my clit.

Shaking my head and stuttering, "You-you're not going to fit."

"Yeah we are, baby. We're going to make ourselves fit." His tone leaves no room for argument.

"You can take it, killer."

I want to insist that I can't. That there's no way, but with the way they continue to fuck into me, and as Adam rubs and pinches my clit, Caine moves up and toys with my nipples. I grind against them, begging for more, though I still don't think I can take it. When my orgasm consumes me I'm crying, grabbing for anything around me, and moving against them trying to get them deeper, harder, and craving *more*.

I turn my head slightly to look at Drew who's been standing there, just watching while pumping his cock in his fist. Somehow, I open my mouth to speak directly to him. "I need you too."

CHAPTER 42
DREW

I've been completely fixated on watching Caine and Adam fuck Max while she gasps, moans, and grabs for them. I'm tempted to shove my cock in her mouth, make her choke on it while struggling to breathe as they fuck her. Instead, I watch while fucking my fist just waiting for the time for me to join.

I know what we're going to try to do, so I don't want to risk blowing my load early. Though, I know I'll be able to get hard for her again almost instantly, I like the edging. She got me close enough with her mouth, tongue, and hands all over Adam and me at the same time.

With his mouth on mine, his hands while she played with us. Fuck, that's one of the hottest moments of my life, but I know it's about to be topped when Max says, "I need you too," while looking directly at me, laying on top of Caine with him and Adam slowly fucking her.

I squeeze the tip of my dick roughly as I step toward her. Hesitating for a second, unsure how this is going to work with the three of us, though I know there's no stopping it. I'm going to make sure it happens, no matter what.

"Get over here, our girl needs you too," Adam instructs and I take in the position.

Adam pulls back slightly, making room for me to fit between Max's spread legs, squatting down to position against her entrance, on top of Adam's cock. Her eyes are wide as she looks up at me, and I smirk down at her, pressing against her just barely.

"You ready, little one? You ready to be stuffed completely full of our cocks?"

She moans as I push in just barely, tensing around us. Caine and Adam both groan loudly as they feel it as well. I feel like I'm going to explode already.

"Push your dick in this perfect little cunt. I can feel your piercings rubbing against me and it's going to make me come," Adam grunts.

"Please! Please give me more. I want it," Max begs under us and I can't help but give her exactly what she wants, pushing in even more. I've never felt anything so tight. I don't think I ever will again. She squeezes around all of us, and I didn't think it was possible for her to be tighter, but she is.

We all groan, feeling the way she squeezes. The underside of my cock rubs against Adam which stimulates the piercings while also being engulfed in Max's tight wet heat and it's fucking *heaven*.

"*Fuck*, your piercings," Adam grits out, thrusting in sharply and Max cries out.

"You guys have no idea how tight her ass is right now," Caine groans underneath her, and I can see the way he grips her hips tightly. I want to see her marked up from us. Bruises and bite marks while she feels the soreness from us between her thighs for days.

We aren't able to fuck into her as hard as we usually would because of how tight she is. My thighs burn from the position I'm in, but my release is already starting to build and I need to feel Max come around all of us. I need to see her fall apart while full of us. I need her to soak us all before we fill her with our cum.

"Give us another one. You can do it," I encourage, pushing into her more, finding the rhythm with Adam and Caine as we all get completely lost in her, and each other.

Max shakes her head, her wild and messy red hair swaying against Caine's skin as she does. Her tits bounce, making my mouth water, but I don't think I can bend down to suck them into my mouth the way I want to like this.

I grab them instead, tweaking and playing with her nipples while she moans and writhes under us.

"Come on, killer," Caine growls.

"You got this, baby girl. Soak us."

Max cries, "I can't. It's too much. I'm too full. I can't."

"You can." Caine moves a hand from her hips to her clit,

rubbing while Adam and I continue to fuck her, pushing her to her absolute limits.

Max continues to insist she can't, screaming and crying that it's too much, but she doesn't tell us to stop. She grabs onto Caine's and my arm, digging into my skin with her nails while tears stream down her cheeks. I don't let up on playing with her nipples, while Caine toys with her clit and we all fuck her.

I'm about to combust and I need her to come first, but I don't know if I'm going to be able to hold off any longer. Though, suddenly her screams get louder, and somehow she gets even tighter as her inner walls pulse around us. It's the sudden flood of liquid as she squirts all over us that sets off my release.

My release takes over while Max falls into complete ecstasy, screaming and crying even harder as her pussy floods around us. I pump my cum into her, mixing with the wetness seeping from her.

Adam and Caine both groan and I think they join in coming but I'm so lost watching Max. Her eyes pinched closed, mouth open, skin flushed, and chest heaving with heavy breath. I can hardly pay attention to anything that isn't her, even my own orgasm doesn't compare to watching her come down from hers.

When her cries turn to whimpers, I finally remove myself from her pussy, immediately missing the tight warmth I was engulfed in. I can't help but watch the way the cum drips from her around Adam's dick. Especially as he starts to pull out as well and the mixture of our cum drips out.

I swipe my fingers through it, collecting some, and watching her while I suck my coated fingers in my mouth. Her mouth drops, and I lean forward to kiss her, shoving my tongue in her mouth so she can taste the salty mixture of us. She moans against my mouth, but I pull back too soon when she gasps after Caine shifts and I think he removed himself from her body as well.

"You're fucking perfect, little one," I tell her.

She smiles a tired, sated smile up at me.

"Come on, killer, let's clean you up."

I help Max up, and she's uneasy on her feet so I pick her up carefully. I want to take care of her. The way she was so good for us makes me want to treat her like a fucking queen. Because I love her, and now she knows it.

And she loves us back. I feel like we don't deserve an ounce of her love. She's too good for me, but she does. She trusts us and loves us and I never want to fuck that up with her. She holds onto me as I carry her into the bathroom. Caine and Adam are close behind, but I don't care about what they're doing, my focus is her.

She leans into me, and I can't help but kiss her forehead lightly and she hums. I don't dare put her down, just shift her slightly so I can turn on the water to the shower. We all aren't going to fit, but if they think I'm going to set her down, they're dead wrong.

Once the water is warm enough, I step in with her, holding her tightly as the water caresses our skin. She wiggles a little.

"Can you stand?" I ask gently. She nods, but I keep a hold on her as I set her down carefully, keeping her held tight against my chest.

She leans against me as I clean her up, washing her hair carefully, and just letting the warm water wash over us. Max hums and sways on her feet; I know she needs to lay down. My own exhaustion is starting to take over and I want to curl up with her in my arms. Sandwiched with Adam behind me if I'm honest. We only share a bed when she's involved, and yet that's exactly what I crave. I want to feel close to both of them. I know Caine is there too, and he always wants to be plastered against Max, but that's fine.

Because she loves all of us.

I can't get over it, and I don't think I will any time soon.

As soon as I open the shower door Caine is there, wrapping a towel around Max, and Adam is handing me one of my own. I give him an appreciative smile, wrapping it around myself as Caine sweeps Max away.

I narrow my eyes at him, but know that this is how it's going to be. If she's going to be with all of us, we all have to share her. I know we will, even if we don't always want to.

We all end up in the bed, I'm between Max and Adam just like I wanted to be, though he lays on his back, only touching with the side of his arm as it's draped across his middle. It's good for me. I don't want to cuddle anyone, I just want to feel surrounded by them.

Caine has her back plastered to his front, so she's facing me. Which means I'm able to watch as she drifts off to sleep easily. I wish I could, and part of me wants to, but I also just enjoy staring at her. It's even better that she's the last thing I see as I finally do drift off.

I wake up a little while later, it's still dark, but the room is filled with deep breathing from the other three people sleeping. I'm still facing Max who's now laying on her back, Caine's arm banded around her like he doesn't want her to leave his side, even in sleep. I remember the night I fell asleep with my cock inside her, and as much as I want to do that again I'm sure she's sore. But I need to touch her.

Feeling Adam at my back also makes me want to touch him as well. I look over to see that he's sleeping how he always does. I think about what would happen if I tried to touch him right now. Then, Max makes a soft noise, pulling my attention back to her, and she's back to being my singular focus.

I want to have her come, but make sure she's taken care of. I slide down the bed carefully, not wanting to wake any of them as I settle between her thighs. I slide them apart gently, nuzzling my nose against her core before running my tongue along the seam. She moans softly and I want to make her come while she's still sleeping. I want to fall asleep with the taste of her on my tongue.

I spread her slightly and flick my tongue on her clit. She lets out the softest, sweetest moan and it only spurs me on. I suck the bud into my mouth and then stiffen my tongue, spearing it into her opening. She whimpers and shifts around as I lick, tasting the remnants of earlier and the new wetness that I lap up greedily.

She starts to move, shifting around on the bed a bit more, and her little sleepy cries have me humping the bed to relieve some of the ache from my rock hard cock at the taste of her. I move my attention back up to her clit and tease her entrance with a single finger because I know she's sore. I push in carefully and she sucks in a sharp breath. I think for a second she's awake and carefully flick my tongue on her clit slightly, but when I look up her eyes are still closed, though her breathing is a little more rapid, and I'm sure she's still sleeping.

I go back to fucking her with my tongue, lapping her clit and when her moans get a little louder I think she may wake up Adam and Caine, but she's close, so I continue. Within seconds she's coming, coating my tongue in her sweetness and I lap it all greedily.

She comes down, and while I want to bury my cock in her, I'm not going to wake her up because she needs to sleep after what she did tonight. I gently kiss my way up her stomach, biting her nipples enough that she whimpers, but still doesn't wake up.

I continue to move up her body before kissing her lips softly, and then settling next to her. Adam shifts slightly when my weight hits the bed next to him again. That's when I decide to be risky, turning toward him and resting my hand on his chest lightly, just my fingers then my entire hand. He doesn't move, and I know he's still asleep.

In a way it's nice touching him like this, something we've never done. It's not leading to sex, it's not for any reason other than to just touch. After a few moments, I slide my hand down, feeling more of him before removing it to turn back toward Max and hold her against me.

As I'm drifting off, I feel Adam move, and I don't dare say anything as his arm comes around me and onto Max, holding both of us at the same time. I smile and this time when I fall asleep it comes a lot easier, still tasting her, hearing her soft and sleepy moans. Having her in my arms, surrounded by more love than I've ever known and the peace that comes with that is something I never want to lose.

CHAPTER 43
CAINE

I'm wrapping my hands at the gym when my phone rings. I want to ignore it, especially when I see it's my mom. I rarely hear from her, usually if my parents have something to say to me it's going to be my dad. I thought I was done with them after his little visit.

I've been happy these past few days after we all talked to Danner. I was ready to commit a murder when we left, but Max knew exactly what I needed that night and distracted all of us perfectly.

I've known I loved her, I said the words after my fight in California. I'm sure she saw, but I didn't say it to her again, only while she was asleep. But the fact that she loves all of us. I shake my head thinking about that night. There's no denying my feelings for her, because clearly I'll give her whatever she wants since I'm willing to share her, and that's something I didn't think I would ever do.

My phone rings again, and I'm annoyed as I go to answer it. "Hello?"

"Hi, Caine, do you have a minute?"

I huff out a breath. "Not really, but what? I thought I was cut off."

She's quiet for a second, and I hear some shuffling before she speaks again. "It's no mystery we aren't happy with the decisions you've made. I do think you should know what's going on even though your father didn't want to tell you."

I sigh, because I'm sure there's a lot going on he doesn't want me to know. Especially in regard to Carson and the case since he and my brother are apparently representing Max's parents. Which is so many levels of fucked up I can't even get into it. "What?" I ask.

"You're involved with the Barclay girl, correct?"

"Mhmm."

"The one who's fiancé was just murdered."

"Supposedly," I murmur.

"You know your father's firm is representing her parents since they are suspects in the case?"

"Mom, what is the point to any of this? I don't care who dad is representing. You guys don't want me in your family anymore so I don't know why you're talking to me."

She sighs. "You're still my son, and you're still an Aldridge. I don't want you to go to prison. I still care even if you think I don't."

I scoff, "You care about the family's reputation. So what? Dad wants to put this on me then?"

"He wants it to be put on anyone other than his clients."

"Well, his clients are guilty. He can try, but he's not a cop, so he doesn't have the pull to put this on anyone else."

"He has connections though, Caine. I don't think you understand."

"So do I. But I wasn't involved. Neither was Max, and if you guys want me out of your life I'm out of it. Don't call just to threaten me or whatever the point of this was."

"The *point* was to tell you I don't want to see you end up in prison. It wasn't my decision to cut you off, I didn't want this."

"Could've fooled me, mom. You will do whatever dad says, it's how you've always been. Don't worry about my life and don't worry about me. I don't need you guys anymore."

She sighs. "Okay. I just thought you should know. Especially since your father reached out to them for representation."

I clench my phone in my fist. Of course he fucking did. I'm sure he's had his nose in this case the entire time with whatever *connections* he has. Good thing Danner has set it up perfectly and we aren't going to get caught. Though, clearly that doesn't mean my dad isn't going to try.

"Of course he fucking did," I grit out.

"I've never liked this fighting thing you do, but didn't think it would lead to murder," she whispers the last word.

"It. Didn't," I say through clenched teeth.

She sighs again. "If you say so."

We hang up shortly after with no words of love between us, which isn't unusual. Like I said I've never had that before. No one said they loved me before Max. She's yet another first. The feeling of it is unique to only her as well.

The positive to the phone call is that I'm ready to practice more than ever, sending my fist flying into the heavy bag furiously as I work out all the tenseness and anger in my body.

Adam comes up to me, and I hardly acknowledge him; he watches me for several seconds before commenting, "Your form is sloppy."

"Don't give a fuck," I grunt.

"You could hurt yourself."

"Don't give a single fuck."

"You will when you lose out on fights."

I stop, huffing with anger. "You trying to piss me off more? Because right now is not the fucking time for it."

"What happened?"

I don't want to say anything. Talking about it is only going to piss me off more, because I don't feel like talking and I just want to get into my training for the day. Then I can go home and fuck my girl again.

Adam doesn't let up because he's a persistent fucker. And because of this relationship we've found ourselves in with the same girl, I think he feels like he has more of a right to know about my life and talk shit out.

"My mom called," I say finally, not wanting to get more into it than that.

"What did she want?"

"To butt into my fucking life, just like you're doing right now," I snap.

"Fuck off with that shit, Caine. Your life is a part of mine, and Max's and Drew's. You have to fucking deal with it. What did she call about?"

"My dad's firm representing Max's parents. Same shit we already know. They want to pin Carson's murder on someone, and they want that to be one of us."

"Why would she call about that?"

"How the fuck should I know? They wanted me out of their lives and I want out of theirs."

He's quiet, seeming to think and I want to get back to throwing my fist into the bag again. Because just like I knew it would, this conversation has pissed me off.

"Danner said it'll be fine, and I believe her," Adam finally says.

"Great, then the conversation doesn't matter."

"We still have one thing to deal with, though." He stops me from throwing my fist into the leather again.

"Yeah, I know, I have a plan for him," I refer to the certain Officer who sold out our girl and is the reason she was taken from us.

"You need to talk about any plan you may have with us because we're not dealing with another murder investigation."

"Sure." I want him to let it go for now and let me get my anger out before it ends up being taken out on him.

"Seriously, Caine, no going off half cocked and doing whatever the fuck you want."

I don't know why they always accuse me of going off half cocked; I'm smart, despite what they think. I may act impulsively, but I'm not stupid. "I know." I tighten the wraps on my hands a bit too tight.

"Later at home we're talking about this. All of us."

"Sure, can I fucking train now?"

He nods, stepping back and I immediately send my fist into the bag knowing today is going to be a training day that ends with me dripping in sweat, and tired enough that my anger doesn't completely consume me.

"Adam," I bark out between hits. "You and me in the cage soon."

He doesn't say anything, but I've wanted to fight him, and I mean *really* fight him for a while. I know that could be just the thing I need.

CHAPTER 44
ADAM

I feel bad for how little I've been home. I know Athena doesn't know the difference, and she only eats every four to six weeks depending on the size of her last meal. It's not like she needs constant affection like a cat or a dog, which has also been a big positive to having a snake for me.

Of course, we've all been spending most of our time at Max's house because that's where Caine decided to move. Drew and I refuse to be left out. Though, she wouldn't do that to us.

She loves us.

The feeling is still so new to me, I'm sure it's new to her as well. Our upbringings couldn't have been more different, though at the same time we both struggle with the same thing. I remember when I was younger I would see families and thought that they all were the same. If you had normal parents, a normal home, siblings, whatever, that you were happy.

I figured you had love, affection, and stability. It wasn't until I got older that I realized that wasn't the case at all and just because you have a family doesn't mean it's a good one. Just because you have parents it doesn't mean you have love or affection.

Good thing none of us need our blood related family. They all are pieces of shit and we are happier and better off without them. That folder in my desk drawer still haunts me from when I had Danner look into my birth parents. I've been curious, I don't know anything about them, and I wonder if it would make me feel anything to get some answers.

I'm sitting at my desk, staring at the drawer after finishing up at the gym for the day. My plan was to get out of here as soon as I completed everything, then go check on Athena before going to Max's for the night.

Though, I've been here staring at the closed drawer for way too long. Maybe I should just look, get it out of the way so the lingering question is no longer there. Or I should throw it away without looking, it won't make a difference for my past or my future at this point.

Pushing away from the desk, I decide to deal with it another time and staring at it is only going to continue to drive me insane. I lock up the gym, and head to my house to check on Athena.

Just as I suspected, she isn't upset with me, and slithers up my arm immediately after I reach in. She moves up to my shoulders, sliding down the other side so she can continue to explore. "I wonder when Max would be okay with you coming to stay as well," I tell her.

I go to my room to get more clothes to bring over to Max's. I'm not in any rush since I know she's there with Caine and

Drew who were more than happy to get out of the gym quickly. As I'm zipping up my bag there's a knock at my door and I'm instantly on edge because the only people I would want it to be wouldn't be here right now.

Athena is slithering on the floor, and I scoop her up to wrap around my shoulders because no one wants to come near someone holding a snake. Even Max didn't, but I made sure to change her mind about the first girl in my life.

The sight that greets me when I open the door has me tensing. It's a good thing I have Athena on me right now, because I'm not about to try and fight a man with her restricting my movements. Though, it may actually give him a fair shot if I did.

"You have a lot of nerve showing up here," I tell the officer standing just on the other side of the threshold.

"Where's the rest of your *crew?*" Doogie asks.

"Not here."

"Well, I'm here to check some things out, so I need to come inside." The bastard tries to step in, but I fill the doorway with my large frame, stopping him.

"You must think I'm an idiot. I know you can't step in here without a warrant. And you're lucky Caine isn't here. We know what you did."

"I don't know what you're talking about. All I've done is my job."

Athena slides across my chest, and I watch how the older man's eyes widen in horror. I smirk. "You know…snakes venom can be deadly, but depending on the snake, it can take days or minutes to kill a man."

He continues to watch Athena move on me. "You wouldn't let that thing on you if it could kill you."

"I wouldn't? I've had her since she was a baby. She's safe with me, she knows I would never hurt her. But someone unfamiliar may not be as safe," I say as she slides down my arm, wrapping around it while resting her head on the back of my hand.

Ball pythons aren't venomous at all and are probably the most docile snake there is, but clearly he doesn't know that and it makes me want to fuck with him a bit more. It's what he gets for showing up to my house for no reason other than to try and intimidate me. It's only a matter of time before he gets what's coming to him anyway.

"You just let her be free like that?" He looks disgusted and terrified. I bite back the smile that wants to spread across my face.

"Sometimes. Want to see if she'll be as nice to you?" I stretch out my arm with her wrapped around it, and he backs up quickly to get away.

"No, I'll come back another time."

"Don't bother. There's no reason for you to come around any of us." I step out toward him and he continues to back up. "The case is with the FBI which means it's out of your jurisdiction, so you can fuck off."

He stutters, looking at Athena again and backing up to his

car. I watch to make sure he drives away. We really need to deal with him; I know we can't kill him, despite the desire we all have to do so.

After I make sure he's gone, I go back inside and put Athena away. Grabbing the bag I packed, I head to Max's because the last thing I need right now is Doogie thinking he can show up there and try to intimidate them. If he's dumb enough to do that, then he probably does deserve to have Caine kill him. More than he already does.

Luckily, I don't see his car anywhere when I pull up and head inside. The TV is on with some movie playing while Max is draped across Caine and Drew, her head in Caine's lap, legs resting over Drew's. The scene looks so peaceful and oddly domestic. It makes my stomach swoop at how...simple it is. How normal.

"You just leave the gym?" Drew asks, rubbing his hand along Max's legs steadily.

I shake my head. "No, stopped at home for a bit to check on Athena." I don't miss the way Max shivers at the mention of my snake, and I smirk. "She misses you, baby girl."

"I can't say the feeling is mutual."

"She was the most important girl in my life before you, and since I have to be okay sharing you, I think you need to do the same."

She chuckles. "I'm more than okay sharing you with her. It's having her on *me* that I still struggle with."

"Really? Because my memory says you enjoyed it." I step

around the couch, kneeling in front of her, where she's giving me a skeptical look. "And I'd love to do it again."

I lean forward, pressing my lips to hers, and she sighs against them, relaxing more on Caine's lap. I pull back when she tries to deepen it and she whines in protest. Smirking, I stand up. "You seem comfortable, don't let me disturb you."

"Damn right," Caine insists, wrapping an arm around her so she doesn't move.

"Disturb me any time." She looks up, her eyes following me. "Just not with Athena."

I chuckle. She says that, but I know she gets off on the fear. Our girl likes to be scared and chased, held down, air cut off and fucked rough.

And we love to give that to her.

Caine has wanted to spar with me for awhile. Though, with everything going on I could tell he needs it even more now. Just like with our girl, we give her everything she needs. I'll do the same to keep the peace with everyone else as well.

Including indulging him in a fight.

"You sure you want to do this, old man?" Caine taunts, and I just shake my head at him.

"Careful with your confidence, you're looking pretty cocky," I retort seriously.

"And you're looking pretty weak over there. When was the last time you actually fought and didn't just hold up the pads for the rest of us to punch?"

"Don't worry about me, worry about yourself."

"Alright." Drew shakes his head. "Let's keep it clean."

"I will, and I won't hurt you too much in front of Max." Caine smirks, sending a wink over in our girl's direction.

"I wouldn't worry about that," I tell him.

"Alright, begin," Drew announces. A big positive I have as Caine's coach is I know his fighting style. I know the tactics he's going to use. While he hasn't seen me fight, he doesn't know anything about mine.

Which is evident how much of an advantage that is when I anticipate his first move, easily dodging it. He immediately acts like it was a diversion and tries to throw a leg, but I anticipate that too.

I'm an expert at his fighting style. About everything with him in the cage so every move he attempts I dodge and deflect and after toying with him for a bit I throw my own hit which lands right in his jaw.

"Mother fucker," he grunts, spitting onto the ground and I know I've pissed him off. I want to smile, but I'll save that until the end.

The thing about Caine is that I see a lot of myself in him. I was a cocky little shit when I was younger too. I learned that's not always the best way to be and managed to check myself.

Except right now I can't help that attitude that comes back because fighting with Caine feels a lot like attempting to play with a lion. I've seen him fight, know how good he is and the fact that I know I can beat him fairly easily makes it difficult to be humble.

Especially when I'm able to get another solid opening that has my fist meeting his face once again. He snarls as the blood drips from his nose.

"Come on, thought you were going to kick my ass." I smirk and I can see how pissed off he is, which is great for me because the madder he gets, the sloppier he'll get.

That becomes even more true with the next combination he tries, and fails. I'm able to get a grip around him to take him down to a submission. He tries to throw me off, both of us grappling for control and even when I get him into the takedown he doesn't tap. I adjust to have him in a choke, and he still doesn't tap. I know the stubborn fucker will let me hold him until he passes out before he admits defeat.

"Tap if you can't get out of it," I tell him, gruffly.

"Fuck off."

I tighten my grip around him to prove that I'm not going to let go; if he's going to let me choke him until he passes out that's on him. I'll let up as soon as his eyes roll back, so it's not like he'll die.

I feel the slightest tap on my leg and I let up immediately so Caine can take in a deep breath. The gym is quiet for a second, then Drew calls out, "Coach wins on a tap out."

I catch Alexander slap Cal's arm. "Pay up."

"Don't bet on fights in my gym," I scold them.

"Hey, I said you'd win." Alexander shrugs like that makes it any better.

"Fun is over," I announce, but my eyes fall onto Max's and I hope she can decipher the look in my eyes that's portraying to her that the fun with her is yet to come.

CHAPTER 45
MAX

My parents have officially been arrested.

It was weird to read about when Adam sent me the article. The pictures they had of my parents in handcuffs should've made me feel happy. Relieved or something. But for some reason, it's only filled me with more anxiety.

I know Caine's dad and brother are their attorneys. I know that the Aldridge's have a reputation for being the best at what they do. They've defended a number of high profile criminals before, some that were so obviously guilty that the public outrage was crazy when they ended up getting off.

I know that them being arrested is only the first step. Sure, there was enough evidence to get them caught, but will it be enough to convict them? Especially having such good lawyers. My head already hurts from the stress of it all and I just want to forget. I would normally seek out my guys and make them fuck me into next week because that always helps me forget everything, but I have my BJJ class at Uncaged, and I actually want to go.

Plus, Drew and Adam need to teach it. Caine also has his own training to do. He has another fight in Portland he has to prepare for. Which is for the best, I can't rely on them to make me feel better, I need to do that myself. I know training will do just that.

I get to the gym after insisting on driving myself because I want to go to the beach after, before I have to get ready for work. I'm a few minutes early and already see that girl Karissa is here. She's always hitting on my men, and it annoys me. I try to brush it off because I know nothing will come from it. It only makes her look desperate anyway.

Of course, she's in one of her tight sports bras, tight shorts, and nothing else like she always is. It's too cold to wear that and not be completely obvious about it. I just roll my eyes, finding a spot on the mats to start stretching. Caine spots me almost immediately, his eyes raking down my body obviously as he wraps his hands, and the simple gesture that I've seen so many times shouldn't be as hot as it is.

He notices me watching and winks, so I roll my eyes looking away to not feed his already inflated ego even more. I focus on stretching out until Adam announces the start of class.

"Alright, today we are sparring, partner up with someone of similar size as you," *Coach* Adam instructs and I'm already turned on from watching Caine, but having Adam be in coach mode only adds to it.

That is until I hear the shrill voice speaking, "Drew, I want to spar with you."

"I have a hundred pounds on you, we aren't similar sizes," Drew tells Karissa, deadpan.

I scowl at the way she sways like she's pouting. While I know I have nothing to worry about, and I may not be anywhere near a professional at BJJ at this point, I know I'm better than her. Which is why I call out, "Karissa, want to partner up?"

She turns toward me with a disgusted look on her face. "No."

"That's perfect." Adam nods. "Max and Karissa, you can go first."

She continues to pout as I enter the cage, and I think for a minute she's not actually going to join me. But she does and I smirk. I even notice Caine pauses what he's doing to watch. Karissa looks pissed off as she enters along with me, and I stretch my hand out toward her which she blatantly ignores so I shrug.

"Begin."

She squeals when I try to grab her immediately and I give her a disbelieving look. Looking over my shoulder to see Drew shaking his head subtly and Adam standing tall with his arms folded across his chest, just watching.

I try again, this time managing to get a grip on her that takes us to the ground. She struggles, and it's obvious she has't been paying attention at all because everything she's doing is not jiu jitsu. I don't even know what it is that she's doing other than squealing and squirming.

I easily get her in a closed guard, and she hardly even fights back, just pushes against me to let her go. When I move from the guard to a choke she lets out a full on scream. I still don't let up because she hasn't tapped, and honestly the bitch deserves to be choked.

Not in a fun way, either.

I tighten my arms a bit more than necessary and she's continuing to flail around as I choke her. Finally, she taps my leg and I let go. She screeches as soon as I do. "Are you fucking insane? You could have killed me."

"That was just jiu jitsu, you know the thing we've been learning?" I look over at Adam and Drew to see their reaction to the madness.

"No, that was you being a crazy bitch trying to kill me," she screams, starting to get in my face.

I chuckle. "If I wanted to kill you, I fucking would."

She gasps. "You psycho, what the fuck is wrong with you?"

Adam enters the cage with us, and separates us with a hand on each shoulder. "Max, good work. Karissa, I don't think you were even trying."

"She was trying to *kill me*," she screams again and I roll my eyes.

"That's the sport; if you can't handle it, then maybe you need to find something else," Adam tells her seriously.

"You're just taking her side because you're fucking her," Karissa pouts and I can't help but laugh.

"I'm taking her side because she's serious about the sport, and just demonstrated that."

She screeches again, and I can't help myself, "If you fucking scream one more time I'm going to *actually* try and kill you. So just shut the fuck up."

"You're such a bitch, think you're so much better than everyone because you're fucking however many of the guys here."

I just shrug. She doesn't need to know the details of my life, and I don't care if she knows who all I'm fucking, or who I'm not. I just want her to stop bursting my eardrums with her shrill ass voice.

"I think you need to leave. It's obvious your intention isn't to learn the sport, and you're taking it out on another student for no reason," Adam tells her, and I bite back my smile.

"You can't be fucking serious."

"Coach is always serious, time to go," Drew insists, standing between us, probably in case she tries to come after me again, even though I would love it if she would.

She storms out with another one of her signature screams and I feel the headache forming already.

"Alright, who's up next," Adam calls out to the class like nothing has happened.

As I leave the cage, I catch Caine still watching me, as always. He nods in my direction, but I don't miss the way he adjusts himself in his pants because of fucking course that turned him on.

And of course, it makes me want to go over there to help him take care of that little situation he now has. Because I'm addicted to these men just as much as they are to me. Their obsession with me has turned into my obsession with them as well, and I plan to show them just how bad it is later.

⚜

"HOLD ON, I need you to repeat that last part, she said what?" Danner asks, laughing so hard I think she's going to fall off the stool she's sitting on at the bar.

"She thinks I'm fucking all the guys at Uncaged, and was pissed about it. I don't know why you're laughing so hard, it's not *that* funny."

"Oh, it's pretty funny. That bitch has had it coming for so long. I'm just mad I wasn't there to see it happen." She shakes her head.

"My bad, I'll make sure to record it next time."

"Could you? Clearly I need to have eyes in that gym all the time for my own personal entertainment."

"Yeah? So you can watch Cal and Alexander as they train?" I raise an eyebrow at her, knowing mentioning them will get her off my back.

The way her eyes narrow proves I'm right and I laugh, turning around to put the glasses I just dried away.

"You're a buzzkill you know that," she says seriously after I turn back toward her.

I shrug. "I'm just calling it like I see it."

"What is it you see?" She folds her hands under her chin.

"They're always trying to talk to you when they come here," I explain.

"And what do you see that *I* do?"

"Not give them the time of day."

She points a finger gun at me and clicks her tongue. "There ya go."

I roll my eyes at her denial. I know it's just a matter of time. I don't think those two are as…intense as my guys. But they seem persistent and I'm sure there will come a time they manage to wear her down.

"Anyway, I saw the news about your parents, that sucks." Her tone is very obvious about how it does, in fact, not suck and we both know it.

"Yeah, it's wild they would do that to Carson." I shake my head like I can't believe it, though I'm holding back a laugh.

"Sounds like they have a pretty solid case against them, too. Even with Caine's fancy pants dad as their lawyer," she explains and I know it's the safe way for us to talk about this in public.

I nod, unsure of what else to say that isn't completely obvious because I'm not great at our code word game we're playing. I change the subject to safer territory. "By the way, we're all going to Caine's next fight in Portland this weekend if you want to join."

"Who's *all?*"

"The guys...me...your guys," I tell her suggestively and she groans.

"Would you let it go? I don't have guys."

"So you coming?" I don't acknowledge her denial.

She's quiet, twisting her drink around. "I'll think about it. But you need to let it go."

I smile widely. "Don't count on it."

CHAPTER 46
CAINE

It's like I can't escape hearing about Carson's murder case, which means I can't escape hearing about my dad since his firm is representing Max's parents. I want to toss my phone in the ocean because every single time I open the internet that's the first thing that pops up. Apparently, the murder of some big shot CEO's son is a big deal.

Especially when the suspects are the ex fiancé's parents.

My dad's defense team is trying to get the case thrown out. I haven't wanted to read more into how or why, but it pisses me off.

The only reason I don't get rid of my phone is that I need it to be able to watch the cameras in our house to make sure nothing happens again. I also need to be able to get a hold of Max at all times.

I do like that she's able to come with me to my fights though. Not only that, but Adam encourages it. I fight better when she's there because I'm not worried about her. I also love the way it feels to have her watching me.

As annoying as it is to keep being reminded of something I would rather forget, now I at least have my fight to focus on. Which is exactly what I do the entire drive to Portland. We all squeezed into Max's Corolla, with Adam driving, Drew next to him while I have Max plastered to my side in the back seat. She tried for a tiny bit of distance, but I didn't let her.

Even with my headphones in, my pump up playlist playing like I always do before a fight, I wanted to feel her close. I want to get in the zone, but also need to feel her. I would stick my hand down her pants right now and make her come on my fingers if it wouldn't fuck up my routine. Even I know that may distract me a bit too much.

But on the drive home, I'll probably have her sitting on my cock the whole time. Actually, that's a good idea. I look down to Max to tell her my plan, but notice she's fallen asleep. That's fine, she doesn't need to know ahead of time. She'll enjoy it when it happens.

I continue to listen to my playlist, staring out the window while my fingers run through Max's soft hair absentmindedly.

WE GET to tonight's venue several hours early and Cal, Alexander, and Danner arrive shortly after us. She insisted she was coming for Max, and refused to ride with the two guys who were practically begging for her attention. I know Cal has wanted her for awhile, and since him and Alexander are practically attached at the hip with how good of friends they are. I wouldn't be surprised if they *both* wanted her.

I, apparently, have no room to talk when it comes to that type of situation. Despite my reluctance, I'm too far in now.

My headphones stay on as Adam and I go to check in. Before I walk away, I make sure to give Max a rough kiss since it's the last one I'll get before the fight and I have to make sure I make it worth it.

When I pull back her eyes are hazy and I know what my girl looks like turned on, which is exactly what she is right now. I lean down. "Don't worry, killer, you'll get my cock in your needy little pussy after I win."

She shakes her head, patting my chest, and instead of walking away, I pull her into me again, taking one of my earbuds out. "I love you."

"I love you too," she whispers between us, like it's still so foreign for her to say, and I agree, but with her it comes way easier than I would have ever guessed.

I can't help but yank her lips onto mine again because hearing her say those words to me has me ready to abandon the fight altogether, though I know she wouldn't let me. If that doesn't show how much I love her, I don't know what does.

Maybe accepting sharing her with two other men.

Before I can get any more distracted, Adam and I head to check in. I turn my music back on loud enough to drown everything out so I can get in the zone. My hands are stuffed in the front pocket of my hoodie, and I refuse to look at anyone, completely focused on the fight.

After we're checked in, we go back to where the fighters go to prepare and do just that until it's my time. I continue everything I normally do, but it's right before I'm about to get called up that Adam looks at his phone, and doesn't do a good job hiding the face he makes.

I know I shouldn't ask, especially when I'm only minutes from going into the cage, but something about the way he's looking and then trying to act like he's not has me asking.

"What?"

He shakes his head. "Nothing, doesn't matter, let's go."

"Fuck that, it's something. What is it?"

"You're about to go out there, you're not getting in your head with anything. I'll tell you after," he insists.

"I'm already in my head, so you might as well fucking tell me."

"It's nothing, Max is okay, everything is fine. Focus on the fight."

I want to argue with him, but knowing Max is okay has me accepting what he's saying for now. Because my name is being called to go out and now, it's time for me to do what I came here to do.

As soon as I enter the cage, my opponent is across from me already acting like he's a lot more dangerous than he is. He snarls through his mouth guard and I just look at him. Though, I make sure to scan the crowd to find my girl. I find her easily, my eyes are always drawn to her.

After I see her, I'm ready to go, turning back to my opponent and the fight begins. He tries to get ahead of me, I play with him a bit, taunting him as we fight. I even let him think he has the upper hand for a moment.

By the way Adam is yelling at me, he knows exactly what I'm doing. It doesn't take long before I manage to get the guy in a solid guard he can't get out of. But I don't want it over yet, so I let him think he's the reason I let go.

We continue and I'm having fun, which isn't always the case. Usually I just want to win, but today I'm enjoying the fight. It's like my own little game I'm playing. At some point it needs to end, so I stop playing around and actually fight. He clearly doesn't see it coming, and I win in a knockout.

My eyes stay locked on Max's as I'm announced as the winner and the way she's screaming and cheering for me has me even more excited to get my hands on her. I know she'll let me do whatever I want. I'll make sure to make it worth it.

I'm so focused on my win and Max by the time we leave that I don't even think to ask Adam about what he didn't want to tell me earlier. Since it hasn't come up again, I assume it doesn't matter.

Plus, once we're leaving, I'm ready to get inside my girl and nothing else matters anyway. Everything else can wait. She's safe, we're all together, and I just won yet another fight. Life is pretty fucking good.

The next morning, I want to sleep in, but never can. My body should be exhausted after a fight and want to recover, but it's like it rejuvenates me and I always wake up early the next day ready for more.

The last thing I want to do is untangle myself from Max, but she needs sleep. I may be a selfish bastard, but my girl needs to rest so she can handle more. Because I sure as shit plan on giving it to her.

I notice Adam isn't in bed on the other side of Drew as he usually is and I remember what happened before the fight. I really consider staying in bed, but if I'm going to figure out what that was about I can't have her awake distracting me.

I get out of bed and when I get to the living room I find Adam on the couch with his laptop on his lap. He looks over at me as I walk out and gives me a small nod.

"'Sup?" I ask.

"Couldn't sleep, usual shit."

I grunt in response, not sure what to say to that. "So, what was up yesterday before my fight?"

He sighs, closing his laptop and running his hand down his face. "I didn't want to say anything, but I feel like we should wait until Max and Drew are up too."

"Fuck that, we can tell them later, what the fuck is it?"

"Apparently, your dad has been dropped from the case and has been put on some sort of leave while he's being investigated."

I can't help the smile that starts to spread across my face, knowing my dad is getting fucked over in some way, and I don't think Danner had anything to do with it. No, this is all him being a piece of shit.

"What's he being investigated for?" I ask, unable to hide how happy I sound.

"That took a bit of digging to find out, but from what I could see, something about bribing judges."

I burst out laughing, and it's probably the hardest that I've ever laughed before. I probably shouldn't, but the fact that fucker is getting what he deserves while my life only gets better is the best type of revenge.

CHAPTER 47
MAX

Danner and I had an extremely fun time at Caine's fight. She never left my side, despite Cal and Alexander trying to get her attention multiple times. She pretended like they didn't exist. Regardless, it was fun and felt surprisingly normal. Like we were just two friends watching an MMA fight.

Everything else faded into the background for a while and we just…enjoyed. Of course, I had even more fun later when my entire body was worshipped by my guys, but that's nothing unusual.

Though, I wake up and only have Drew next to me, which isn't entirely unusual. Caine usually wakes up early and doesn't always stay in bed. I look past Drew to see that Adam isn't in bed either, and wonder where they both could be.

I'm a little surprised to find them both in the living room, Adam is sitting on the couch with his closed laptop next to him, and Caine is standing with his large arms folded across his chest looking weirdly giddy.

"What's going on?" I ask, looking between them.

"Turns out my dad has been bribing judges, which explains why he's won some of the cases he has," Caine tells me.

"Wait, what?" I shake my head, this was not the kind of news I was expecting this early and I don't know how to process any of it. "What does that mean?"

"He's suspended, so he won't be representing your parents," he explains. "Hopefully getting his ass handed to him so every shitty thing he's done can catch up to him."

"That's...good?" I question because Caine is extremely happy about this, which is unusual for him and I'm still trying to catch up.

"That's very good, killer, he's a piece of shit and is getting caught for it."

"Is that because of Danner?" I wonder.

Adam shakes his head. "Doesn't seem like it, but I wouldn't put it past her."

"Who the fuck *is she?*" I can't help but ask. They both shake their heads.

"Someone who we're lucky to have around," Adam says.

"That's true. So what does this mean for my parent's trial?"

"They're getting another attorney, but luckily my dad's

whole firm is being investigated so it won't be someone there. Including my asshole brother."

"That's good, but does that mean they may have a higher chance of getting off?" I flinch at the thought.

"I don't think so. They have a lot of evidence thanks to your friend; I wouldn't worry too much about it, baby girl."

I drop down on the couch, next to Adam, and he pulls me into his side, which is always so calming when he does. I know we both have our trauma and his struggle with physical touch makes it more special when he initiates it in a not sexual scenario.

"Okay, Daddy." I smile up at him. He groans, squeezing my shoulder.

"Don't start something you don't want to finish," he threatens.

"Oh, I'll finish it." I smile.

"Damn fucking right you will, killer, let's go to bed."

I look at Adam, hoping he'll join. And I manage to drag them both to bed. Hoping they're right and that we don't have anything to worry about. I can't take anymore setbacks in life. I need everything to work out from now on.

I feel like I've earned a bit of peace in my life and I would like that to be with my three men and myself. No risk of prison, no risk of crazy family kidnappings. The only crazy can be between the four of us. And that's the type of crazy I prefer.

"You really didn't have anything to do with Caine's dad being investigated?" I ask Danner as we sit on the beach, which has become one of my favorite routines. We walk some, watch the ocean some. We talk, but sometimes we're silent. Danner knows what I need just like my guys do.

Of course in different ways.

"No, I really didn't," she insists.

"You sure you didn't use some of your little vigilante powers to get him caught?"

She chuckles. "I'm not a vigilante."

"Undercover cop?"

"Absolutely not."

"Connected to the mob?"

She shakes her head. "Will you just drop it and accept me for who I am without needing to have all the answers?"

I huff out a breath. "That wasn't a no about the mob."

"Max," she practically scolds and I roll my eyes.

"I'll figure it out one of these days," I insist.

"Yeah, okay. Anyway, no I didn't have anything to do with that, but I may have had something to do with another thing."

"What is it?" I'm partly excited, but also worried about what else could happen.

"Don't worry, you'll see." She smiles. "Now, let's backtrack a bit because you never told me exactly what happened when you kicked Karissa's ass."

"I hardly would say I kicked her ass." I laugh.

"That's not what Drew said."

"Oh my God, he would." I roll my eyes because of course he would exaggerate what happened when telling my friend.

That's okay because it's just another thing I love about him, but I do make sure to tell Danner the real unexaggerated version of what happened during that class.

༄

ADAM SENT me a text while I was with Danner asking me to come by his house. I didn't question it, because why would I?

When I arrive, I'm greeted by him in the doorway looking as attractive as usual. Hair slightly disheveled and I wonder if Drew and Caine are waiting inside as well, but when I enter the quiet house, I realize it's just us.

"What's going on?" I ask.

"On your knees, baby girl," Adam instructs, though it feels like more of a demand.

"Yes Daddy," I sass while doing what he asks. His eyes flare before roaming over my body.

"Take off your shirt." This time it truly is a demand.

I swallow roughly, reaching down to pull my top off as he walks away, and I don't dare ask what he's doing. Not even when he's at Athena's tank and opening it. I stare at him, clenching my thighs together, the fear and arousal a lethal mixture.

Even when he turns back around toward me with the snake in his hands, my mouth drops in shock, but nothing comes out. He steps closer and I try to back away, but the wall behind me stops the movement.

"Remember the last time you held Athena?" he asks.

"I don't think that counts as holding her," I retort, keeping my eyes on the slithering creature.

"Close enough. I remember how much you enjoyed it."

"I don't." I shake my head.

"Aw, baby girl, don't lie. You're going to hurt her feelings. She likes you."

I shake my head even more, "No. Nope, not again, Adam."

"You two are my special girls, it's important you get along." He moves to drape her across my shoulders again and I freeze the second she's against my bare skin.

"Adam," I whimper, especially as Athena starts to wrap herself around my neck again, but not tightly. It's like she thinks she's a scarf. A scaly, slimy, scarf.

"She won't hurt you, baby girl." He swipes some of my hair off my forehead. "Did she last time?"

"There's a first time for everything," I squeak out.

He lets out a soft chuckle. "Yeah, this can be the first time you take my cock in your pretty little throat while wearing Athena as a necklace."

My jaw drops, but I close it quickly because I don't need the snake to take that as an invitation. I shake my head.

"Aw, baby girl, I thought we were done with you denying us." He chuckles softly.

"I also thought the snake was a one time thing," I squeak out.

"We're a package deal, just like you are with Caine and Drew."

"I think this is a little different," I gasp.

"Maybe, but if you didn't love it so much the first time we wouldn't do it again."

I don't have a retort to that because I remember the fear. I remember not being able to breathe and how I was convinced I was going to die. On the other hand, I remember how turned on I was. How badly I wanted his hands on me. How the feeling of having my air cut off only added to the release when it finally hit me.

I remember how much I fucking loved it.

Even if I would rather wear his hand as a necklace than his snake, the danger only adds to the moment. Which is why I do want it.

Despite all the reasons I shouldn't, I open my mouth, silently telling Adam exactly what I want. He smirks down at me, taking his time to unbutton his pants. I start to close my mouth, but he shoves his thumb in, pushing down on my tongue and forcing my mouth open wider.

"Keep this open for me, baby girl. I want to see the drool fall from these pretty little lips while you wait so patiently for my cock to fill it up."

I whimper softly and Athena tightens slightly around my throat making my eyes bulge, but I don't move. Adam keeps his finger pushed in my mouth while he works his pants off with one hand.

"Look at you, already so desperate for me, is it getting hard to breathe?"

I nod slightly.

"Good, let me see some of that drool, make sure your mouth is nice and wet for me."

I do my best to push some out and it must satisfy him because he lets out a low groan, collecting the saliva on his finger he removes from my mouth and swipes it along his length. I keep my mouth dropped open because the sight is so fucking hot, and also I want to be good for him. Which is a thought I never would've imagined having, but here we are. My entire life has been flipped on itself all thanks to these three men and I can't do anything about it.

I reach forward to get him to come closer. He grabs my hand, stopping me. "That's not being patient."

I narrow my eyes.

"There she is, there's my spitfire I love to see," he coos.

He rewards me by pushing his thick cock into my mouth, letting me taste every inch of him as he pushes to the back of my throat. I try not to gag around him, wanting to take more. Wanting to do everything in my power to be so good for him. Even as Athena starts to tighten slightly around my throat.

I work through my fear, though it's still there and only makes me wetter knowing what's happening. I know it's fucked up. I know I'm so wrong for feeling this way, but these men make it feel like it's okay. My men.

Closing my lips around Adam, I hollow my cheeks and suck hard which makes him groan loudly above me. His hands fist the hair at the top of my head, holding me in place.

"How're you feeling, baby girl? How's your breathing?"

I hum around him in response. I swear if he tries to stop this I'll bite down so he's unable to leave my mouth. I've liked fighting back, telling them no, trying to escape, but right now in this moment I don't want to do any of that. I want him to know that this is exactly what I need right now.

That I'm scared, but doing it anyway because I want to. Because I'm beyond turned on. He seems to understand, and uses his grip on my hair to fuck into my mouth harder. I take everything he gives me, hitting the back of my throat while my air is constricted.

"So good for me, baby girl. Fuck you're perfect," Adam grinds out while fucking me even harder.

"I knew I'd be missing something." Drew's voice pulls me back to reality slightly. I didn't hear him come in. Or maybe he was here and I didn't know.

Or maybe I'm hallucinating from lack of oxygen.

"You want to join her?" Adam asks.

Drew hums, coming closer. I look up at him, blurry through my tears but he's standing right next to Adam. So close I think they may touch, but both of them are focused on me instead.

"Nah, I'm going to enjoy this," Drew answers, not moving from his spot, and not taking his eyes off me.

It's like something switches in Adam and I thought he was rough before, but it only increases now as he pulls back so it's just the tip of him between my lips. I lick around the crown before he thrusts back in almost completely. This time I'm unable to fight the gagging sound I make and it makes Athena tighten so my air is completely cut off.

My eyes bulge as I look up at the two men looming over me.

"Can you breathe, little one?"

I make a small sound, and he looks at Adam, then back to me. "You better not kill our girl," he threatens.

"Not gonna kill her, she loves this, don't you?"

I hum, closing my eyes to try and blink away some of the tears so I can really see them. They look so good together. So tall, attractive, and in love with me. I think there's more, though. There's more to them, more than they want to admit.

Adam swells inside my mouth, moaning loudly before he floods my throat with his release and I struggle to swallow it all. He pulls himself from my mouth, and I stand. Incredibly wet, but I look between them and I want to see if what I'm suspecting could be real.

Adam removes Athena from my neck and I grab my shirt and tug it back on, looking between them. I know there's no way either of them would ever admit anything on their own. I have to force feelings out of them. So if that's what I need to do for them to admit what I now feel is completely obvious, then that's what I'm going to do.

CHAPTER 48
ADAM

"You both love me?" Max questions.

"You know we do," I respond easily, answering for both of us, putting Athena away.

"What about…each other?" She hesitates and I look over at Drew who's just as surprised by the question as I am.

"What're you getting at, baby girl?"

"I think you two have more feelings for each other than you want to admit, but you should." She places her hands on her hips, looking between the two of us.

"I think you're seeing things, little one. We're in this for *you*," Drew insists. I can't explain the way I feel when a small part of me was wondering if he would have a different response. Like maybe she was right and there is more between us. But it's all because of her.

Neither of us would have let anything progress between us

beyond the physical if we weren't in this situation with her. With her pulling the emotions from us, albeit unwillingly.

"Am I? Because I've seen how you look at Adam when you don't think anyone notices." She raises an eyebrow at him, and I do the same.

"Like what?" I question.

"You've always been a bit overly protective when it comes to him, you don't think that means anything?" She swings her gaze over to me.

"I show the same level of protectiveness to all my fighters that get injured," I insist, folding my arms over my chest.

"You both can stay in denial, but I know it's not true and you should just admit it. Make things easier." Max shrugs.

"Makes what easier, baby girl?"

"You two realizing it's okay to have feelings. It's even more okay to admit them."

"We did," Drew insists.

"For *me*."

"We aren't going to lie," I tell her, seriously.

"Would it be a lie?" she questions.

I open my mouth to say something, but snap it shut as I really think about it. How I feel about Drew is different than how I feel about Max, but not entirely. With her, the love I feel is easy, it's natural and like it should have always been there. With Drew I feel…out of control. Like he tests me, but I want to protect him. I want him to succeed, just not at the expense of ruining his body.

At the base of it all I want them both happy. I want them to do things that make them happy, be around people that make them happy even if it's not me. Even if they are it for me.

Oh fuck.

I do love him.

With the way he's acting, though, I don't think he feels the same way and I'm not about to force my fucked up feelings on him. We've forced enough on Max, I'm not about to do that to him. We're all in this relationship and it works, there's no need to do anything to alter it like she's trying to do.

"Why does it matter, little one? Is this not enough for you?"

"Of course it is, but I don't want you two walking around with suppressed feelings because you don't think you can admit them," she insists.

"Then what if we did?" I say suddenly.

"Did what?" she questions.

"Admit we have feelings." I try to keep my voice even.

"Do you?" Her eyes widen.

"Yeah, do you?" Drew asks, his own shock written all over

his face, but he does a good job hiding any other emotion he may be feeling.

"Would that be the worst thing in the world?" I stand tall, ready to defend and deny if I need to.

"No, I just...Do you?" Drew shakes his head with the question.

"Yeah, do you?" Max goads slightly.

I grind my teeth, regretting saying anything. I struggled enough admitting my feelings for Max, and I haven't even considered feelings for Drew. So, instead of anything else I turn to what I know is a distraction for all of us. Especially at times like this when I don't want to talk about emotions or anything resembling them.

Which is always.

"How about you two stop with the questions and do what you're told. Max, go over there." I nod toward a chair across the room.

I see defiance shine in her eyes, but before she has a chance to say anything I speak again, "Drew, strip."

He has his own internal battle about arguing with me, and I silently dare them both to do just that. They can either argue about this. Or they can let it happen on my terms and we all end up happy in the end. Up to them.

Luckily, for all of us they decide to listen. Drew reaches behind his head, pulling his shirt off revealing his toned chest. Max stares at him, and is still unmoving.

"Max, go get the lube."

This time, she goes, listening like the good little girl she is for me. For all of us. Jumping into action to go get the bottle of lube from my room. When she comes back she hands it to me, and then goes to sit down, squirming slightly when she sees Drew is down to only his boxers.

"We always said this doesn't mean anything," I say to Drew.

"Never has." He nods.

"But what if it did?" I reach behind my neck, pulling my own shirt up over my head.

"What if it did what?" he asks with narrowed eyes.

"Mean something."

"Does it?"

"You tell me." I step forward, teasing the waistband of his boxers, but not pulling them down or reaching in yet.

"What would it mean?" he asks weakly.

I raise an eyebrow.

"Is this only for her?" His voice drops quieter, almost like it's just for us, but I know Max can still hear.

"No. This is for us," I admit, hoping he understands.

"So, does it mean something then?" Drew reaches down to my pants, popping the button on them.

I swallow roughly, the song and dance we've always played around this has been the same for awhile. Though, it has been different for awhile this is the first time it's being spoken. And I finally do.

"Yeah. It does."

His mouth drops open, but I don't allow him to say anything, grabbing the back of his neck, and pulling his lips onto mine roughly. I faintly hear Max's gasp, but my focus is solely on Drew. On proving to both of us that this can, and does, mean something. We may have been lying before, but I'm done lying now.

He better be too, because I'm not going to be the only one putting myself out on a limb like this. He meets my fierce kiss with one of his own, and I know this means something for him too. It has to. We can deny it all we want, but this isn't nothing.

It hasn't been for awhile.

I yank on his waistband, pulling his boxers down, immediately wrapping my hand around his cock that's hard, and already dripping from the tip.

"You want this, don't you?" I ask into his mouth, pulling his bottom lip between my teeth roughly.

He groans, thrusting forward into my hand and I squeeze tighter around him. "Yeah, you do. Gonna show Max what a good boy you are for me."

Drew snarls, but it quickly turns into a moan when I rub against his piercings. "Not a fucking good boy for you."

"Yeah you are, you fucking love listening to your coach," I grind out with another rough tug on his dick.

He grunts in response, and starts yanking at my pants, trying to get them off my body as quickly as possible while I continue to work my fist over him.

"How about you tell our girl over there what she's going to do while she watches me fuck you," I demand.

The small amount of control I give him has him smirking over at Max while I run my lips along his throat, continuing to let him use my hand as he thrusts into it.

"Let's see you touch that pretty little pussy of yours. I want to watch you come apart while coach fucks me," Drew tells her, and she sucks her bottom lip in between her teeth, barely concealing the small moan she lets out.

I take my hand off Drew to help him push down my pants the rest of the way, joining the rest of our clothes on the floor.

"This what you want, baby girl? Want to see us admit our feelings for each other while you rub that sweet cunt for us?" I ask, guiding Drew over to the couch, instructing him without words into the position I want him in.

"This is even more than I wanted," she admits, "But I want to see more before I dare touch myself."

"See more of what?" I question.

"All of it."

Drew is bent over the arm of the couch, while I settle behind him, already pouring some of the lube between his cheeks, spreading them apart and rubbing the area between them with the liquid. Then, coating one of my fingers in it I press against the tight bud, just barely pressing the tip inside and he's already groaning, trying to push back and get more.

"So fucking needy, aren't you? Such a desperate fuck toy for me," I groan, pushing my finger in all the way.

"More," he pleads. "If this means something, I want everything you're going to give me."

"That so?" I ask, pushing another finger in and he clenches, groaning loudly with the invasion.

"Yeah, fuck me," he moans loudly.

"I'm going to, and you're going to say how it feels. No holding back."

"Fuck, okay, yes. Whatever gets you to fuck me," he practically begs and I love when he gets desperate like this. The only thing that would make it better is Max begging alongside him.

I like that she's just watching like a good little girl. My eyes look up to meet hers, and she's clenching her thighs tightly together, eyes locked on us and barely even looks like she's breathing. It seems like she doesn't want to do anything to disrupt this moment and knows that it's for Drew and me. Even if she was the reason for us coming together in this way. This moment is about us. This is just *us*.

"You sure you're ready?" I ask Drew, scissoring my fingers and he tries to push back onto me more.

"Yes, so fucking ready," he says through clenched teeth.

Instead of teasing him more, I pull my hand away and start to coat my dick in the lube before dripping more onto his ass for good measure.

"This what you wanted to see baby girl? Wanted to see me fuck him, knowing that for once it actually means something?" I ask Max, lining up against Drew's ass.

"Yeah, but I want you doing this for yourselves and for each other," she encourages.

I grip Drew's hair tightly, yanking his head back. "What do you say, is this for us?"

He nods against my hold. "Yeah, it's for us."

"So good for me." I can't help but tease him a bit, but then I'm pushing into his tightness that any retort he may have had dies on his tongue.

Our moans mix together as his heat envelopes my cock and it feels so fucking good. I never would've thought it would actually feel different knowing that this is more than just sex, but it does. Somehow, in someway, it really does.

When I'm fully seated, my pelvis pressed completely against him we both let out a loud moan. My eyes look up to find Max to see her reaction. She's completely fixated on us, unmoving, barely breathing as she watches us.

Knowing she's here, knowing her feelings for us and the fact that she knows our feelings for each other only add to the moment, and I pull my hips back before thrusting forward roughly. Grabbing onto his shoulder, I pull him back as I thrust forward and fuck him harder than I feel like I ever have.

"How does it feel?" I groan.

"Feels like your type of love is fucking brutal. Which is exactly what I need," he moans and fuck if that doesn't make me fuck him harder.

"You saying you need my type of love?" I can't help but ask. The word a lot less scary coming from my lips than it was before.

"Yeah, just like you need mine." I see the way he's gripping the couch with white knuckles as he takes everything I give him.

"I do," I grunt in agreement because I do.

Our lives wouldn't be complete without each other in them. We have Max, and it wouldn't be complete without her, but if we had to walk around denying each other forever, something would always be missing. We may fight to admit it, it's the truth.

"I need your love that pushes me, that fights back and that also accepts every fucked up battered and broken piece of me," I admit, leaning over his back to wrap my hand around his cock as I keep a steady pace of thrusts, matching them with my fist.

"Fuck yes," he moans, dropping his forehead down and I know the time for talking is done, he's going to come and I'm not going to be far behind.

I look up and see Max has finally moved her hand into her

pants, and is touching herself watching us. It's like she needed us to admit that to each other. That is the final straw she needed.

Drew groans loudly, pushing into my hand and back against me seconds before he's coming, I feel the warmth coat my hand as he shudders underneath me. I'm unable to hold back any longer myself, pushing in deep while moaning my own release, coming louder and harder than I think I ever have.

Max's cries mix with ours and in this moment nothing necessarily changed, because it's how it's been. We've just finally admitted it. That within itself is enough to acknowledge that everything changed.

That this isn't just fun for us. This is everything.

CHAPTER 49
DREW

I never thought I'd see the day.

Well, I really hoped I would, because he's been a shady fucker the entire time I've lived here, but I never truly thought anything would happen to him.

Which is why the notification on the community social media about Officer Doogie getting fired is extremely satisfying. It didn't go into details, but we know what they are.

Though, it's not enough. Especially not for Caine.

Or me. We could run him out of this town, he could get arrested for what he did and it still wouldn't be enough. It doesn't matter that Max, Adam, and Danner insist that we drop it, and let him live out his miserable life without the made up power to fuck with us anymore.

We aren't going to listen.

Caine claims he doesn't react without a plan, that's almost

exactly what we're doing. Mostly because we have to sneak out while Max and Adam are sleeping, and be back before they wake up.

I managed to get the ex-officers address from Danner, though it took a bit of convincing.

"No way," she insists.

"We won't kill him," I tell her.

"Somehow, I still don't believe you."

"That's fine. If we do, we won't involve you."

"Now I really don't believe you." She shakes her head and looks over at Max who's behind the bar, not paying attention to us. Which is good because I don't want her overhearing and knowing about this half assed plan.

"I won't ask you for anything ever again," I try.

"You're not doing very well convincing me."

"What will it take?"

"Tell your buddies to leave me alone. It's not going to happen, and they're wasting their time."

"Who? Cal and Alexander?" I act clueless.

She gives me a look that tells me she doesn't buy my nonchalant act.

"Fine, I'll tell them to back off," I relent.

"Fine, I'll see what I can do."

I figured she still wouldn't follow through, but she did, writing the address on a piece of paper she slipped me the last time she saw me, telling me to burn it right away.

Now, Caine and I are headed to the house that turns out to be a little shit hole on the edge of town. It's perfect because there's not many people around to hear him beg for mercy.

Caine and I don't say much as we cut the engines on our bikes down the street, and go around the back of the small shack looking house. He ends up picking the lock of a side door we find and I really wonder why that's a skill he developed. Though, it helps right now so I guess it doesn't matter.

We find the older man asleep, and he clearly isn't someone who's on guard because we aren't quiet as we stomp through his house, or as we enter his room.

Or when Caine kicks him in the stomach.

"Get the fuck up." My tone is stern, but not loud.

"Wha—" He grunts, trying to get his bearings, but I don't let him get far, grabbing the back of his shirt, and slamming him down onto the ground, face first.

"Don't fucking act like you don't know who we are." Caine kicks him in his side again.

"I'll kill you," Doogie spits, and I laugh, continuing to hold him down by the back of his neck as he attempts to get up weakly.

"Should I let you up so you can try?" I taunt.

"You let me up I'll either arrest you or kill you," he groans, and I see Caine is pressing his foot on the small of his back.

"Can't arrest us, you're not a cop anymore." Caine smiles, and it's so sinister I would be afraid of him if I didn't know him. "If you want to try to kill us, then go ahead."

He lets up at the same time I do, and we give the older man a chance to get up off the floor. He struggles, coughing and wheezing as he does. But we just wait, standing tall, waiting to see what he'll do.

As soon as he's standing, he continues to stay slightly hunched even while raising his fists like he's actually going to attempt to fight us. I can't help the laugh that bursts out of me at the sight.

Caine just looks entertained. Especially when Doogie actually starts coming toward us like he's going to throw one of those fists. Before he gets the chance, Caine moves quickly, jabbing his own punch forward right into the man's face.

Doogie's hand flies up to his nose that's pouring blood while he groans in pain.

"What was that you were saying about killing us?" I can't help but tease him.

"You're fucking dead men."

"Yeah, okay," I scoff. "Pretty sure that's you. Maybe you should think about what a fuck up you are getting paid off to help get our girl hurt."

"I don't give a fuck about you or your girl," he spits.

"Good." Caine throws another punch to the man's face and this time I hear the crunch of his nose breaking. It should disgust me, but all it does is make me smile.

"You motherfucker," Doogie groans, hunched over in pain and somehow still standing.

"Anything else you want to say? Or are you actually going to fight us like you said you would?" I ask because frankly, my own fists are tingling with the urge to feel the crunch of bones underneath them.

"Yeah," he says weakly, raising his fists again and a loud laugh bursts out of me.

"Okay." I shrug, and Caine and I let loose on him. It's not a fair fight, but we didn't come in here expecting one.

I did think that maybe we could toy with him a bit more. Maybe he would beg for his life some. He continues to hold his ground, and that only makes us go harder, beating his face in. Once he ends up on the ground, unable to fight back anymore, Caine is on him throwing his fist into his face over and over.

I end up having to pull him off once Doogie isn't moving any longer, and I think he may have actually killed him. The scene is so familiar to me. The rush of panic in the back of my mind tries to take over at the familiar feeling I had when my dad looked like this man on the ground.

"Enough," I tell Caine who's breathing heavily as he looks down at the unconscious man.

We're both quiet, looking at him, wondering if he's going to move.

"Think he's dead?" Caine asks.

I shake my head, not sure how to answer. I really take in the scene and how similar it was to the day I ran away from home. The shitty house, busted up floor. The old man beat to shit on it, blood on my knuckles and clothes splattered around.

Though, this time I'm not alone. And this time, I'm less afraid. I know I have a place to go that's safe. I know I have people who make it safe. And I know the man isn't dead. Because he groans again, trying to turn onto his side, spitting blood onto the floor.

I kneel down by his head, making sure he can hear me. "We weren't here. We have an alibi, and if you even think about fucking with us we *will* kill you. Get the fuck out of this town before we decide to come back and finish what we started."

With that, we leave. Though, it may be stupid, I have a feeling he's going to listen. He has nothing for him here anymore. No job, no friends, and it won't take much to turn everyone who lives around here on him.

I'm pretty sure half the town already hates him anyway, so it wouldn't be that hard.

"You know, there could be worse guys to share my girl with," Caine grunts out and I'm pretty sure he's joking, which is why it shocks me a bit. The guy doesn't joke.

"Wow, was that you saying something nice?" I hold my hand against my chest dramatically.

"Don't get used to it."

When we get back to Max's house, both her and Adam are still sleeping peacefully. Caine doesn't even bother washing off the evidence of where we've been, he just sheds his clothes. I think he at least wipes off his knuckles with his shirt before he slides into bed, pulling Max into him.

Though I'm dying to do the same, I jump in the shower to quickly wash off the dried blood. I don't linger because the only place I want to be right now is between my two favorite people.

That's when it really hits me, that I've felt that way about Adam. This whole relationship has been new for all of us, but Adam and I have another layer. While what we had before was just sexual, when it's all of us together it feels like more, even between us.

I want him, just as much as I want Max. None of this would be complete without the four of us. Even Caine adds to the relationship in a way I never would have guessed.

When I get into bed, I'm careful not to jostle them, but Adam ends up speaking softly, "Where were you?"

"Don't worry about it," I tell him. He doesn't say anything else, but I'm sure we'll hear about it in the morning.

Which is fine. There's nothing they can do about it now. Adam settles back, keeping his arms resting on his stomach like he always does. And even though Caine has pulled Max against him, I can't help but do the same.

As I'm falling asleep, I swear I feel Adam scoot closer to my back. Eventually, I feel his tentative touch on me, and I relax even more. After we admitted more of our feelings something has shifted between us. We aren't lovey people, but it still feels good to know that this is what we have. All of us. Together.

CHAPTER 50
ADAM

"I thought we talked about going off half cocked." I shake my head at the two other men sitting across the island from me while we eat breakfast.

"And I told you, I'm never half cocked," Caine retorts.

"Yeah, I think you kind of did exactly that," Max says, cupping her mug of coffee close to her chest.

"Did you guys at least wear masks or anything?" I ask them, and the look on their faces tells me they didn't. "I don't think Danner will help you guys get out of this one."

"We won't need her," Drew insists. I just shake my head again at them.

They were so proud to tell us what happened last night when we all got up this morning. I know Max and I both feel the same way about their little adventure. There's been a lingering worry ever since Max has been back about what was going to happen and I feel like it was just starting to get better with Max's parents getting arrested for it.

Now, we're going to have to worry about if Doogie is going to do anything or if he'll listen to them and actually leave town like he should.

"If your not-plan ends up working, then I won't lie. That was pretty sexy of you guys." Max smirks.

"Don't encourage them," I grumble.

"Please encourage us, little one." Drew yanks her into his side with an arm wrapped around her waist.

"Okay, well, who's coming to the gym today? Unless you end up arrested, that is." I give both men a glare.

"Since I'm working, I will," Drew says, pulling Max tighter against him when she tries to walk away, and giggles at the movement.

"I am. Alexander wants to spar with me," Caine adds.

"Take it easy on him," I insist.

Caine mumbles something I can't quite hear, but I think it's something about being too bossy.

"Daddy's on a roll today, what demand do you have for me," Max sasses.

"I'll have plenty for you later, baby girl."

She doesn't suppress the shiver that runs through her body

and Drew nuzzles into her neck, which only makes her squeak a small moan. I know that if we all get started, we won't end up leaving the house.

"Let's go, we have limited time before you two are carted off to prison," I half joke.

"I know you're new to joking, but that's not funny," Max scolds.

"Aw." I pull her out of Drew's grip and into me, speaking against her ear. "You can come up with a punishment for me later."

Her eyes light up when she looks at me, but then they narrow. "That's another joke."

"Now you're catching on. I'll be the one doling out punishments." I wink. "I'm heading to the gym. Feel free to join me, any of you."

I know they will, which is why I have no problem walking out to get on my bike and driving the short distance to Uncaged. All while thinking of exactly what I can do to our girl later.

⚚

AFTER CLASSES ARE DONE for the day, Caine and Drew are both working out. I think they may be competing a bit especially because Max walked in here about thirty minutes ago since she got to go home early from work apparently.

She was toying with them, teasing so bad I thought they were going to fuck her while I was still teaching the last class of the day. That is until she followed me into my office, and I watch the way both guys stop what they're doing to stare at her ass.

Max closes the door behind her when we're both in my office. "What're you doing, baby girl?"

She shrugs, her back resting on the now closed door.

"You trying to fuck with them?" I can't help but ask.

She shrugs again. "Maybe a little. They deserve it for what they decided to do without us."

"They deserve more than getting to stare at your ass as you walk in here," I tell her and she smirks.

She sways her hips, walking toward me, and climbing onto my lap. I welcome her attention, loving the way it feels to just have her alone, even for a moment.

That's when I remember the folder in my desk drawer that's been bothering me for so long, and with Max here with me, I get an idea. Keeping an arm wrapped around her, I lean forward toward the drawer, opening it and pulling out the simple folder, dropping it onto my desk in front of us.

"What's that?" Max asks, turning in my lap slightly to look at me. "Don't tell me that's some in depth report on me or something."

I breathe out a small laugh. "No, it's not on you, baby girl. It's info I asked Danner to get for me…on my birth parents."

She sucks in a small gasp, and I can see the worry written on her face. "What does it say?"

"I don't know. I haven't looked at it."

"How long have you had it?"

"Awhile."

"Do you want to look at it?"

I grip her thigh, running my hand along her soft leggings, enjoying the feel of them and her as I try to stay grounded. "I haven't been sure. But I think I should."

"You can if you want to, but it won't change anything either way," she says, and I know she's trying to comfort me. I appreciate it more than I could ever explain.

"I know, I just feel like I should know once and for all. I think it'll help if you stay right here." I clamp my hand down on her leg, though I don't think she's planning to go anywhere.

Max nods. "I'm here for you. I'm always here for you."

I can't help myself, reaching up, I grab the back of her neck tangling my fingers in her hair there and pulling her mouth down to mine. "Fuck, I love you," I groan.

She kisses me back; I push my tongue into her mouth to caress hers and she melts against me. When I part our lips she sighs, "I love you."

Before I can talk myself out of it, I reach forward and open the folder, pulling it toward the both of us so I can reach it a bit easier. I make sure to keep Max on me, not that I think she's going anywhere, but I need to feel her sitting on my lap as I read.

There aren't any pictures, which I half expected to see. I'm somewhat disappointed, since I have no memories of either of my parents and I thought that maybe I would see what they look like. But I don't.

My eyes dart all over the page, unsure where to look first. I'm looking around so much, I'm not able to read anything. It's all jumbled together before my eyes finally settle on one of the top lines. It's information on my birth mom, her name being the giveaway. *Talia Hayes.* Her last name was the one thing I have known.

I try not to show any reaction to seeing her name. Instead, I try and remain focused on the rest of the page. My eyes catch on the dates just a little lower, and the way my stomach drops is my only reaction.

I was fifteen when she died and had no idea. She was only thirty-one.

I don't know how to feel about it, about any of this. So, I keep reading until I see *cause of death.* I don't know what I was expecting, but seeing the words *drug overdose* makes complete sense. I knew she had a problem, that's why I was never in her care, but part of me hoped maybe she got sober and regretted never getting to know me.

Knowing now she was only sixteen when she had me and died before I even reached that age hits a weird spot in my heart. It's not exactly pain, but I'm not entirely numb either.

Conflicted, I flip to another page to see any information about the man I truly know nothing about. I see his name at the top of a page, Lukas Woods. The dates on the page catch me off guard.

Math was never my strong suit, but this is pretty obvious and my blood boils.

He was ten years older than her, twenty-six with a sixteen year old. What a piece of shit. On top of that, he got to live into his sixties while her life was stolen so much younger by the battle to addiction she lost. It pisses me off even more, and if the bastard wasn't dead I would kill him.

"Hey." Max's soft voice and gentle hand on my cheek pulls me from the blinding rage taking over my body. I flinch at her touch, and she tries to recoil, but I grab her wrist, keeping her hand on me. I like it there. Grounding me.

I tighten my hold on her, still not saying anything, just feeling her.

I don't even know if I want to see how he died, because if it wasn't some violent way that made sure he suffered, I won't be happy. I need to believe my own version of his ending to make myself feel better, even if it's just barely.

"Hey," Max says again, a little louder this time and I move my eyes up to meet hers this time. The concern evident in her voice as I look at her. "Are you okay?"

I shake my head, not sure how to answer. All I can say is, "She was sixteen. He was ten years older than her."

That's when it really hits me, how similar I am to him. The woman on my lap is seventeen years younger than me. I'm sick just like him. It doesn't matter that we're both adults and that I would have never touched her, or anyone else, underage. I'm no better than him.

"Stop," she commands. "You're not like him."

I wonder for a minute if I said that out loud, but I know it's just Max being able to read me so easily. Understanding me better than anyone else ever has.

"I'm disgusting just like him." Shaking my head, I try to move her off my lap because I don't know why she's here. Why she would want to be with me. She has two men that are age appropriate for her and here I am, the son of a sick man who turned out just like him.

Max latches onto me tightly, not removing herself from my lap. "Knock it off. You're nothing like him. Would you be with me if I was seventeen right now?"

"Of course not." I grimace at the thought.

"What about any other girl underage?"

"Never."

"Then don't compare yourself to him. You're not the same. We're both consenting adults. The *four of us* are consenting adults," she insists.

"You could have so much more. You have them, you don't need me."

"Adam, stop." She grabs my face in between both of her hands now, forcing me to look at her. "I love you, none of this is wrong, I struggled for a while because it's unconventional, but none of that had to do with your age. You didn't groom me. You didn't force me. Understand?"

I swallow roughly, struggling to agree with her, but when she leans forward, her lips grazing mine. "I love you, and I've never loved anyone before the three of you. That can't be forced, trust me."

I close the distance between us, falling into her. Getting lost in her. Which is exactly what I want right now. It's what I need to erase the information I just found out. She's right, it doesn't change anything. Both of them are dead, so there's nothing I can do about it now.

Grabbing the back of her head roughly, I yank her hair there hard enough she gasps, and it pulls our mouths apart, though she tries to seek mine out, I don't let her, just pull harder when she tries. Whimpering when I don't let her.

"Remember that day in the forest, baby girl?" I growl.

She sucks in her bottom lip between her teeth, trying to nod against my grip in her hair.

"I think we should have a repeat, but I don't feel like waiting to get you out there."

She gasps when I pull harder, arching her neck back even more.

"I'm going to let you go, and you're going to run. Just remember what happens when we catch you." She thrusts her hips slightly against me, already seeking friction. "Such a naughty girl, already wanting to be filled."

"*Yes,*" she moans.

"But only if you run. Make us work for it, baby girl, or you won't get what you're wanting."

I let go of her, and she struggles to stay balanced as she drops off my lap when I stand up. She backs away from me toward the door, and I prowl toward her.

"Run," I say darkly, and she doesn't wait any longer, turning quickly to run out of the office into the open gym. I know Caine and Drew will know this game we're playing. We all have a weakness for her when she runs.

CHAPTER 51
MAX

I don't waste any time darting out of the office and into the gym. I wonder for a split second if I should run outside to try and get away. But the thing is, I don't actually want to get away from them. They all know it. Though, I still make a serious effort to run within the limits I have.

Drew and Caine were focused on whatever they were doing when I come barreling out of Adam's office. It doesn't take them long to catch on. I'm dodging and avoiding three different men who are all trying to hunt me down.

It's harder than anticipated, the gym isn't necessarily small, but it's also not big. There's really not many places to hide. Despite that, I hope this is doing what it's intended to, and distracting Adam from what he just found out. He need to know he isn't like the man that played a part in his conception. Our ages are different, and I want him. I want *this*.

I duck behind one of the hanging bags, breathing heavily in anticipation. It's too quiet, and the only thing I can hear is my own rapid breaths. Then there's a banging of chains against metal that makes my heart rate kick up in my chest.

The steady beat of the chains swinging slows down. Silence surrounds me before a face appears right in front of me. Drew smiles. "Found you, little one."

I squeal, going the other direction to run away again. He doesn't immediately grab me and I know it's because he's enjoying this. They love toying with me, and though we all know how this is going to end, it's still fun to feel like there's an element of danger being chased.

One of them is closing in on me as I race around and head toward the cage. I feel the large presence right on my heels, and I know I should probably go in another direction, but I'm pretty sure it's my subconscious telling me I want to be caught. Right. Now.

Though, it's not on purpose, I stumble slightly, which gives Caine the opportunity to grab me around my waist, yanking my body against his. He carries me in the direction I was already headed. I thrash haphazardly in his arms.

"Come on, killer, you can do better than that," Caine taunts against my hair.

I let out a frustrated noise, attempting to throw a leg back to kick him, but he just laughs. Dropping me onto my feet, but not letting me get away as he's grabbing my wrists and holding them up in front of my face.

"What the fuck are you doing?" I snap, trying to yank my arms free, but his grip is tighter than a pair of handcuffs.

"Making sure you never get away from us," he answers, holding up the unraveling roll of hand wraps.

"You going to wrap my hands for me?" I raise an eyebrow.

"Yeah, but not how you're thinking." He backs me into the corner of the cage, stretching one arm out, securing my wrists to the metal one at a time. I don't even have enough brain capacity to consider fighting back.

I'm fixated on watching the way he expertly restrains me, so I don't notice Adam and Drew joining us in here. They both crowd me on one side, it should feel claustrophobic. I should feel restricted considering I'm completely at their mercy. But I don't. I feel comfortable. Like them all being so close to me is the best way to make me feel the most like myself.

"How's that feel, baby girl?"

"Not enough," I complain, shifting, rubbing my thighs together, realizing how turned on I am from the chase and now the fact that my wrists are bound, my arms outstretched to my sides.

"You need more, little one? Need us to touch this greedy pussy? How wet is she for us? I bet you're *dripping*, aren't you?"

I let out a soft moan, my head dropping back against the chain. "Find out."

Caine grabs the waistband of my tight leggings, pulling them down along with my panties at once. The cool air hits my drenched core and I whimper at the sensation. Especially when both Drew and Adam reach down, Adam's hand on top of

Drew's while they collectively shove a finger inside me, and I gasp at the intrusion.

Caine takes advantage, grabbing the back of my head, pulling my mouth onto his, pushing his tongue inside my open mouth immediately while the other two pump their fingers. I'm a completely needy mess as two of my men work me with their joined hands, and the other fucks my mouth with his tongue like I wish he would do somewhere else. But also don't want him to go anywhere.

Especially when his hand collars my throat, tightening just enough for me to feel the pressure, but not take away my air. Though with the way his tongue plunders into my mouth, and Adam and Drew's fingers are curling inside me, I'm at risk for forgetting to breathe and passing out from lack of oxygen on my own anyway.

I pull at my restraints, wanting to touch them, to rip their clothes off and feel their strong, hard bodies under my fingertips. I growl in frustration that I'm not able to break free, and it only makes them tighten a bit more around my skin. I feel like I'm going to have some marks left over after this, and I crave them. They can be my reminder of this moment, and I know it's going to be one I won't want to forget any time soon.

"Please," I beg against Caine's mouth.

"Please what, killer? Their fingers not enough for your desperate pussy? You need to be filled by something bigger?"

I nod against him. "Yes, I want more. I need more, please."

"You heard her. Caine, give her what she wants," Adam says, grabbing my face, pinching my chin between his fingers. "Then we can each have a turn with you, fucking and filling your pretty cunt."

I gasp, clenching around their fingers, loving the sound of that. They pull away from my body and I cry out at the loss, but it isn't long before Caine has pushed his shorts down, grabbing me by my hips and lifting me so I can wrap my legs around him, though he's so tall and my arms are still stuck where he tied them up. Yet, any ounce of discomfort is gone as he presses the blunt tip of his cock against my entrance.

I buck against him, silently urging him inside.

"So fucking greedy, killer. It's a good thing I'll give you whatever you want and need," he growls, pushing himself in to the hilt in a single thrust.

I scream at the sudden stretch, but also feel myself constrict around him, wanting to keep him there, Like I need him to be a part of me. Turning my head to the side so I can see Adam and Drew, they're watching with rapt attention.

"Touch each other," I instruct them desperately. "But don't you dare come unless it's inside me."

"Oh fuck, killer," Caine groans. He pistons his hips roughly and I cry out as they slam into mine.

My eyes don't leave the sight of Adam and Drew who are now shedding each other's clothes, mouths locked while they desperately wrap their hands around each other's dicks, pumping furiously while kissing and Caine fucks me at the same punishing pace.

It's almost too much, watching them and feeling Caine, but

not being able to touch. I'm at their mercy. They can do whatever they want to my body, and I've never loved the loss of control like I do right now.

"Oh please! I'm so close, *please.*" My release is teasing me, teetering just out of reach, and when I see Adam drop down to his knees in front of Drew I almost lose it. Seeing the way he sucks Drew's dick into his mouth, I moan.

"Getting me nice and wet to fuck you, little one," Drew groans, thrusting forward to bury himself in Adam's throat even more.

"Oh God," I cry. Caine tightens his grip on my hips, fucking me so hard I think I'm making sounds I've never made before. Especially when my orgasm starts to take over, and it's like my body knows it's going to be the first of many tonight because it's over too soon. My hands desperately latch on to the cool metal chains above where I'm tied.

"That's it, killer, choke my cock, you've got this," Caine encourages and somehow that only makes the aftershocks of my release hit me even harder.

"Caine," I moan. "Come inside me, I want to feel you fill me with your cum."

"Shit," he groans, his grip turns painful as he fucks me even harder, groaning only seconds later as he does just that. He's coming and shooting ropes of cum so deep inside me it seems impossible.

"Fuck," I hear Drew groan, and it draws my attention back to him as he pulls Adam off his cock. "I'm going to come and our girl had a demand about that."

Adam stands up. "Then you better get over there, and give her what she's wanting." He nudges Drew toward me and he goes easily.

I expect Caine to argue, or refuse to let me go, but to my surprise, he drops my weak legs down gently, presses his lips to mine, more gentle than he has before. "I fucking love you, killer. I hope you realize how much."

"I do." I nod with a smile. "You're willing to share me even if it kills you. Of course you love me."

"Don't forget it, either," he growls with another rough kiss before letting me go.

My body is cold for only a moment before Drew is there. But instead of picking me up like Caine did, he lifts one of my legs over his hip, runs his spit covered cock through my folds before angling up against me, and pushing in slowly so I feel every inch and every single one of his piercings.

I moan, and once he's fully seated, he smirks down at me. "Remember what I told you about getting off when you first counted my bars?"

Nodding, I whimper, already feeling close. Having Caine's cum already inside me, while my body is already primed from the first orgasm, plus watching the two of them together will always get me worked up. Every. Single. Time.

"I'm going to prove it to you."

I want to sass him, tell him there's no way, but I don't even have time because he drops his hand to where we're joined, rubbing my clit with perfect precision as he positions himself so he hits the perfect spot on my inner walls with each thrust.

I cry out at the way he's quite literally pressing all the right buttons of my body, and I'm not keeping track of how many seconds pass, but it isn't many before my body is crying out with its release.

"Yeah, that's it. Come all over my cock, little one. So fucking pretty falling apart for me. So"—thrust—"Fucking"—thrust—"Perfect."

His words only make me continue to cry out, and the way he's fucking me and rubbing my clit prolongs my orgasm.

"Damn baby girl," Adam groans.

"So fucking pretty coming all over him," Caine growls and my eyes roll back at the overwhelming sensations. Their eyes on me, hands on me, the dirty words being spoken. *All of it.*

"Fuck," I moan, not sure what else to say. I don't have anything to say. My body comes down from the pleasure overload. With the way Drew is still touching me, it's impossible to come down completely, even as I feel myself become weaker.

"Knew it, you're so fucking perfect," Drew groans, pushing my back flush against the cage as he slams into me roughly and I can only take it. Though, I wouldn't want to be anywhere else right now.

Drew's face drops down to my shoulder as he groans, holding himself against me, his own release barreling through him as he fills me as well. My jaw drops on a silent moan as he does. I don't know if I can take more, but when I look over at

Adam, and see the way he's gripping his cock tightly, desperately, I know I need him where Drew is. I need to feel all of them. And even more than that, I know he needs it too.

That's confirmed when he steps up next to Drew, clapping a hand on his shoulder before dropping down to his knees and I'm not sure what he's doing. Until Drew withdraws from my body and Adam buries his face between my thighs, in the spot the other two were. And he licks the mixture of release that's there.

I groan at the sensation, knowing he's tasting all of us makes it even hotter, even though everything he's doing with his tongue feels amazing, it's knowing that he's not just tasting me that has me going over the edge another time and this one has me feeling like I'm going to lose all sensation in my legs.

I'm screaming as I come, gushing out my release and soaking Adam's face, I'm sure of it. The moan he lets out that vibrates through me lets me know that I'm right.

"Fuck, killer, that feel good?" Caine rasps, and I nod furiously.

When Adam stands in front of me, I'm barely able to stay upright so when he picks me up I'm not even able to wrap my legs around him tight enough, but it doesn't matter because Adam holds me up with pure strength.

I cry out when he pushes into me because I'm overstimulated. I've been stretched and pushed to the absolute brink of pleasure from the back to back orgasms. All I can do is hang on as he fucks me.

The one thing I can't help but tell him is how perfect we all are and that this shouldn't feel wrong. I don't want him to be worried anymore or question anything about this relationship.

"I love you, Adam. You complete all of us, and no one is going anywhere," I insist.

"I love you, baby girl. This is how it's always going to be."

I nod in agreement.

"Now, you're going to need to come for me again. I need to feel your sweet little cunt come on my cock like you did on my face."

"I can't," I cry.

"Better listen to coach, little one," Drew adds, coming up to one of my sides.

"I can't," I insist again, louder and more of a whine.

"You can, killer, come for him, you can do it," Caine encourages, coming up to my other side.

I cry out in frustration at all of them because I really don't think I can. I'm overly sensitive to the point it's almost painful and I don't think it's even possible for me to come again.

"Come on, baby girl, give it to me or I'm going to force it out of you."

"*Agh, Daddy,*" I scream.

Drew reaches between Adam and me, rubbing my clit and I moan, Caine grabs my head, turning it toward him and crashing our mouths together. All of them being here, touching me, loving me, I'm sure it's the only reason I'm able to come again, even though I didn't think it would be possible.

But I do. With a loud scream that I'm sure everyone in this whole fucking town hears, but I don't even care.

It triggers Adam's release and with a loud groan of his own, he's filling me as well, pushing in deep with little thrusts like he's making sure every single drop stays inside me.

My vision is fuzzy, my breathing rapid. My skin is slick with sweat, body exhausted, and yet I've never felt better. Especially when they take care of me, untying me from the side of the cage. Making sure I'm okay before taking me home.

I hardly register everything that happens after we leave the gym. I'm half asleep as they take me home, clean me up, and tuck me into bed. As soon as my body is engulfed in comfort I fall asleep, dreaming of how perfect my new life is with three amazing, slightly psycho men who I love more than I ever thought possible.

CHAPTER 52
CAINE

It's nice to see updates on Max's parent's case and *not* see my family name attached to it anymore.

It's even nicer the day the verdict comes in.

We've all been slightly on edge despite Danner's insistence that it'll be fine. Max has continued to be worried, even though she tried to hide it from us. Too bad I can always tell what she's thinking. What she needs. She's my girl, and I know everything there is to know about her.

Our girl.

Apparently I need to get better about saying that, though I still think of her as mine, and I always will.

"Verdict is in," I call out, seeing the headline, but not daring to click on it until we're all together. Especially because if it's not guilty, I'm worried about how Max will react and I want to be right next to her for it.

She's hiding how nervous she is and I wrap my arm around her shoulder, pulling her into my side immediately.

"You okay, killer?" I ask, and she nods, the little liar. I press a rough kiss to the side of her head, wanting her to relax, but she's so tense I don't think it's going to happen.

Drew and Adam join us, and I don't hesitate before clicking the link so Max can either chill or have a breakdown that we will all help her through. My eyes skim the page, searching for the words to make or break this moment, and they appear bold and definite.

Guilty.

I feel the whoosh of air leave Max when she sees it too. Of course there's talk of appeals, but that's common with any case like this and I doubt they'll get them. It's done. She's free. We're all free.

Doogie ended up listening to us, and left town without trying to pull anything stupid. Which I was happy about, because we could've had him taken care of a bit more, but I know Danner is sick of our shit.

She's been a good friend to Max, and that's all she should have to be instead of constantly covering up crimes for all of us. Though, it's still nice to know we have access to that kind of skill if it's needed.

I hope it's not.

Max told me to keep our fighting in the cage.

"*You too, killer,*" I told her.

"So, that's it then?" she says, turning her head to look up at me.

I nod. "Guess so. How do you feel?"

"Weird. I feel like I've been paranoid and worried my entire life, but knowing they won't be able to do anything to me again…" She hesitates. "I guess it's going to take some getting used to."

"Don't worry, little one, we'll make sure you're distracted enough while you get used to it." Drew winks.

"Well, now what do we do?" she asks, looking between us.

"I have a few ideas." I yank her into my chest roughly.

"Later," Adam scolds. "Right now, we all have lives to get to since no one is going to prison today."

"Today, but never know about tomorrow." I lean down to try and steal a kiss, but she stops me with her hand over my mouth.

"Too soon." She shakes her head.

I groan against her hand, biting the skin enough that she yelps, pulling it away with a scowl. One I'm quick to kiss away, and she doesn't stop me. Her body melts into mine, and a hand slaps down on my shoulder.

"Come on, we don't have the time," Drew tells me.

"I'll be late," I reply against Max's mouth. She smiles into the kiss, and I suck her bottom lip between my teeth.

"Might not be a good idea," she rasps once I let go of her lip. "The boss is pretty demanding."

"I don't have a fucking boss," I growl, diving in for more of her.

"You have a coach, though, and he's going to make your life a living hell if you don't knock it off," Adam's stern voice says.

"Worth it," I try to kiss Max again, but she stops me, and I'm getting real tired of her doing that.

"Go, and I'll reward you later." She winks.

"I don't need a reward, I'm not a good boy like Drew."

A hand slaps the back of my head, and I smirk, knowing I pissed him off. Good, I hope it riles everyone up so we don't have to leave.

"Watch it," Max threatens.

I lean down, whispering, "The only thing I'll be watching is you bouncing on my dick later."

She sucks in a sharp inhale, and I back up. "Alright, let's go, fuckers. I have important plans later."

"I'll see you guys after I'm off work since there's no point in any of you showing up to The Tavern anymore."

"Nice try, baby girl, we're still making sure you get home safe." Adam drops a quick kiss to her lips even though she narrows her eyes at him.

"When will you guys trust that I can handle myself? Do I need to be a black belt or something?"

Drew laughs, pulling her into him. "Do you know how long it would take you to get a black belt?"

"Oh you don't think I can?" she challenges, and for some reason, my half hard dick is now at full attention at her tone. I fucking love when she gets feisty like this.

"Of course you can," he relents, and I see the flash of pride on her face, though it's true about the time it would take for her to get a black belt. Honestly, even then I think we would still meet up with her to make sure she gets home safe.

She's our girl to keep safe. To take care of.

She's our girl to love, and it doesn't matter if the dangers we knew about are gone, there'll always be more. She'll never be taken from us again. We'll make sure she's safe, cared for, and loved for the rest of all our lives and she's just going to have to deal with the way we choose to do that.

"Love you guys," she sighs, and I can't help but look back at her before leaving. I never would've pictured my life like this, but I wouldn't take it back.

She has us, and she'll never get rid of us, even if she wanted to. We'll always be obsessed, but it's a good thing she's just as obsessed with us as we are of her.

EPILOGUE

MAX

SIX MONTHS LATER

Walking into Uncaged, I have a surprise for the guys. It's small and probably silly, but it's something I would have never thought I would do, and it means so much to me. I know they'll be proud of me.

Though, I already know they'll be mad they didn't join me. They haven't let up on worrying about my safety, but they still let me have a level of independence. That will always be the difference with their level of controlling compared to what I came from.

They want me to be happy, I'm the priority and always will be. Even when I'm chased, tied up, held down, or at the mercy of them in and out of the bedroom, I'm in control and my needs come first.

They're overbearing, protective, but loving and caring to a level that I never saw coming.

I came here to get away, to find myself, and escape my old life. I didn't expect to find three men to fulfill every fantasy I ever had, and support me in finding out who I am. But I did. I found everything I never knew I needed and more.

There aren't any classes going on right now, but I walk in on Cal and Alexander in the cage with Caine and Drew in opposite corners acting as their coaches. They yell out instructions while the fighters exchange blows.

I look around for Adam because I'm not going to disturb them, and see his office door open. I sneak over there, entering and shutting the door behind me.

"Hi, baby girl, what're you doing?" he asks with a small smile as soon as he sees me.

"Came to see you, Daddy." I smirk, especially when he narrows his eyes at me. I know what it does to him when I call him that. He prefers I keep it in the bedroom because it makes him want to bend me over and rail me into next week.

Which, of course, I always want, but I know it's not going to happen with the other two guys here. Still, I come around his desk, sitting on the edge in front of him, draping my legs on either side of his lap. He leans back in his office chair, his eyes raking over me and I shiver under his gaze.

"What about Caine and Drew?"

I shrug. "They're busy."

"Hm, did they see you come in?"

"I don't think so."

"Should I take advantage of having you all to myself?"

I try to clench my thighs together, but he stops me from being able to with a grip on each of my knees.

"Or should I make you wait until we get home? Especially since you came in here trying to be in control when you know that's not how this works."

"I think you should do something about it now." I bat my eyelashes at him.

He smiles, rubbing his hand over his mouth, looking me over. "No, I think you want to be punished and have to wait."

I groan, tossing my head back, but then the door opens, revealing Caine and Drew standing there.

"Told you I could tell our girl was here," Caine insists.

"I never said you were wrong," Drew insists.

"No fighting, I just didn't want to interrupt you," I tell them to stop the fight before it can progress further.

"Interrupt us any time, little one, we want your interruptions."

"I don't think Cal and Alexander would like that," I tell them.

"If Danner walked in, they would be distracted too," Drew says.

I roll my eyes. I keep telling her they want her, but she continues to insist it's not going to happen. Though, if they're persistent like my guys I'm sure it's only a matter of time before she gives in.

"I actually have to go to work soon, but came by to show you something," I announce because as much as I would love to take advantage of an empty gym with them, I really do have to go soon. They've tried to convince me to quit The Tavern and work here instead, but I like my job. That may not be a normal feeling to have about working, but it is for me.

"I hope it's your pussy," Caine groans and I give him an unamused look.

"You saw that this morning," I sass.

"And I'd happily see it every second, every day for the rest of my life," he tells me seriously.

For some reason that makes me melt a little, and maybe I can be late to work.

"What do you want to show us, baby girl?" Adam brings me back to what I actually came here for.

I adjust slightly on the desk where I'm still sitting. "I did something."

I catch the way they all look me over, probably trying to figure it out before I show them. For some reason I start to get nervous about it, maybe they won't like it, and will think it's dumb.

I shake away the fear because that's not who they are, that would be something that would happen in my old life, but not with them. They wouldn't ever make me feel anything less than perfect.

With that thought, I grab the hem of my shirt and start to pull it up, and Caine can't help himself saying, "Fuck yeah, your tits work too, killer."

I pause my movement to glare at him. I shake my head, but continue to pull my shirt off, knowing my boobs may distract them, but I'm hoping what's between them is enough to draw their attention, since that's what I'm here to show them.

Should I have gotten the tattoo done in another spot? Probably. But I wanted it to be front and center on my body, just for this moment.

The snake tattoo runs up my sternum, the head reaching just above my boobs. They all look at me, taking it in, and it takes a minute for them to catch the abstract markings on the snake.

"Is that an A?" Adam asks, and I smirk.

"And a D?" Drew joins in.

"I know that's a C." Caine smirks.

I nod at all of them. Hidden in the markings are each of their first initials, it's not obvious at first glance, but they're there. Imprinted on my skin, just like the three of them have embedded themselves in my soul.

"That's so fucking hot, killer, I'm going to get your name tattooed on me as my first tattoo," Caine growls, reaching for me.

"Where?" I ask, not sure how I think about him doing that, but also liking the sound of it.

"Anywhere. On my fucking dick if you want."

I huff out a laugh. "If you do that, I don't think you can use it until it's healed."

He grimaces. "Good point, I'll get it somewhere else."

"If you're getting her name, then so am I. But bigger," Drew announces.

"I'd find space and get it too," Adam joins.

I shake my head at all of them. "You guys don't have to do that. I got this for me. Someone told me that snakes mean rebirth, and I thought it was the perfect symbol for me to get." I wink at Adam. "Plus, I looked into it and snakes also mean immortality and healing."

"It's fucking hot." Drew pulls me into him and I giggle.

"Glad you think so, but I do really need to go to work, so you all can show me what you think about it later."

"You're going to *work* with that under your shirt?" Caine asks, dumbfounded.

"Well, it's stuck to me, so yes." I roll my eyes.

Adam takes my hand and yanks me into his lap, and my bare chest presses against him, the scrape of his shirt against my nipples have them hardening even more. "We'll make sure to show you exactly how much we love this new ink of yours later," he tells me.

"You better." I smile, reluctantly getting off his lap and pulling my shirt on, making my way toward the door while they all watch me like predators who are ready to pounce. "Be good boys, and be ready for me after work."

"Watch it, baby girl, you're going to get it," Adam threatens.

I wink, leaving them staring at me, and I can't wait for what is going to wait for me when I get home.

The mother fucking end.

ACKNOWLEDGMENTS

This duet.

Holy shit.

Going into these books I didn't anticipate it would turn into two, and when I tell you I fought against it for awhile, I mean it. Until Desires was getting pretty big and I realized these characters had much more to say. I am sorry for the cliffhanger before, but also…not really ;)

Of course these books would have never been completed without all the help I have from so many amazing people who support me constantly and I don't think any amount of thanks will ever be enough.

Maeghen - When I say these books (especially this one) wouldn't be done without you. I mean it. Thank you for continuing to talk me off the ledge….multiple times. There were many days this book was going to go in the garbage and you had your back up saved, ready to swoop in if I decided to do it…and who knows, maybe I still will! Thank you for sticking by me this entire journey I love you!

Chelsey - Thank you for being the best PA I could ever ask for and of course my bestie! You also talked me off the ledge and stopped me from deleting this book many times. Thank you for sticking by me through every meltdown, spiral and ridiculous thought that comes to my mind. I love you forever and you're never getting rid of me!

Ashley - You're my forever Booha and you support me so

much it's insane. I love you forever and ever. Also I'm still sorry this wasn't the book you wanted me to write next, but I promise Jameson and Sutton will be!

Sarah Beth - Girl...the fact that you've been with me since my very first book is insane. And you're still with me and still stand by me I can never thank you enough. Your love and support has been everything to me and I truly wouldn't be here if it wasn't for you!

Mikaela - Thank you for taking the chance on me with Chasing Books PR! Thank you for being there for me, everything you've done, the advice you've given and being there. You're the actual best!

Kay - Thank you so much for always being flexible with me and putting up with my chaos when it comes to editing. You're stuck with me for life and you know that.

Kim - Thank you for the gorgeous covers you've made for this duet! Seriously you kill it every single time and these ones are everything I could've wanted and more!

Thank you to all my beta readers, your comments and feedback kept me going! Anja, Emily, Lanae, Dani, Erin, Jaeann, Jessica, Katelyn, Leslie and Tiffany.

Of course thank you to my ARC readers and every single person that has shown my books and me love over the years. I couldn't do this without you all and I'm so incredibly thankful to have so many amazing people supporting me!

If you made it this far, just know that I'm a mood writer so you may never know what you're going to get from me next, but let's just say it may be on the sweeter side so I hope you're ready!

ALSO BY MADI DANIELLE

Denver Dragons Series:

The Hat Trick - A hockey why choose romance

The Power Play - A forced proximity hockey romance

Cross Checked - A friends to lovers novella

The Break Out -An enemies to lovers brother's teammate hockey romance

Uncaged Duet

A dark MMA why choose romance

Uncaged Desires

Uncaged Obsessions

The Falling series

When They Fell - A friends to lovers romance

Who They Are - A cop romance

What They Feel - An enemies to lovers age gap romance

Signed Books available on my website:

www.madidaniellewrites.com

ABOUT THE AUTHOR

madi danielle

Madi is a romance author, wife and mother to one daughter and several animals. When she isn't reading or writing you may find her watching hockey or some cheesy movie. Madi has been writing since she was a teenager, but it took a backseat when she went to college and got her degree in Family and Human Services. After working as a social worker, she got back into writing as an escape and hasn't looked back since. Madi is originally from Arizona, but moved to Oregon to attend UO, which is where she still resides with her family.

instagram.com/madidaniellewrites
tiktok.com/@madidaniellewrites
threads.net/@madidaniellewrites

www.ingramcontent.com/pod-product-compliance
Lightning Source LLC
LaVergne TN
LVHW011942060526
838201LV00061B/4183